NALS

By

M.D. Nuth

NAILS

By

M.D. Nuth

Published by
Crimson Cloak Publishing

ISBN 13: 978-1-68160-764-1

ISBN 10: 1-68160-764-6

Cover by Carly McCracken

Edited by Denna Holm

Publisher's Publication in Data

Nuth, M.D.

Nails

1.Fiction 2. Literary. 3. Political Fiction

PROLOGUE

Gerald sits quietly in a simple, generations-old Chippendale chair that has been reupholstered so many times over its life that nobody knows what the original material looked like. The chair is not particularly comfortable, but it reflects wealth and, more importantly, the permanence of the family. Except for his monotonous humming, there is no noise in the room. Although others find the humming bothersome, he appears completely unaware of his peculiar habit. He always hums when he ponders difficult situations, proud of his ability to come up with solutions that elude other, lesser people.

He reaches for his cup of tea on the small table that separates him from his wife, but his hand stops short, instead falling to rest on the highly polished maple, his thumb slowly tapping. Suddenly, the humming and tapping stop. He leans forward to focus on his wife, bringing his face close to hers. She has seen him use this tactic numerous times in business negotiations. It is intended to intimidate, and it almost always works. Almost always. It never works with her.

But today is different. Gerald is angry … truly angry. If not for his cultured upbringing, he would have grabbed her by the throat and squeezed until her breath stopped. But Gerald is not a murderer, per se. He is not capable of taking a life with his own hands. A shortcoming. He is unable to do the hard, dirty things, instead relying on underlings to do the nasty stuff that life requires. She hates him for his inability to be uninhibited, to be rash, to be violent. Sometimes a little violence is required in life; it makes people afraid to cross you. Certainly, Gerald is respected, but feared? He relies on others in the family to create fear. She considers him a weakling—a genius, but still a weakling. She does not fear him.

"Lizbet, what were you thinking? You are going to destroy everything, flush away everything our family has worked for over the past three centuries."

"You miss the point, dear husband. I am destroying nothing. I am saving everything: our family, our power, our world. You men have done nothing more than accumulate money and power. Sure, we control many of the largest and most profitable companies in the world. We own more real estate and have plenty of money. We drive the economies of whole countries, and they know it, even though they will never admit it. You have been successful, but you ignored the plight of the world. What purpose is there to being the most powerful family on Earth if the planet dies? You should be bowing down to me and the rest of the Committee for finally doing the hard, right things you ignored."

"Your killing of two-thirds of the people on Earth is the hard, right thing? Are you mad?"

"Is it mad for a director to fire employees who fail to contribute to a business? Is it mad for a surgeon to amputate a gangrenous arm to save the body? Is it mad to push people off a lifeboat to ensure it remains afloat? Of course not. It is mad to think the planet can endlessly support a rampant growth in population. It is mad to allow those who make no meaningful contribution to breed like rabbits and expect us to care for them. The Committee is ending this madness before the world rebels and destroys us all. You have failed the planet. I will not."

BOOK ONE

"Shhh! They can hear us."

Tau—We Were Hammers

What makes me better than you? Nothing … and everything. You drive by me in your fancy cars and you sneer at me, you laugh at me, you abhor me, but when you walk by me, you fear me. Fear is everything.

Rubbing the back of my fist against my mouth and nose, I draw in air through my nostrils to catch the metallic scent of blood, sweet blood. I pass the sticky crimson staining my hand across my face and open my mouth to get a taste. Sure, the stuff might be diseased, but I lick it anyway. It's my reward for the battle victory. True, it really wasn't much of a battle.

Hell, the old man might have been sixty-five, maybe seventy. He was no match for me or my gang. And it was his fault. He forced me to beat the shit out of him. He would not turn away. How could I let him disrespect me? Well, he won't be disrespecting me or anyone else for a long time, if ever. Now he lays at my feet in a small pool of his own blood. I don't know if he's breathing, and I really don't care. The crowd is crying out for me to kick him again. I do ... again and again. I think he's dead, but there is no one here making me stop, so I continue to stomp him. The crowd—the mob— have become my people, my posse, my kin. I do whatever I want. I'm like God.

How did I become so powerful? Simple ... people gave their power to me. Now when I yell, they turn away. When I push, they walk the other direction. When I punch, they run. They are chickenshits. They can't stop me. This old man thought he could. He couldn't, and now he's dead. He is a sign to the rest of these little shits. I am here.

CHAPTER 1: Good Morning

My head aches like crazy from partying last night. I don't want to move. The smell of vomit stings my nose. It overwhelms the stench of rotten food, urine, and BO that I have become so accustomed to. I open my eyes just a crack to let in a little of the late morning light, allowing my pupils to adjust before I open them fully. I hate the day.

Even though I know it's almost noon, the overcast skies filter the sun, leaving my room a dingy gray. It matches my furniture and my mood. My bed is nothing more than an old twin mattress stained with feces, blood, and dirt. Padding extrudes through at least a dozen spots where the fabric has given way. It's dirty and beaten, but it's soft, at least softer than the ground in the park where I had been sleeping before. Before what? Before becoming judge, jury, and executioner.

I don't need much. I have power, and isn't that all anyone needs or wants? I don't want to make it sound as though I don't have any physical things of value. I do. In addition to my bed, I have a couple pairs of construction shoes with steel toes, some clothes (all black), a kitchen cabinet and a stove. Granted, the cabinet is really nothing more than a beat-to-hell end table, and the stove is a kerosene single-burner cooktop I pulled from the trash behind the local Goodwill. Even the poor didn't want this piece of shit. For me, it is a godsend. I can have hot food now.

"Godsend?" Did I really use that term? There is no God. How can there be? If there was one, he wouldn't let me exist. I am an anti-god. God is supposed to be good and powerful, but I am more powerful. I know this because people cower and turn away when I yell at them. And I am not good. I never have been, and I don't expect to ever start doing good, at least to others. In my book, I am the only thing that counts. You should listen to me when I walk by you; it might save you a beating.

I open my eyes and sit up in bed before standing. One of my gang is snoring on the floor beside me. He's my right-hand man and I call him "Boots." Maybe it's because he has walked the path with me for years, or perhaps it's because he has always worn these old black leather biker boots, or perhaps it's because he uses those size fourteen boots to kick the life out of anyone who gets in our way.

This morning I'm going to let him sleep for a while longer. I'm not ready to listen to him banter and brag about the carnage we caused last night. I need a handful of aspirin and a joint to numb my head and quiet my stomach. More importantly, I need some quiet. Once Boots wakes, there will be no quiet until night, or until he zones out on drugs.

I'm Tau. Not my real name, at least as far as my parents are concerned, but now it's all I will answer to. I loved Tau when I first heard it was the name of an evil, chaotic spirit in some South American tribe. I don't even recall the name of the tribe, but the story stayed with me. Tau was sneaky, smart, and the personification of evil here on earth. How apropos that this is what I am. It is me. I am Tau.

My posse has been with me for years, at least it seems that way. In reality, we've only been together a few months, but we have become family. I never had a real family before, at least the type most people have. In my case, I never met my dad, and Mom was typically strung out on drugs. I don't remember ever living in a house. Mom, my sister, and I bounced from dirty, bug-infested apartment to dirty, bug-infested apartment, until eventually we landed on the street. It wasn't so bad. It's where I learned to roll other strung-out pricks for their dope money. It was easy and, more importantly, fun for me. I would beat these helpless souls until they bled and then leave them on the sidewalks for the cops to arrest. Funny, they got beaten, and that gave them the privilege of spending a night in jail. At least they got a couple of free meals. Me? I got nothing but the pleasure of taking out my frustrations on someone who had even less than me.

That didn't change until Mom didn't wake up one morning. She was blue and stiff; the night cold finally got the best of her. My sister OD'd later that morning. She never got the needle out of her arm. I guess she'd had enough heartache, and this was a way to put the pain behind her. Lucky bitch.

I have already introduced one of my new family members, Boots. He, too, was raised with drugs, but in his case, his family pushed as much as consumed. They made enough money to stay off the street, but they didn't have it easy. Boots told me his folks would move from town to town as they tried to stay ahead of the fuzz and their suppliers. The cops wanted them behind bars. The suppliers wanted them buried—his parents made a habit of skimming money from their drug sales and trying to stiff those upstream. Sometimes it worked, sometimes it didn't. The suppliers caught up with them before the police. Too bad for them. They ended up as fertilizer in a couple of tomato fields down in the central valley just north of Bakersfield. Boots escaped the punishment by passing out in the backseat of his parents' car. The drug lords never even bothered to look.

Boots, who is twice as old as me and twice as big, is a huge man. I mean HUGE. He dwarfs my six-foot-two frame, and, at more than four hundred pounds, he is almost twice as heavy. His tanned arms are thicker than my legs and are covered with a reddish-brown curly hair. His body hair is so thick it is difficult to make out the tattoos covering his forearms and shoulders. These aren't the tattoo decorations of the posers we terrorize. These are the real thing. They each mean something bad; however, the scariest tattoos aren't so big. The first is just five black dots on the back of his hand next to his thumb. He doesn't talk much about it, but I know it relates to his time in prison. The second tattoo is a small cross just below his eye. It is a mark of pride for killing at least two men. I know these are real. Hell, I've seen him kill two people in one night. He's one malevolent dude.

I adopted two other brothers, or should I say, they adopted me. The first is a twenty-something crazy Irishman I call Salmon. His skin is so white and translucent I can see the blue veins below the surface. That is until he gets into the sun for few minutes or drinks a few pints, then his skin glows pink, as pink as salmon flesh. I said he's crazy. He is. He gets his jollies watching people hurt. Whereas Boots and I enjoy beating and kicking the senses out of folks, Salmon likes to quietly watch until our targets give up, then he pulls out his knife and begins to carve on them. He slaps them to keep them conscious while he cuts into their faces. He's too chicken to hurt them when they can fight back. He's also a white supremacist. None of us like the guy, but he makes my posse even scarier.

My last family member is B. Just B. He's my hammer. He's a big black man, not as big as Boots, but a hell of a lot larger than me. I don't know how old he is, but I think he can't be much older than me. He came with Boots. Unlike me, he's quiet and deliberate in his devastation. His weapon of choice is a pipe he keeps strapped to his thigh. When he attacks, he looks lugubrious, almost as if he wants none of it, but has no choice but to kill and maim. It's in his nature. He hates Salmon. I look forward to the time he buries his pipe in the crazy Irishman's head.

I'm hungry and thirsty. I tackle the hunger by digging into food I lifted from the gas station market next door. They call the market "Quik Serve" so that's exactly what I did. I stuffed a couple bags of Hostess mini donuts into my coat pockets and headed out. The clerk saw what I was doing, but fear has a way of making one ignore theft. So it cost him a few bucks. It saved him his front teeth.

Between donuts, I greedily gulp water directly from the bathroom faucet. The water tastes metallic, and it smells, but it hasn't killed me yet.

The sun is high in the sky and hot, and my posse is finally rising from slumber. After a long night, everyone is moving slowly. Nobody speaks until we have completed our ritualistic punching and jostling as we push our way onto two picnic table benches to eat. Once situated in our places, we are ready to tackle whatever the day brings us. We raise our coffee mugs and yell.

Today we'll ride the bus north to stroll through the UC Berkeley campus. These privileged kids love to act as though they are anything but privileged. They saunter between classes with their hundred-dollar backpacks, their thousand-dollar iPhones, their two thousand-dollar iPads, all while carrying five-dollar lattes from Starbucks and wearing clothes that run another grand. These kids have it so tough. They think complaining of injustice and repeating soundbites from MSNBC makes them worldly. They have no idea. I like to go to Berkeley to remind them what it means to be unprivileged. They'll cower like the posers they are.

*   *   *

A small group has gathered next to the steps in the Sproul Plaza. They are listening to a masked individual I'll call

"Speaker" who is dressed all in black. He's too far from my posse for us to hear what he is preaching. It's funny. These kids are giving him a lot more attention than I suspect they provide to their teachers. As they listen, they also look to be consuming information being texted to them. They are responding in masse. Then, as one, they pull out facemasks from their pockets and backpacks. I doubt any of them belong here. They look too old, or too pimply, or too dirty, to fit in. They are actors and nobody seems to notice.

One by one, they secrete away their phones and move up the steps and into the modern, pristine student center. They are quiet as they move, not even acknowledging the individuals standing beside them. Before moving inside, they pull on the masks to hide their identities. One of them holds open the glass door as the rest run inside, disappearing from my view.

Motioning for my posse to follow, I take the steps two at a time to catch up with the kids. They look to be up to no good and I want to be part of it.

As my hand hits the door handle, Speaker stops me. "Where do you think you're going? You don't belong here."

"Fuck off." I nod to Boots, and Speaker backs away.

"You don't want to be here, and if you screw up my operation, I have friends who'll make sure you don't eat solid foods for months."

Although he doesn't frighten me, it's obvious we've already missed much of the fun. I hear the crashing of glass and the blare of microphone feedback that is quieted by more crashing, some yelling, and the then silence.

Speaker smiles at me. "Go on in and enjoy the fun. By the way, I'm called Ten."

"Who the fuck cares? My guys will show you some real fun. At least it'll be fun for me. After the fun, I'm going to let that crazy ass bastard..." I nod to Salmon. "...chop off your nose."

Speaker never flinches. "If you want a battle, I'm more than—" He stops mid-sentence and walks south, down the steps to the plaza.

I motion to my posse to follow him. He's moving quickly, so we break into a trot to keep up. I can hear Boots breathing hard before we even get across the courtyard. His puffing disappears behind me as I turn down a tree-lined walking path in pursuit of Speaker. The walkway exits the campus and deposits me back into the land of real people. I know Boots has given up. His tonnage serves him well in beating up folks, but it is a huge liability when we chase prey.

The walkway is empty save for shadows and a couple of kids who look as though they might be interested in school. They appear out of place. Speaker is gone. It's as if he's been absorbed into the ugly stores lining the street. I motion for B and Salmon to return to get Boots. I'll continue my hunt for Speaker and meet up with them at the student center in a half hour or so.

As soon as I'm alone, two huge hands grab my shoulders from behind and throw me into an empty doorway. "Why are you following me?" Speaker stares into my face. He is not alone. Several of his buddies have me surrounded. Some I recognize as the fake students from his little speech in the plaza.

He hits me in the face with the back of his hand, once, then twice. I spit blood. "I'm not following you," I lie. I look at his entourage, his buddies, his warriors. They are quiet, waiting for word from Ten to fuck me up. Turning my eyes back to Ten, I accuse him, "You set me up."

"You set yourself up. Who are you and what are you doing here?"

This is not going to go well. I'm outmanned and Ten looks as though he has hurt people before. His hands release their hold on me. Now they are made into fists. I begin evaluating where he will hit me so I can prepare to defend myself. He brings his knee upward into my groin. I wasn't expecting that and I fall to the ground. He lets me lie there a while, holding my manhood, gasping in air until the pain subsides. He kneels next to me and brings his face down to mine. I smell his breath, the stench of stale cigarettes.

"You stupid fuck. From now on you will address me as Ten. It is not my name, but it is what I am called, and what you will call me. I take that back. In your case, you will call me 'Ten, sir.' Do we understand each other?"

I have no idea what he means by 'do we understand each other?' I don't understand this guy at all. I have no idea what he wants from me.

"DO WE UNDERSTAND EACH OTHER?" He pushes me over on to my face and kneels on my hand. "Let me try this again. You will refer to me as Ten, sir. Is that plain enough?" He pushed harder on my hand until I growl with pain.

Well, maybe it wasn't much of a growl because Ten's friends start laughing. Ten smiles and again brings his face close to mine. "So, what the fuck is my name?"

"Ten."

"Ten, what?" He pushed harder on my hand.

"Ten, sir!"

He lifts his knee from my hand and stands. "Get up." He reaches his hand toward me to help me up from the concrete. "You'll never know my name or the names of any of these fine gentlemen." He pauses to look at his partners. "And you don't want to know."

That was my first meeting with Ten.

CHAPTER 2: ReAlly?

Boots, B, and Salmon are sitting at a concrete table in the plaza when I return from my impromptu meeting with the man I now know only as Ten. "Cute. Geez, I hope I'm not interrupting your little study group. You guys look just darling." They don't look up at my sarcasm. They don't look darling at all, but then again, they don't look very fearsome sitting quietly among the quiet, self-isolated students playing with their iPhones.

"Time to raise some hell. How about it, boys?"

Boots raises his eyes to me and nods to the doors entering the student center. "Maybe later, Tau. They got campus police all over the place. I think that guy you had us following and his cronies beat us to the fun. Sounds like they broke into a "Future Business Leaders of America" lecture and pretty much tore the shit out of the place."

"Well, time for us to head inside anyway. Let's see what happened." I'm already on my way to the doors, and I know my posse will follow. The campus police step aside to let us pass; what a bunch of pussies. As soon as we step into the hall, the damage becomes apparent. What was once a door and conference room wall made of tempered glass now litters the floor. A couple TV news crews, one local and one national, are already on sight filming the damage. I see a gray-haired man sitting inside what's left of the room getting some type of physical attention. Though the old man is covered in blood,

I don't think he's badly injured. Even superficial head wounds bleed like hell. Having caused plenty of them, I'm kind of an expert.

We stand back and listen as the on-sight local newscaster does his duty.

"…interrupting what is considered by some to be a conservative diatribe against those less fortunate. The group taking credit for breaking up the biased talk is the national Reform All organization. We know them as ReAl, and they have stated their intent to stand against any campus lectures or talks that do not first get their endorsement.

"The targeted speaker is a local business leader and long-term advocate for the university. ReAl asserts his purpose is to generate a cancerous environment on campus, separating the haves from the have nots and fomenting discontent.

"I'm still waiting for comments from school officials, but it is disheartening to see they failed to provide protection for a local supporter who was invited to present to undergraduate and graduate business students. I'll be back next hour for an interview with the speaker who was attacked…"

I have to give Ten credit. His guys did wonderfully in creating chaos. I'm jealous. I would never have thought to break into a meeting like this. We've limited our fun to bullying individuals. This was so brazen, so confrontational. I loved it.

Beyond the conference room, the second TV reporter is busy interviewing students. I assume they were either attending the lecture when hell broke loose, or they were outside and heard the commotion. I've seen this guy on TV before, but I don't recall his name. I might be smart as hell, but I suck with names. Slipping around the cameraman, I walk just beyond where the interview is taking place, trying to get into the picture. It'll be a blast to see myself on TV tonight.

Finally, giving up on getting in the camera's picture, I stop to listen.

"Let's try that again." Then, looking at the young female student he's interviewing, the reporter says, "I need you to be a little more concerned. You know, like you're afraid. Otherwise, this just won't play well for our reporting. You get my meaning?"

The girl nods and smiles. "Sure, I can do that, but can I make a comment about why I think the students stopped the talk?"

"Why not? Keep the camera rolling. Why do you think the students stopped the lecture?"

"Well, it's obvious, isn't it? It's because anything coming from this group is racist and classist."

"You mean, coming from 'Future Business Leaders of America,' right?"

"That's right. They had to be stopped before they could infect us with their ideas."

"So what was the subject of the talk?"

"How would I know? I wasn't there, but I'm sure it was divisive and promoted old capitalistic ideas that just don't make sense anymore."

"Why is that?"

"Because they don't."

"Cut the camera, Bob. I think we have enough to go on here. Let's see if we can get to the University President for some comment."

Bob lowers his camera. "You want to see if we can catch someone who was actually attending the talk?" He motions to the conference room.

"Not now. The network isn't going to be very interested in their perspectives. They're just going to bitch about being targeted again. It's what they always complain about." He pauses and walks toward the room and the gray-haired man dripping in blood. "Maybe just a few minutes won't kill our timetable. This might be interesting even if it doesn't make it to air."

I can't help laughing as I stare at the girl who'd apparently just screwed up her shot at fame. She looks back at me and winks. "You think this is funny, big man? They will televise the first answer. The rest doesn't matter. Ten's got it all planned out."

I'm speechless as she stands up and is absorbed into a throng of students. It's obvious Ten's gang is a hell of a lot more organized than my posse, and they're interested in more than just their little act today. I find myself wanting to be a part of whatever they are doing.

Boots taps me on the shoulder. "Let's get out of here. I'm feeling way out of place. Like I'm waiting to get arrested or something."

Behind him, I see B nodding in agreement. Salmon is standing off to the side, oblivious to us. I follow his eyes to where the coed disappeared into the crowd after her interview.

"Salmon, what's up?"

"Tau, that girl just ran out the door and is walking arm-in-arm with that fuck you had us following. I think she knows the damn guy. What you think's going on?"

"Let's find out." I head to the door with my entourage in tow.

Moving quickly, Ten and the girl exit the plaza down a path that passes through half a block of trees before leading off campus to a city street filled with traffic. Ten is talking on his phone as he walks, but we're too far away to hear his conversation. As soon as they step onto the sidewalk paralleling the street, they are met by a white van. The van, though not new, isn't old enough to look out of place in Berkeley. It pulls up to the curb, the side door with its darkened windows sliding open before it comes to a complete stop. Ten and the supposed coed slip inside without a beat and close the door. The van accelerates from the curb within seconds of arriving. I'm shocked at how quickly and easily Ten escaped us.

We turn to head back to campus as a second white van pulls to the curb and honks its horn.

We freeze, waiting for someone to exit the van. Nothing happens. Finally, the driver's window lowers. "You waiting for some special invitation? Get the fuck in and don't say anything." The window closes as quietly as it opened. The van also has darkened windows, shaded to a point we can't see inside the vehicle.

Salmon smiles, runs up to the side door and slides it open. "Gentlemen, your carriage awaits." He smiles again and hops into a back seat without waiting for us. He's crazy. He hasn't any idea who this guy is. Stupidly, we follow without saying anything. B goes in first, sliding next to Salmon. I'm next. Boots crawls in last. The van literally sinks to the side under his weight.

Inside, I can see the driver is not alone. Once Boots closes the door, a second individual in the passenger seat turns halfway around to us. He looks past me, speaking to Salmon. "What part of 'don't say anything' didn't you get?" He waits for an answer. The van doesn't move. It's obvious we're not going anywhere until the prick in the passenger seat has made his point.

I can see Salmon is stunned. I can't recall ever seeing Salmon speechless. It's precious to behold, but it pisses me off, too. "He can speak if he wants. It's my posse and my rules. You don't like it? Then let us out and go screw yourself."

The man in the passenger seat pulls up his hand in a fist and extends the index figure and thumb, pretending his hand is a gun. "Pop" at me and "Pop" at Salmon. "This time you'll get away with your mouth, but not again." He turns around, facing forward. "Let's get out of here."

The van lurches forward as the driver steers the van from the curb and accelerates into traffic. Like good little kids, we remain silent for the rest of the trip.

*   *   *

After a couple hours of stop and go traffic stuffed next to Boots, I'm hot and need to take a leak. The inside of the van reeks of body odor. I suspect Boots is the source. He's dripping with sweat, and I see the dirt lining the little rivulets as they course down his face, disappearing into his beard. We should stop, but I don't want to push it with the driver. I may have gotten away with acting tough when we climbed in, but I don't want to try it again. Although the driver and his co-pilot are not large men, for some reason they intimidate me. I can't show fear to my posse. I close my eyes in hope I might be able to sleep through the rest of the trip.

The van skids to a stop. My eyes snap wide open just as the side door is wrenched agape from outside. Bright light and heat rushes in. It takes a moment for me to recall where I am and for my eyes to adjust to the bright sunlight. How long was I asleep? I have no idea.

"Get out," is all he says.

Slowly, we exit the can on wheels in the opposite order we had piled in. I'm stiff from being squeezed between Boots' huge girth and the hard, steel sidewall. The van's bench seat would normally be wide enough to accommodate any two adults and a child, but Boots is as wide as any two average men, so I'm happy to get out to stretch. Boots is, too, but he has an ill-looking pallor to his face. The heat has gotten the better of him. B and Salmon look fine, though concerned. If I were as smart as I think I am, I guess I should be concerned, too.

"Welcome to your new home." Ten held out his hand, gesturing to a small older home situated next to a small public park of some type. Beyond the house, I see a couple of fast-food joints and a grocery store. Behind us is an image that could have been pulled from almost any small downtown USA. It is quaint, if not beautiful.

"We have this place and the one next door. You will be quiet and respectful when you are here. One fuck up and you're gone. If you are gone, you're dead. We can't afford to be noticed. Here we can be invisible."

CHAPTER 3: Winnowing the Herd

The sun is just beginning to slip below the hills to the west of us. It must be past eight in the evening, but it remains unbearably hot as we sit to eat. At least the wind has started to subside somewhat. It's been blowing all afternoon, making this little household miserable. The hot breeze has been flowing in through open windows where we quietly sit. Ten has refused to close the window, saying the house doesn't have any air conditioning, so closing off the airflow would just make the heat worse. I don't believe it could be much worse. It must be approaching a hundred degrees as we try to enjoy a late dinner.

My arms are clammy with perspiration that fails to cool me. My hair hangs in strings while sweat runs down my forehead and into my eyes. It burns. I can't wait for the coolness of night to bring some relief. B and Salmon both look as miserable as me. Boots has laid his head on his forearms and looks to be asleep. I thought he might be dead, but his shoulders rise and fall with each breath.

"Where are we?" I quietly ask Ten. I feel as though talking loud just takes too much energy. My voice is barely a whisper.

Ten appears unfazed by the sweltering heat. "Never mind for now. You'll know soon enough."

"Look, can we get out of here to get some relief from this heat?"

"Tomorrow. We'll be evaluating you tomorrow in the house next door to see how well you'll fit in with us. That place has air, so even though the evaluations are tough, you're going to be thankful. *Comprendé?*"

"Hell, yes. Why don't we move over there now?"

"Because you don't get relief until I say so."

I push the scrambled eggs and potatoes around on my plate with my fork. It looks like it should taste okay, but the heat has killed my appetite. None of my posse looks very interested in eating, either. I pull open my large plastic bottle of water (we each have one), but instead of drinking, I pour it onto my head before taking a swallow. It tastes like shit, but I know I need some fluids. I'm beginning to feel sick from the heat. B takes my lead and brings his bottle to his lips to drink. He empties his bottle without pausing to breathe.

I nudge Boots. "Dude, wake up and drink some water. You'll feel better."

"Forget him. He doesn't have a chance of making our team," Ten says.

"So what the fuck does that mean?"

"It means, I'm sending him back home tonight. Don't worry, he'll be glad to get out of here."

"He's my right hand. Why can't he make it?"

"Too old, too big. Can you imagine him being able to blend in with the crowd you saw today on the campus? No fucking way. Remember, we're invisible."

"So why bring him here in the first place?"

"To get you."

I stare in disbelief. "You don't know anything about me."

"Tau, we've been watching you through your smartphone for months. I know who you've rolled. I know where you've been sleeping. Hell, I've even listened into your conversations with the rest of your fucks." His voice was escalating in volume. It was obvious he didn't care if the rest of my posse heard what he was saying.

"You two are still in the running…" He was now almost yelling at B and Salmon. "…but you got a lot to prove tomorrow."

Salmon could not restrain himself. "Maybe I don't give a shit about making your little team. I'll bet Tau doesn't either. Do you, Tau?" He waited for me to say something. "Tau? You don't really want to let this fuck push us around. Do you?"

All I could muster was a "Shut the fuck up, Salmon." I never took my eyes off Ten. "He has a good point. Why should I or any of us want to join your team?"

"Because we are the future. We are the muscle behind a movement in this country that will change everything. I'm going to be a general and you're going to want to be on my side. I'll be the police, the judge, the jury. Anyone who's not with me runs the risk of me stepping on them. What you saw today is just the start.

"We are ReAl, Reform All, and by that, we mean all. Kind of catchy, huh? Fucking kids eat it up because "reform" sounds cool to them. Well, fuck them, too, and their rich parents. When we're done, the downtrodden will rule."

I don't know what to say. Spittle is flying from Ten's mouth as he completes his tirade. I'm now more afraid than intimidated. If I'm not with him, I'm probably a target. I will be with him. I could relish the power, too.

"Salmon, B, we are going to enjoy this." I hope my face doesn't give away my fear. I'm convincing though because I believe this really is going to be fun. A little voice inside me tells me we're getting the means to ramp our terror-making to a whole new level.

*   *   *

For the next half hour or so, the van is bumped and tossed as it rolls down the dirt road. Boots can barely make out the shadows of small scrub oaks and wild berry bushes in the moonlight. He remains silent the entire trip, preoccupied with contemplating what he'll do next. He's spent months with Tau and B. They are like brothers to him. Even Salmon had begun to grow on him. Now it's all gone. He's being returned home alone. And just because he's big and a little older than the rest. It isn't fair.

"Hey, when are we getting off this piece of shit road and back to the highway?" he barks at the driver he knows only as Ace.

Ace glares back at Boots in the rearview mirror. "Look, big man, the boss wants to make sure we aren't followed, and that you don't know how to find us again. This is for your own good … and the good of the movement." He leans over to his co-pilot. "And this dude doesn't get why he doesn't fit in."

"This is bullshit. Get me to a gas station and let me out. I don't have a fucking clue where we are already. I'll find my own way home."

Ace slows to a stop and pushes the parking brake to the floor. Turning back to face Boots, he says, "Even better, just get the fuck out here." Pulling a pistol from the console beside him, he points at Boots' forehead and fires. Boots never had a chance to release his seat belt. His head flies back and then recoils to a stop with his chin against his chest. A small, red dimple just above his nose leaks red. The back of his head is gone.

"Shit, Ace, why'd you do that. This is going to take forever to clean," says the co-pilot.

"Yep, just push the beast out for the coyotes. Consider it my gift to the environment. We'll hose out the back and leave the windows open to dry once we get back to the compound."

"Ten is going to be really pissed. We were supposed to dump him in the estuary."

"Then fucking don't tell him."

"But we're supposed to dump him in the estuary."

"He doesn't give a shit where we dump him as long as he can't be linked back to us. There's no fucking way we're going to be able to drag his carcass through the muck far enough to get him to the water. If you want to try, go for it, but I'm not."

"Okay, okay, let's just dump him fast, and then we need to clean up the van."

Ace gets out and slides open the side door while his co-pilot slips between the two front seats to position himself on the other side of the big man to help push him from the van. While he pushes, Ace grabs two handfuls of shirt and pulls. Slowly, the mountain of a man begins to slide to the side, picking up momentum until his upper body rolls off the seat, slamming against the door sill before continuing its fall to the ground. Boots' legs are stranded in the doorway while his head and shoulders are crushed into the hard, dusty dirt of the roadway.

Ace tugs at Boots' pantlegs to pull him from the doorway to no avail. "Screw this." He climbs back in the driver's seat. Putting the truck into gear, he moves forward, dragging Boots until the friction of the dirt and rocks pulls him from the door onto the ground.

Both men climb out of the van to roll the body from the rarely traveled dirt road. The co-pilot is first to speak.

"You think we need to hide him?"

Ace laughs. "No way. He's too fucking big to hide. Just leave him. We've got more important work to do."

*   *   *

Boots left our compound hours ago with Ace and Arrow. I hated to see him leave, but I get it. He can't go anywhere without being noticed. It's why he was so important to me. He made people afraid just to see him. But in my new world, we need people who can meld into the crowd. They must be able to disappear. Boots is anything but invisible. The other challenge with Boots is that if he hits you, you might die. Ten is adamant we are not to kill, yet. The whole idea is to create fear: push some folks around, you know, be disruptive, and then move on. We want to incite the mob to attack for us. "Can't arrest a whole mob," he said.

"So, I guess, the Re in ReAl might also mean Revolt." Ten smiles when I suggest that.

Now Ten has been closed up in the next room with B and Salmon for the past half hour or so. I have no idea what they are discussing, but I'm beginning to get concerned. Maybe I'm just being paranoid, the dope gets me like that, but then again, maybe Ten doesn't think I'll fit in either and I'm being excluded from his plans. I slide my chair closer to the door in hopes I'll pick up some of what's being said. The rest of Ten's team ignores me.

Although the voices are muffled, I think I hear Ten asking, no, telling Salmon to shut up. That dude never could get control of his mouth. I don't know what drives the guy, but he always has a comeback. He makes you want to smack him upside the head. Salmon is yelling now, something about he'll talk whenever the fuck he wants to. He's going on and on now. Ten is quiet. B is quiet. It's just Salmon yelling and banging on a table or something. Then there's silence.

"So, Salmon, you done now?"

"I guess so."

"Then I think it best if you get some rest. I'll have a couple of my team show you where you can bunk down next door."

The door opens and Ten looks completely unperturbed, happy even. Nodding to a guy sitting on the floor to my right, who I know only as Rock, and then to me, he says, "You two take Salmon next door and find him a place to sleep."

Salmon slips out the door, purposely bumping into Ten on the way out. His face is covered in a grin. I suspect he thinks he's established his place with Ten. Somehow, I think he's wrong. He grabs his jacket from a chair and heads to the front door.

"Not that way." Rock's voice stops Salmon instantly. "We have a gate in the back to connect the two places. We stay away from the front. We don't like to give neighbors a chance to see us if it can be avoided. Make sense?"

"Perfectly." Salmon spins around and pushes by me and Rock to the house's sliding glass door that empties into the back yard.

Rock is smiling as he follows Salmon into the darkness. "So, Salmon … that's your name, right?"

"Yeah, you know it is."

"That's fucked-up. What are you, a fish or something?" Rock stops. "So, fish-boy, stop a minute. You get to sleep out here."

"Go fuck yourself. I ain't sleepin' in no grass."

"Wanna bet?" In one motion Rock pulls a small handgun from under his shirt. Its barrel length is accentuated by a silencer. There is a quiet pop. I swear there is hardly any noise, and blue smoke oozes from the tip. Salmon stops talking and falls to his knees, teeters a bit, and then falls onto his face in the grass. "Tau, you owe me one for getting rid of that punk."

"Why?"

"He didn't fit in."

I think of Boots. "Is that what happens when you don't 'fit in?'"

He turns to face me. I can barely make out his smile in the dim light that escapes through the windows. This is exactly what happens.

I know then my friend Boots is dead. "What about B? What about me?"

"You both made the grade. You're okay."

"Who decides?"

"Ten, I guess … and his boss. But Ten says you're part of the team now."

"Well, hallelujah, I'm saved. God must be watching over me."

"God's got nothing to do with it. Trust me." Rock turns to walk back inside the house, leaving me with Salmon. "I'll be back with some plastic to wrap around him. We have to dump him before it gets light."

The thought of murder has never bothered me until now. It just became very personal because I know it can happen to me, too. I'm no longer in control.

CHAPTER 4: Invisible

I'm sitting shotgun in the van for today's fun. B is riding in a second van that will serve as backup. Hopefully, the second van won't be required, but it and its occupants, B and Ace, will be waiting at the other end of campus in case we need to make a run from the police after we start our violence.

Ten, the young woman I saw interviewed at the campus named Lulu, Arrow, Rock, and I are going on a destroy mission to break up another speech by the same businessman, Aldus Simmons. Aldus Simmons is to give a talk on the importance of capitalistic ideals for our inner cities' prosperity, and ReAl is going to ruin it. Ten has told us how this man is dangerous, how his message contradicts everything we stand for, how his words step on free speech. We cannot allow him to spew his evil. We will stop him and make anyone following him afraid to speak up again.

I'm shaking with excitement as my feet hit the pavement. I can't wait to try out the rules of engagement Ten has been drumming into me for the past several days.

The first rule was simple, hit low. Never strike above the chest. Hitting high is too easy to see; plus, people bleed when you hit them in the head. The blood brings sympathy from onlookers and forces police to respond. Whereas kicking someone in the legs or pushing someone with your chest rarely gets caught on camera, and it typically ends up eliciting a violent response from those you push or kick. The response almost always gets caught on camera. If we do our job right, we get away and the assailed looks like the bad guy.

The second rule is to yell loudly. Get into the face of those we hate. They will almost always back down. If they don't back down, incent them to hit you. It might hurt, but we'll catch it on camera.

Rule three: ALWAYS video. We can always edit once we get home. But video streaming the assailed striking back and making it look as though they are the assailant is precious. Even if you end up with a broken nose, it's worth it.

The fourth rule is simple. Attack the defenseless. Make them fearful always. Bullying worked as a kid. It works as an adult. The lesson—people always speak tougher than they are. A successful bully understands that. A little push and they shrink away.

The last rule is the most important. Name calling is your best weapon. Calling a person fascist or racist is more effective than any physical harm. It doesn't matter if it's true, it'll still work. Ten stressed that most folks don't even know the definition of fascist, but they do know it's bad. Therefore, calling someone a fascist proves they are bad.

When I asked Ten if this Aldus character was a racist or a fascist, he looked at me incredulously before he answered. "What part don't you get? It doesn't matter."

So, we are back here at Berkeley to crash a lecture. We are here to stop free speech under the guise of protecting free speech. We are here to hurt people. I'm okay with this.

By the time I start for the student center, I'm alone. My team members have already split up and made their way to their assignments. Lulu is screaming at a campus police officer that he is part of the fascist machine that raped her time and time again. Students have stopped to watch. She's good.

The poor officer doesn't stand a chance. He is quickly surrounded by gen-Z'ers happy to have some reason to skip class. They are beginning to yell and throw papers and coffee cups (some of them full) at the cop. I see Rock screaming in the background, trying to amp up the crowd.

Behind them, Ten and Arrow are making their way up the steps to the student center to once again crash Aldus' talk. I jog to catch up. It's my job to rally kids just outside the door of the lecture hall. Once I have a crowd, I'm to push open the door and let the sheeple pour into the hall. Ten and Rock will be part of the throng and are armed with cups of hot coffee to throw at the unsuspecting speaker. My next job will be to ensure videos are taken of the response. Nothing like scalding coffee to create animated and aggressive actions. It'll look great on the news tonight. Aldus and his ilk will look like crazed individuals threatening those just exercising their free speech rights.

Once inside, I realize I have no idea how to get these kids going. I start to yell and call the man inside names, but I soon realize apathy is as prevalent on the American campus as is activism. I'm getting nothing but snickers and eye-rolling as the kids move through the hallway. I feel as if I'm nothing more than comic relief to these humanoids, until … Ten slips up beside me and calls me a fucking faggot. He yells at me again and looks to the kids in the hallway. They stand there frozen. His eyes scan across them and he yells, "You faggots and queers are not welcome here! Not now, not never!" He stops, turns, and disappears inside the room. It was magnificent.

I turn to the crowd that has instantaneously assembled. Rock, who is in the back, yells, "Let me in. I'll show that racist hater who's not welcome here."

I push open the door and a crush of twenty-something year-old people flow in. People are yelling at the speaker.

Dozens of iPhones extend into the air, recording the events as the panel speakers attempt to escape through a side door. A cup of coffee hits the guest speaker. A chair flies, hitting a student who'd also been on the panel. She is down and bleeding. There are no police to be found. The crash is on.

I'm grabbed by the arm. "Gotta go." It's Ten. He's happy.

I don't want to leave. The violence is glorious. I stand gaping at the crowd for too long. A fist slams into my face and I spit blood. "Gotta go, now."

I follow Ten out. Rock is already out of the facility and moving across the plaza. I don't see Lulu or Arrow, but I suspect they're waiting for us at the van. We created chaos and vanished before anyone knew who we were. We are powerful. We are magic. We are invisible.

*   *   *

Dinner is quiet. Today's excitement has wiped us out. All I want to do is finish my burger and fries and hit the hay for the evening. Ten hands out dinner, compliments of the local burger joint on the corner. It's amazing what a little shop will do to avoid trouble. Along with our individually bagged meals, Ten hands each of us a sealed envelope. I start to tear the envelope open, but I'm stopped by Ten's hand grabbing back the gift.

"That's your pay for today. Each of us gets some, but I decide each of your shares. You can't tell anyone your share if you want to stay here. If anyone finds out how much you got, I'll know you don't belong. You get my drift?"

I did. I folded the envelope and put it in my pocket.

I watch Ten as he passes through the rest of the team, handing out his presents like a skinny, hard Santa Claus. He makes a point to address each individual and thank them for their contribution to today's success. His team fears him, but I also think they love him. I can see why. He's giving them something to live for, something to be a part of, something for which to be thankful. It doesn't matter if what they did was right or wrong. They did it because he asked them to do it.

Ace was last in line for tonight's meal and pay-out. "Ace, you want to join me outside to eat?" Ten asks.

Ace looks into Ten's eyes and waits a bit before answering, then almost reluctantly agrees and follows his leader into the back yard. Through the glass, I can see the discussion is not a pleasant one and ends with Ace opening his envelope. Although I can't see the contents, it's obvious from Ace's face that he's displeased. It's the look of a kid opening a present, hoping for a toy and instead getting socks. I guess it's a matter of perspective. I never got any presents, so socks would have been wonderful for me, but not for Ace. They eat their meals sitting facing each other without muttering another word. After they finish their burgers, Ten comes back inside. Ace makes for one of the vans.

Within minutes, I see the beam of headlights cut across our front lawn and through our windows as Ace leaves on an assignment.

Ten flips the light switch off and on again in the small living room. He has our attention. "Our friend, Ace, has forgotten that when I ask him to do something, I mean it. He has forgotten how serious I am, and he has now gone to make amends, fixing what he fucked up. I'm not sure if we'll see him back this evening. If he's not here by morning, Arrow, you'll join him in doing what he and you should have done a week ago. Do you understand?"

Arrow remains silent. I get the feeling he doesn't like Ace, but he fears Ten. I have no idea what they did, but I know I never want to get on the bad side of the boss.

Ten flips the lights out again and exits through the back door, leaving the rest of the team in the dark. A faceless voice breaks the silence. "I guess this means nighty-night."

The comment is followed by whispers as we break up to go to our respective rooms. B and I don't need to move far. Since we are the newest members of this gang, we get to sleep on the floor of this room with just a thin blanket. It's hard and uncomfortable, but it's good to have some time with the only remaining family member from my posse.

After everyone has left our sleeping quarters, I whisper into the dark, "So what was that all about ... with Ace?"

"Dude, how would I know?"

"You were with him all day in the van. Didn't he say anything?"

"Tau, let it go, man. It don't matter no more."

"Fuck that! What gives?"

"Ace killed Boots because that Ten-fuck told him to, and he just dumped him somewhere he wasn't supposed to. Arrow was with him when he did it. These dudes are fucking crazy. I think Ace just got a second chance to hide Boots the way he was supposed to. If he screws this up, maybe he ends up like Boots. I hope so." Then there was quiet. "Boots was my brother, man."

I pull my blanket up around my chin, roll onto my side and try to sleep. Impossible. I'm too afraid to even close my eyes. I listen for footfall noise in hopes it'll provide me and B some heads-up when one of Ten's fuckups decides we need to be eliminated. How can Ten be trusted?

Giving up on the sleep, I push myself up from the floor and walk outside into the cool night air. After the dry heat of the day, the relative cool and humidity are refreshing. I unzip my pants to take a piss in the backyard.

As I zip up, Ten calmly says to me, "I killed Boots. Just thought you should know."

I don't know what he wants me to say. I remain quiet, wanting him to continue. I can't grasp why it was important to end my friend's life. He understood why he didn't fit in, and he would have been fine with that. And he certainly would never squeal on us, but I guess Ten didn't know Boots the way B and I did.

"Look, we never leave loose ends. Never have, never will. I answer to a boss just like you guys. If I fuck up, I die. No second chances. I give you guys second chances all the time."

I'm lost in where he is going with this.

"But that all stops tomorrow. Tomorrow, we start anew. We are getting ranks to reflect our positions of authority and to make it clear who the boss is."

"What the fuck, Ten. I'm not in the military. Why would I need a fucking rank?"

"That's the point. You, me, we are in the military, just not in the same sense as what we are used to. Think of us as CIA. We are secret. We work in the shadows. We are at war.

"Tomorrow, I become Captain Ten. You'll be my Lieutenant. The rest of these fucks will be corporals."

"What about B?"

"What about him?"

"He's not a fucking corporal."

"You're right. I don't have a clue what his rank is. He's going south to LA tomorrow morning." He pauses. "Don't worry, he's not being eliminated like Boots or Salmon. The 'Syndicate' has special plans for him."

"What the fuck's the syndicate?"

"It's not what; it's who. They pull all the strings. The ones who pay our bills. They put those dollars in your pocket earlier this evening. They are your reason for living ... but I have never even seen them. Maybe if I get to the rank of general?" He laughs. I hear the hiss of a butane torch lighter and blue light illuminates Ten's face as he brings the flame to his face, lighting a joint. I've been longing for some dope and wait to see if he offers to share. He does.

CHAPTER 5: The ReAl Syndicate

It's already hot. The morning sun is beating against the window with a vengeance. I wish we had drapes to mute the light and the heat. I'm not ready to get up. I roll onto my back and then to my side to face B. My back screams as bone rubs against the hardwood floor. The floor won the battle last night. I can barely move.

B is gone.

Ten is sitting on the sofa, watching me. I have no idea how long he's been there. His face is stern, and he appears to be barely breathing. He's as still as the dead air in the room.

"Time to get up and say hello to the real meaning in your life." He rocks forward to his legs and stands. He walks out of the room to the back patio. I feel that I'm supposed to follow him, so I do. I'm too frightened not to.

We are still alone on the patio. Ten is sitting at a PC that is set up on a splintery picnic table. An old, faded umbrella has been opened to provide some protection from the sun. Even with the shade, the screen is still difficult to see. I can barely make out an individual shielded in darkness on the screen. I have no idea where this individual is located.

Without facing me, Ten answers a question I have not asked. "This is our future. Do not say anything unless he asks you directly. Your opinions are not solicited."

"Why am I here, then?"

Ten ignores me and taps the PC's mouse.

"Captain, good to see you. I've heard you were successful in your mission."

"That is true, sir."

"Is that Tau behind you?"

"It is"

"Tau, welcome to ReAl. You are part of our new generation and our army. Welcome. I am your General. We are responsible for knocking our enemies from their feet. We ensure they never get a fortified position from which to fight back. We emerge from the shadows to attack and then fade into the background before society's nemesis even knows we exist."

"Thanks," I answer.

Ten turns his head to me and shakes his head just slightly, as if to remind me to be silent.

"Ah, yes, well, 'thanks' is not what I'm looking for. I'm only concerned with results. So, Tau, what did you learn from yesterday's mission?"

I pause, having no idea what he is asking. I'm sure I am being castigated, but for what? Then it hits me. I failed at getting the students riled. Ten bailed me out by assailing not the strong, but the weak with a series of invectives. He got the crowd engaged by thinking they were doing right.

"I learned people can be led around by the nose if they think they are defending the helpless, if they think they are righteous. I didn't get it until Captain Ten showed me the way."

"Good. Maybe you are smart enough to be with us. Do not let me or the movement down again."

"Sir? What is the movement?"

"You mean Reform All?"

"Yeah."

"This is not an appropriate place or means to discuss this. Did not your captain make that perfectly clear? I will not be questioned. Ever.

"Captain, make sure Lieutenant Tau understands his place, would you? Now for the real reason we are on this call…"

The general informs us that our physical connections will be dissolving. We need to move out of our house. We are to be funded by ReAl's parent organization, but the name of that entity is kept secret. Each of us will be paid through deposits in personal digital wallets, and one has already been set up for me. If I need the cash, I am to use an ATM that handles contactless transactions with my new smart phone. The pay will be from a meaningless, faceless, non-profit organization.

The pay is good, almost too good, until he outlines what we need to be prepared to do for the money. We will each receive communications via smart phone as to our missions. We need to act independently and instantly to these orders. Any failure will result in separation from ReAl. I hear 'Separation,' but I think it really means 'Elimination.'

After the general's introduction, I'm ordered to pick up my new smart phone from the kitchen counter (it's already marked with my name and password) and to pack up. I'm to leave the nest, so to speak, and find a place to stay, somewhere that will still enable me to respond in less than two hours to any mission within a radius of fifty miles of Berkeley, day or night. The missions will be like those we accomplished yesterday, but no longer will I have the luxury of having a support team, at least as far as I know. In any case, I'll have no idea who is from ReAl, and who are just protestors caught up in the fever of a cause, regardless of what that cause might be. I'm informed there will be ReAl captains at each of the missions, evaluating performance, but I'll never know who they are. It's clear that if I fail, I can't say anything about the organization or the Syndicate or I'll be separated. The last item is easy because I really don't know anything about ReAl. I can do this.

Finding a place to stay is my problem, but the "Syndicate" will make sure I have sufficient enough money deposited into my account for some type of modest rent. I have no idea what that means, but I'll find some place as cheap as possible with the money I received from yesterday's attack. Each mission will come with a bonus. I'm excited at the prospect of getting paid for violence.

I'm dismissed with a wave of the general's hand, so I step back into the house to gather my things. As I pack, I can see Ten now has Lulu out on the patio. I suspect she's hearing all the same directions.

When complete, she, too, is dismissed and the next pawn is summoned. I use the term pawn because I have a feeling that is just what we are. We are to act when asked to act. Failure to get the job done correctly means we will be removed from the chess board. We are of little value beyond our mission. I can live with that. I don't want responsibility, per se. Sure, I loved pointing my posse in a direction and watching them terrorize the innocent, but I hated planning for anything beyond the present. Our only organized task was exercising a little protection racket to scare up food money. Everything else we just stole from our victims.

These guys are serious planners. Not only do they seem to have a long-range plan (that I am unaware of), but they also have the resources to pull it off. The envelope full of twenties in my pocket and the new iPhone on the counter are proof. I'm a part of something big.

Lulu looks shocked when she enters the kitchen in search of her iPhone.

"You want to hitch a ride with me to find a place in the city?" I ask.

"No reason to. I take a plane to DC tonight. They have me going to DC with Ten, for Christ's sake. What can I do there? I've never lived outside of California. What did…?" Her voice trails off to silence. Tears run down her cheeks. "What if I fail?"

"It can't be so bad. You know how to rev up the crowd. You won't fail." I have no idea what I'm saying. To some extent, I'm just fooling myself into believing that none of us will fail. It's easier than having to confront what will happen if I don't make this work. I'm also jealous of her. Shit, even though I get a rank, she gets the honor of going to DC. Somehow that must be a good thing for her.

I'm heading back to my old stomping grounds in Oakland. I can't imagine anyone has taken over my place, and if they have, I think I can make them see the wisdom of giving the place back to me. It might not be the Ritz, but it's been home to me for the last several months, excluding the brief time I've been with ReAl. Plus, it gives me the opportunity to save some bucks while keeping me close enough to Berkeley to fulfill my missions.

I punch in the address to the Uber app that's already been loaded on my phone. It's enabled and already linked to a ReAl credit card. My ride will be here in minutes. I love this. I stuff my few clothes into a plastic grocery bag and go outside to wait on the front lawn for my Uber driver, just like I'm a normal Joe.

CHAPTER 6: Could I Care Less?

W hat the fuck? The iPhone alarm pierces the quiet of the night. There is a text message that demands I call in to conference in a half hour. It's only five in the morning; the sky is still dark. I pull up the message to confirm the time and conference call-in instructions, then roll off my old shitty mattress and head to the common bathroom down the hall. I need to take a leak and throw some cold water on my face to wake up. It's silly to use the adjective "cold" as if it were a choice. There is no choice of temperature here. The building has no functioning water heater, so the rust-colored liquid that comes out of our faucets ranges from cold to tepid, depending on the weather outside. Looking at my gray, sleep-wrinkled face, cold is exactly what I need.

Repulsed by my own smell, I jump into the shower for a frigid scrub before the call. It's doubtful I'll get the opportunity to shower once I get my assignment.

The purpose of my missions no longer interests me. I fulfill them without passion or understanding. They just pay the bills. My only joy exists in those brief moments of violence right before I need to escape into the crowd, my mission accomplished.

A few weeks ago, I made the mistake of questioning my new captain on the purpose of a mission. She responded that it was the same as always: to interrupt and disrupt, to create fear.

I didn't think she caught my question, so I clarified myself. "I get our objective, but why are we doing this? I mean, what is it that we're attempting to stop?"

From her face, I could tell I had stepped into some serious shit. On her phone, she made a couple keystrokes, then she was gone, or should I say, I was gone. She'd ejected me from the conference. When I attempted to dial back in, I got a message that I was blocked. This was not good.

Half an hour later, my phone rang for a video call and I'm given the opportunity to talk one on one with someone who chose to hide in the darkness. I call him the Dark Man. At first, I thought it stupid to make a video call and then not show his face, but as the call went on, the intimidating nature of the shadowy picture became ever more ominous. This man was playing with me.

He never introduced himself, but it was clear he had a level of power and authority that went beyond our normal rank structure. It was as if he played outside of ranks and could inflict damage on whomsoever he chose.

"Tau, your captain tells me you are having second thoughts about our mission. Is that so?"

Trying to steady my voice to sound brave, but failing, I answered, "It may have sounded that way, but it isn't what I meant. It's just—"

He cut me off. "So, tell me exactly what you did mean. And take your time so your meaning is not in any way misinterpreted by me. You would not want me to misunderstand your viewpoint."

"Ahh, yeah, I get your point. I just didn't know why we were going to make someone's dinner a nightmare. I mean, it isn't like they're giving a speech on something we don't agree with, right?"

"And what is it that we do not agree with?"

I'm struck dumb, having no idea how to respond … and the man just waits. Finally, I spurt out one of the slams we typically use against our enemies. "We don't agree with racism." And I stop, thinking I had made a good answer.

"So, if the people you are terrorizing at a restaurant are racists, is that not good?"

"Are they racist?"

The man explodes on me. "What do you care if they are racist? If we say interrupt their dinner, you interrupt. We say fuck them over, you fuck them over. If we say kill them, you kill them. Do you understand? I will not have you questioning our tactics. Are we clear?

"You have exactly forty-five minutes to be in place for your mission. You have wasted a lot of time with this foolishness. I suggest you get going now or this conversation is meaningless." My screen went black, and I was off to the races.

It was the last time I questioned my superiors on the assignments. I've become a tool only. What little humanity I may have had is gone. I now exist to damage and destroy anything I am pointed at. I do have to operate within some set rules, however. For example, if cameras are on, I must look as though I am just a peaceful demonstrator, invisible and indistinguishable. When the cameras are off, or I have my face covered, I can act according to my nature. I may be as violent as I desire. Sure, ReAl prefers that I not hit our targets above the shoulders—bloodied heads seem to create sympathy—but then again, if it creates fear, they can live with my tactics. They do dock my pay, though. I can live with that. I'm making more as their muscle than I ever made on my own. Plus, I have respect. On the calls with the captain, if I talk, the other participants listen. They address me as Lieutenant Tau. I am somebody now.

Shivering from the water and the cold of morning, I towel off with the tee-shirt I'd slept in. I squeeze the water into the sink and dry some more, then slip on my blue jeans. They are beginning to take on that brown/blackish look of dirt so I'll need to wash them in the shower when I get home. Hopefully, they'll be dry enough to wear the next day. I need to buy another pair as a spare.

Hustling back to my room, I'm in plenty of time to call into the conference and be one of the first callers. I've learned there are advantages to being one of the first on these calls. I can tell from the greetings who is doing well and who needs to step it up. I've stepped it up. I want to be Captain Tau soon. I do not want any more calls from the Dark Man unless it is to congratulate me.

"Welcome. Let's start." That was as much preamble as we ever got from the captain. Our target today is an enemy. This man has the audacity to question our validity as a voice of the people. For this, he and his followers must be punished.

"We know he's having breakfast with his wife at Rocio's in San Francisco this morning at 8:00 a.m. You can pull the address up on your phone on your own time. It's a photo-op. We think he's getting ready to ratchet up his run for the Senate. There'll be camera crews from a couple of TV stations. You will close the restaurant and keep the patrons holed up inside."

I ask, "You mean the guy and his wife?"

"I mean everyone. Nobody gets out of the place until you get a message stating 'free.' I want everyone in the place to understand why they are scared. I want them to hate the very man they now respect. They need to know that to be his supporter makes them a target. They'll run away from him in the future and ostracize him. They need to realize they could be next. This man and his message must wither and blow away like a dead leaf in autumn. Lieutenant Tau will be the ranking member on the outside. Each of you have assignments included in your text messages. We've only one hour to act. If any of you cannot make that time-window, respond now with a 'NO.' We can't afford to be surprised by any no shows." The captain waits a moment, then says, "Go," and our screens go blank.

As I go down the steps to the street level, I'm already inputting a location where the Uber driver is to pick me up. I'll need to sprint a couple of blocks to get to my rendezvous location as no intelligent driver would ever make a pickup in front of my building.

My ride is just pulling to the curb as I jog up to it and rap on the window. I can tell the nonplussed driver is not comfortable with me climbing into his vehicle. It might be the fact that I look dirty and disheveled, or that I'm sweating profusely from my two-block sprint, or that I look like someone escaping a crime scene. I hear the door-locks click and he rolls his window down maybe an inch, asking my name. After confirming my identity, he reluctantly unlocks the rear door and I climb in. He'll need to open his windows for some fresh air before his next ride. I'm all too aware of my own stink. Too bad for him he didn't notice before I sat on his freshly wiped seats. I really don't care, it's not my car. I just hope he doesn't rate me so low that other drivers avoid me. I'll need to give him a large tip for his trouble.

"I need to hurry. Any chance of getting to Rocio's in San Fran by eight?"

He looks at me in his rearview mirror. I can tell he's uncomfortable. He doesn't answer my question, but responds with a question, "You want some music or the news?"

"Neither." I close my eyes in hope of getting a little rest before it's show time. The car speeds from the curb.

*   *   *

I chuckle every time I see the crews from the news stations that are sent out to kiss the asses of the famous and the wannabes. They seem to be the same crews every time. Hell, even their clothes never change. I swear the reporter standing next to me—I think they call him Jamison—has worn the same sports coat and tie every time I've seen him, and that must be at least a dozen times. I can't believe they all fail to recognize me. It's as if they never really see what they report. They're just going through the motions.

There are two news crews milling about this morning, waiting for their opportunity to stick their microphones in the face of the future political hopeful, as if they're going to get a scoop on some ground-breaking story. So boring. Today, their luck is going to change, because I'm going to give them some excitement for their tired, humdrum lives.

Jamison can't possibly be completely oblivious to me, nor to the fact I've been handing out signs to the folks gathering in the street outside the restaurant. The funny thing: park a news van in the street and you're guaranteed to draw a crowd. Half of these folks are hoping to hear a few words from their potential candidate, while the rest are clueless and just want to get their faces on the nightly news. The clueless are my targets.

I doubt Jamison recalls that I've been a crowd instigator on several of his assignments. Or perhaps he does, but he chooses to not call me out, hoping I'll do it again. When I get the crowd going, he gets additional airtime in the morning, or even an occasional spot on the evening news.

Reporting accurately is not important to him. His only objective is his fleeting shot at fame. If we riot, his coverage gets infinitely more interesting, and he is one step closer to an opportunity as a news anchor somewhere. One thing is consistent with all these crews, they believe this job is a steppingstone to something better. Well, perhaps not for Jamison. Even though he doesn't know it, he is old. His opportunities for a cushy anchor job are long gone. Even if he had the looks at one time, he no longer does, and he certainly doesn't have the smarts. He begins some idle talk with his cameraman about where to set up for their shot, as if he cares. The cameraman's eyes roll about unfocused as Jamison prattles on and on.

The other news team is a surprise. The reporter is a fellow I've never seen before. The crew is not from San Francisco, but from LA. Interesting. Perhaps this fledging politician is a bigger deal than I thought. On this crew, the guy with the microphone has all the looks for TV. He is tall and athletic. I think he's young, but his dark hair has just a touch of gray around the temples, giving him a distinguished, wise look. In contrast, Jamison's hair looks to be a color not found in nature, but in a spray can.

The crew from LA has already set up and is waiting. They are all business, while I suspect I might need to help Jamison's crew know where to point their camera.

Jamison pats me on the shoulder. "So what's up with the signs?"

I have royally fucked up. My first rule … be invisible, and here I am being questioned by a news guy. Invisibility is impossible, so I turn my visibility into an asset. Ultimately, I know I need to attack the individual inside eating a peaceful breakfast, so I launch into my rant. "We are ReAl, and we are the people. Inside, hiding in this restaurant is an enemy of the people. His racist and fascist views cannot be allowed to stand." Turning to the crowd, I make a fist with my right hand and hold a sign in my left. I have no clue what the sign says. "Reform All. People unite now!" I yell. The crowd cheers and begins to chant 'Reform All.' We have a movement, and the cameras are rolling … and we don't know what the fuck we are yelling about. It's wonderful. I've succeeded even before starting.

I reach to the ground to pick up a stone to throw, but before I can launch it indiscriminately into the developing mob, the portable podium set up for the candidate's speech is hurled through the restaurant's window. I have no idea if the individual who shattered the glass is ReAl, but they may as well have been. We have a riot, and the candidate hasn't even shown his face. I fade into the back of the crowd and look for my next option to help ratchet up the action.

CHAPTER 7: Captain Tau

We all desire to be rewarded for success, and I have been successful, perhaps more than I deserve. My last assignment has already become legendary as a victory for the movement, whatever that might be. Not only did the breakfast degrade into a bloodletting, but it also resulted in a death. Everyone seems elated, but not me. Don't get me wrong, I love to impart fear, and I truly enjoy hurting people, but I feel guilty at how things spun out of control. The businessman turned politician lost his wife when a shard of glass slid down the side of her face as she tried to protect herself by turning away from the shattering window. The glass, sharper than a scalpel, sliced neatly through her ear and passed through the skin covering her jaw before embedding itself in her neck. She bled out as sick onlookers with smartphone cameras hovered in for close-ups. The blood was dark, too dark, and stunk of metal. For some reason, this surprised me. I'd never noticed it before. But then, there was so much of it. It soaked the woman's summer dress before dripping to the floor into a broad crimson, almost black, thick lake.

I couldn't help myself. I should have immediately escaped the scene, but I felt compelled to look. I saw her husband's face as he held her in his arms, the glass still protruding from her body. He had to be distraught, but his chiseled countenance showed something else, a combination of anger and determination. He glanced at my face, and I sensed his recognition. I had seen this man before at the campus months ago, and he had seen me. That morning, I think ReAl got its first true enemy, one who would fight us to the death.

Perhaps I mostly feel bad at the woman's death because it was unintentional, or maybe because, for the first time in my life, I feel as though I have become the target. I've become the hunted.

I have no reason to mention any of this to my superiors, nor a desire to, although I'm sure my indiscretion is already known to my captain. Certainly, one or more of the ReAl participants in the crowd could not wait to inform on me. To them, I am an anachronism. I still understand loyalty and hierarchy. My captain pointed me in a direction, and I attacked. For the rest of the ReAl minions, they are merely ideologues who somehow think our terrorism accomplishes some type of good. I have no such expectations. There are serious consequences for not adhering strictly to the plan, and I screwed up. My bosses will be pissed if they learn I was recognized by the stupid reporter, and the target. Best I keep this to myself, and hope my captain does, too.

My mind stops drifting back to that morning as soon as I hear the voice of the Dark Man on my phone. I have feared ever hearing his voice again, and yet, here it is, praising me. His dark and threatening demeanor is replaced with an almost giddiness as he recounts the death of the target's wife. In his words, it "was more than any of us could have wished for." I have no idea who the "us" is he refers to, but I know it has nothing to do with those of us who were at the restaurant. Apparently, the Dark Man has no idea I wasn't the one who shattered the windowpane. The fact that the ice-clear glass stiletto that managed to pierce the jugular was just a fortunate stroke of serendipity did not matter. It had escalated the game for ReAl and made me famous in the eyes of the organization, and infamous in certain public political circles.

I guess I am now somewhat a star. I have crossed over into a new level of importance. The Dark Man informs me I've been promoted. From now on I am Captain Tau, the assassin. No longer will I be chasing public speakers, or professors, or students who have some small message my superiors do not like. Instead, I'll be in the shadows, ensuring those who don't heed our warning will never make the mistake a second time. This even includes those who have second thoughts about joining ReAl. From now on, once in ReAl, always in ReAl. I can't help thinking that someone just like me had been waiting to ensure I never questioned the Dark Man. I've been lucky.

In the future, I will no longer answer to anyone except the Dark Man. He has never shared his name, nor his rank, but there is no question regarding his authority. After acknowledging my promotion, my old captain congratulates me and drops off the call. It is just me and the Dark Man.

"First, Tau, do you mind me foregoing on the rank? Of course, you don't. Tau, I know what you did that morning. I know you didn't throw the podium through the window, let alone the rock you held in your hand. That is not important. What is important is that now the world knows your face.

"That stupid reporter with whom you spoke managed to get you on video as you stared through the broken window. He told the world you are the murderer. He has made himself into somewhat of a hero even though he did nothing more than stand on the sidelines as his camera crew shot him watching that poor lady die. You, on the other hand, are wanted for a murder you had little to do with. And because of this, you now need to become a murderer. Funny, isn't it. Luck has taken away your choices. You now work for me and only me. You are now a hammer for us.

"Your first assignment is easy. You get to eliminate the two ReAl members who could not wait to tell your old captain what really happened."

I must be dreaming as the Dark Man goes on to describe the individuals I will be assassinating. He is annoyed that he needs to go over the directions a second time for me. He stresses these killings need to occur the following day so he might communicate to the larger community of ReAl members the consequence of disloyalty to any of our members: death. I will not be mentioned in the communication. In fact, my name will never be mentioned within the confines of ReAl again. From now on, I'm a part of ReAl's parent group, GAL: Global Acting Locally. I am one of many "hammers" in GAL.

"And Tau, do you not get enough money from us?"

"Of course."

"Then get a real apartment and clean yourself up. I can't stand filth. You don't want to become a target, do you?"

Before I can answer, the phone call drops. I'm left thinking I have two marching orders: first, kill two cancerous members of ReAl, and second, look respectable when I do it.

I pull several ReAl envelopes filled with cash from under my mattress, stuff them into my jacket pocket, and head out to open a bank account, and then to buy some new clothes. A new apartment will need to wait until I've turned out the lights on the two pricks who finked on me. I think the Dark Man will understand.

As I walk down the steps to the street, my hand thumbs the envelopes in my pocket. I can't help but wonder how much a captain makes in this organization. I laugh to myself. I would gladly do this first job for free.

*   *   *

It's hot and dark while I lie awake, waiting for my delivery. My building is never quiet, even late at night, though tonight is different. The music of the city is muted. There is no banging or yelling in the hall, no blaring car horns on the street, and no staccato gun shots. The sweltering heat has thrown a blanket of peace and quiet over the city. I can't stand it, and yet, I can't escape it.

There's a knock at my battered door before it slowly opens. The dim illumination from the hallway light creeps as the door pushes inward. I lay still as the silhouette of a man slides a paper bag into my room with his foot. I feel him staring at me as he pushes the bag further until it butts up against my mattress. He never turns from me even as he backs through the door to leave. My heart is racing. I wonder if he can hear it pounding in my chest.

As soon as the door closes, I jump up from my bed and turn on the light. Even before checking the battered grocery bag on the floor, I open the door to try to get a glimpse of the delivery man. The hallway is empty and quiet. I run back into my room and open the blinds in time to see a big black man in the street nod to my window and salute. I swear it is B. He climbs into a dark sedan that is waiting for him, and he is gone.

Inside the sack are two small semi-automatic pistols and a box of ammo. I toss one pistol and the bullets onto the bed and inspect the remaining gun. It feels good in my hand, but it's so light. It is small caliber, a .22. I'll need to get very close to my prey if this is going to be effective. The second pistol appears to be an exact copy of the first, except for a silencer that has been threaded onto the end of its barrel. I have rarely shot a gun, and never one with a silencer. I feel like a secret agent.

I drop the gun onto the mattress, grab a soiled towel, and head out the door and down the hall to shower. My goal is to surprise both of my targets before the sun comes up. There is no way I will disappoint the Dark Man on my first assignment. The two snitches are as good as dead, and yet they don't even know what they did wrong. I can't keep the smile from my face. If someone were to see me now, they would think I was touched, mentally unstable. Maybe I am, but I'm thinking so clearly now.

The cold water of the shower shocks me into coherence. In my head, a plan crystalizes. I shiver and groan as the frigid liquid flushes over my face. This should be easy.

CHAPTER 8: Hooked

This is not fair. I cleaned myself up for the kill and now I'm waiting in the heat, sweating like a pig, for my Uber. When has it ever been this hot and muggy before the sun comes up? Sweat beads on my forehead and runs into my eyes, making them sting. My shirt is already damp and sticks to me. Making it worse, I'm wearing a light windbreaker to help hide the pistol I stuck under my belt. The driver is going to think I'm crazy for wearing the jacket in the sweltering heat. I won't be surprised if he or she drives by without stopping, deciding to leave me standing on the curb to wait for another driver.

A Prius pulls up to me and the driver-side window lowers. "Tau? Who are you waiting for?"

I welcome the driver by his name. He smiles and unlocks his rear door for me to enter.

"Kind of early to be going to work, huh?" He answers his own question before waiting for my response, then continues with the one-sided conversation even though it appears he is including me. "Yeah, it sucks to be heading out before the sun gets up. So, can you ever remember it being so farting hot and humid? No way. I think it's all that global warming stuff. You want to listen to classical music? It's all I play in the car. It keeps things running smooth." And so on and so on. He is making me tired even though I've not said a word.

Finally, I interrupt his incessant, meaningless drivel. "Look, I need to head up to Berkeley. You got the address, and I need some shut eye on the way. You mind?" He got it. I can see him in the rearview mirror, pouting like a spoiled kid. He's pissed, but at least he's quiet. Who cares if he likes it? The trip is quiet for the remaining twenty minutes of driving.

He drops me off next to a place called Indian Rock Park in the north section of the city. Even though I'm hardly dressed for climbing, I make an excuse that I'm meeting a friend here to shoot a video of him as he climbs. The driver seems to buy it. What a moron.

I hop from the car and walk west for several blocks until I'm left standing in front of an old house that's been converted into apartments. This is the home of target number one. I climb the exterior steps to the second floor, pull the little .22 from the back of my pants and knock on the door. There's no sound from inside. I knock slightly louder, but this time I continue rapping on the wood without stopping. I can be annoying when I want to be. In a few moments, I have won. I hear "What the fuck? Stop already," and the door flies open. I'm facing a man, or, more accurately, a boy who thinks he's a man.

"I'm going to pound you for—"

He stops as I raise the pistol, the silencer resting on his forehead. I see no point in making this dramatic, so I pull the trigger. The gun makes almost no noise, even in the quiet of the predawn darkness. The boy-man staggers backwards, slumps to his knees and collapses, face down in the entry.

From inside, I hear another voice. "Make them shut the hell up, Billy. I gotta get some sleep."

Billy wasn't who I was charged with taking out. Too bad for him. I walk into the apartment and follow the voice down the dark hallway, stopping at an already splintered door. I kick it open as I raise the pistol to complete the first half of my job. My target throws his legs onto the floor and jumps from his bed. My first shot takes him in the belly. It looks as though he barely feels it; however, he slows just enough, looking to where the little bullet has punctured his abdomen, so I can be more intentional with my aim. The next piece of lead hits him in the right cheek, leaving just a small dot where it enters. I step closer and put the last shot between his eyes. He falls back onto his bed.

I'm unconcerned about picking up the shell casings. I loaded the magazine wearing gloves. I couldn't care less if they were found. I'm sure that even though the bullets left no exit wound, they'll be too damaged to ever trace back to my gun.

I walk quietly back up the hallway, step over Billy, close the door, and head down the steps. I check windows of the building, looking for shadows of observers or to see if my noise has pried someone from their sleep. There's no movement and no lights. I've been a ghost, slipping in and out as quietly as a spirit. Instead of heading back to where I started, I head north to get lost in a section of town littered with nondescript stores and restaurants.

At a Starbucks, I order a coffee and some egg bites to kill time while preparing for the second half of my challenge. I love Starbucks. It's the only place I can sit next to someone and remain completely invisible. It's as if I don't exist. And to these wannabe grownups, I guess I don't. Unless I have an iPad or a PC or am enthralled playing with my phone, I'm no more interesting than the table these boring people sit at. I'm tempted to pull out my little gun and begin depositing lead into their brains. I wonder how long it would take for them to realize what I was doing.

I stop fantasizing and pull out my phone to set up the next phase of my morning. I text the remaining target and introduce myself as his new captain. It's still early, so it takes him time to respond, too much time. I use this to knock him off balance by berating him for not being responsive to my message.

I set up a conference call and wait for him to call in. Little does he know this conference includes only the two of us. I provide a fictional mission that starts less than two blocks from where I'm seated. My snitch will need to travel more than thirty miles south to get to this location, and he'll have less than an hour to get here. I can hear the anxiety in his voice as he struggles to figure out how to make it here in time. It's important to have him defocused and not thinking once he arrives. I only want him to fear being late. He's breathing hard on the call; wind from his mouth strikes the microphone. He's already on the move. I struggle to avoid laughing when I stop the conference call. He'll be here in time, but it'll be a frantic trip for him. Little does he know that I'll be his reward for making it.

I provide a text to my prey outlining his fictional mission. I take my time and drink the last bit of the coffee I've been nursing for the past hour or so. It's cold now, but the bitter taste is heaven for me. I leave the cup and the little paper bag that delivered my breakfast on the table when I leave. Screw them. For the price I paid for this cup of coffee, they can bus their own fucking table.

Outside, it is already getting warm. It's going to get hot today. On the bright side, the individual I will kill gets to avoid this heat.

I stretch and wait for my eyes to adjust to the bright sunlight. Turning to my left, I walk to the building where I'll set my trap. My prey has been instructed to position himself behind a small restaurant called Alphonso's, next to their trash dumpster. From here, he thinks he will team up with another member of ReAl to intercept my fictional character, who will be entering the business by 9:30 through the rear door for a secret meeting. To add a little urgency, I suggested media will be showing up no later than 9:00, so he needs to get here early.

Within minutes, I'm standing at Alphonso's, looking through the darkened windows into the dining area. It's not much of a place, certainly not the type of place in which one might expect a high-power political meeting to take place. I may have screwed up royally on this. If my target thinks this through, he'll begin to question the mission and potentially sense he's being set up. I know I would. Even more concerning are the hours posted in the window. The place doesn't open until 11:00. I should have been more careful. My quarry will see this and run. I can feel I have failed … until a car pulls up behind me and a young, frazzled-looking man with a headful of strawberry-red hair jumps from the rear door and runs around the corner of the restaurant. Perhaps luck is with me.

I follow the man around back to find him pushing the dumpster away from the wall. I assume he intends to hide there until the fictional quarry shows. I grab a corner of the stinking, greasy, rolling container and pretend to help. "Where are you going to move this?"

"Don't push that side. I just want to push this corner out far enough to hide behind. You go find your own place."

"Sure, sure. Oh, and by the way." I pull out the pistol and fire once, twice. The first shot strikes him in the belly, the second takes him in the throat. His hands rise to his neck and his mouth starts moving frantically, but no sound comes out. I move around behind him and place the muzzle into the red mane of hair, resting it against the back of his skull. Pop. Almost no sound at all. He falls to his knees, wedged between the steel garbage bin and the wall. I push the dumpster back against the wall as far as it will go.

I pull off my jacket, wrap the gun in it, and slide it under my arm before returning to the front of Alphonso's. I don't know if there really is an Alphonso, but if there is, he has a six-foot-long surprise package waiting for him behind his trash.

I dial the Dark Man as I walk away from the scene of the crime. I have no desire to have my Uber pickup be trackable to this neighborhood. It's better to walk a few miles before looking for a ride.

The phone seems to ring forever without passing over to voice mail. I'm just getting ready to hang up when the voice oozes from the speaker. "And tell me that you have wonderful news, Tau."

As I jump into bragging about my two successes, he cuts me off and suggests we talk once I am in a more secure area. For some reason, he seems concerned about having this discussion in public, even though nobody has a clue with whom I am speaking on the phone. He says he'll call me in the evening and hangs up before I can ask what time. I guess he doesn't give a shit if I have something else planned. It's obvious I'm nothing more than a cog in the machine. Perhaps I needed to be reminded.

I take my time getting home. Whatever time the Dark Man meant by "evening," I still have several hours to kill. I walk a few miles to the west before breaking down and ordering an Uber to take me to the neighborhood just to the north of my apartment. There can be no trail to my home.

*   *   *

"I don't care how you accomplished it. I just need to know that it's done. Do you understand?"

I nod to the camera on the phone. Even though I can't see the Dark Man's face, I know he can see me perfectly. He made me turn on the lights in my room so he can see even subtle changes in my expression. I feel naked, inferior, and disadvantaged. I have no doubt this is what he intends.

He is quiet. I assume he is going to wait until I acknowledge him verbally. "Yes, I get it. I'll try not to bore you in the future."

"You would do well to not patronize me. You do not have the ability to play on my field, but I'm feeling magnanimous today, so I forgive you. You removed two objects of my disdain today. Do not replace them with yourself. I'm rarely generous with those who try to piss me off. That said, if you look under your mattress, you'll find an envelope. Inside you will find a token of my munificence."

I don't have a clue what magnanimous or munificence means, but I slip my hand under the bed and slide it around until I feel the envelope. It's thicker than normal, much thicker.

"Go ahead, look."

The envelope is filled with twenties. There must be a couple grand. I look back into the camera and mouth a "thanks."

"No thanks necessary. Those two had outlived their importance to the cause. We can't have loose ends, right? So, they needed to be eliminated. One thing I never leave is loose ends. Consider what you did basic housekeeping."

I can feel his eyes burrowing into me. "You never want to become a loose end. So, tell me, where did you dump the guns?"

"I didn't. I have them here with me."

"Were you not told to get rid of them? You need to dispose of them somewhere they will never be found. I will always have new weapons delivered for your next assignment."

I ignore his question, not wanting to get myself or B in trouble. "And when is that? The assignment, I mean." I finger the bills in the open envelope. I can't wait for my next job.

"Soon, soon." Even though I can't see his face, I'm sure he is smiling. He knows he has me hooked.

CHAPTER 9: Friend or Foe?

It's been weeks since my last job and my bank account is getting lean. I need to generate some income quickly if I'm to avoid getting thrown out of my flat. I'm concerned the Dark Man has forgotten me, or worse, that he no longer needs me. His comment about "loose ends" is keeping me awake at night. Out of fear, I sleep with the same pistols I was supposed to get rid of. I wonder if GAL knows I kept them. I suppose they do, but I don't care anymore. If they want to get rid of me, it won't be without a fight. Sure, it might be a fight I lose, but I'll take them with me.

I have no food in my mini fridge so it's time to roam. That's become my term for hitting the streets in search of someone I can roll for a couple bucks. Tonight, I'll roam close to home. One wouldn't think the money would be good in this poor section of town, but they would be wrong. Here, I can hit a lowly junkie or his pusher and bank a couple hundred in twenties and tens. The only downside: I need to kill them to ensure they can't finger me to their suppliers. I've adopted the Dark Man's policy of no loose ends. That's easy in my neighborhood; nobody gives a shit about my targets. As far as the police are concerned, one less pusher or junkie is fine for them. Even the suppliers don't seem to care about losing the occasional pusher, as long as I leave the drugs and don't take too much money. It's the cost of doing business.

The silenced .22 works great, compact and quiet. I'm so glad I kept it. No one knows they've been shot until it's too late. Just a quiet "phht" and I have my money. Hell, their bodies make more noise collapsing on the sidewalk than my pistol.

Tonight, I'm set up in a dark alley. Leaning against the wall, I hope to pass as a pusher to a passing customer in search of a hit. I make eye contact with my first potential prey of the night. He is a young white kid who doesn't belong here. His clothes are too clean, too expensive. I can tell he's afraid, but his habit has given him the fortification to enter a bad section of town in search of a couple cheap hits. I consider passing on him, thinking he looks as though he might be missed by someone. I don't want to invite trouble. I need to stay invisible. Unfortunately for him, he also looks to be carrying a fat wallet. The temptation is too great to skip this kid.

He approaches me. Even in the dim light, I see he's young, very young, maybe not even old enough to drive. He would be a good-looking kid except for his pimples. Over the next couple years, he would have grown out of them. How he got here, I don't know, but I do know he won't need to worry about getting home. Before he opens his mouth, I raise my gun and fire twice into his forehead. He stops, blinks, and falls on his face.

I stuff the gun back into my jacket pocket and kneel to pull the wallet from his pants pocket. There's plenty of cash. Too much for a basic junkie. This might have been a big mistake. Rich kids don't get ignored by the cops. I keep the wallet and disappear into the alley, walking to a street on the opposite block. It's important to establish some distance between me and the crime before I can be seen.

My phone rings. It's the Dark Man.

"Having fun?"

I have no idea how to respond. "You see my black sedan in front of you?" Before letting me answer, he continues, "Get in. Now."

The rear door pushes open. It's dark so I can't make out anything inside other than the dull orange glow of a lit cigarette or cigar. I hurry to the car and climb in, pulling the door closed behind me. My eyes adjust to the dimly lit interior just enough to make out a face. It's my first look at the Dark Man. Although I don't know where, I have seen this face before. The man is wearing a suit, not an expensive one that screams successful banker, just a generic, non-descript type. Dark, no pattern, it reminds me of the detectives from every cop show I watched on TV when I was a kid. Okay, he may not be stylish, but he is still scary.

"Give me your gun. I should have you killed now, you stupid SOB."

I'm tempted to jump back out of the car. I even move my hand up to rest on the door handle. I sense he knows exactly what I'm considering. He doesn't move, so he must have someone waiting outside.

I give up and lower my hand to the pistol. I remove it slowly so as not to invoke any violent action from the Dark Man. He reaches across the seat and grabs my gun before I've even pulled it completely from my pocket.

"You are even dumber than I thought. You understand the kid you just dispatched was not our enemy? He was just another fuck-up of a generation, just like you." He stopped talking, letting his words sink in.

I've never thought of myself as a fuck-up, but maybe I am. Apparently, my boss thinks so. I wait, letting the silence become overwhelming. Years ago, someone told me that whoever speaks first in times like this loses. I'm not going to lose this time. I think my life might depend on it.

The Dark Man reaches into his sports coat and pulls out an envelope and tosses it to me. "If you need cash, you need to ask. You pull another stunt like tonight, you better save a bullet for yourself because I will make damn sure you wish you had never been born. Understand?"

Rather than acknowledge him verbally, I nod. He pushes no farther. Instead, he pulls up a thin satchel that's been sitting on the floor between his feet.

"This is your next job. It's the most important job you will ever have. One you cannot fail. This defines how you will fit into the organization for the long haul. You succeed, you and I will have a long friendship. I don't think I need to say anything about what happens if you fuck it up."

I don't reach for the bag. I wait for him to hand it to me. Why? I don't know, maybe it's just a power game. I'm not sure I even want it. Once I have it in my hands, there's no turning back, as if there's any chance of that anyway. I guess I can pretend.

He pushes the leather pack across the seat and waits for me to grab it. He gives me no choice, so I pull it onto my lap and open the flap. His hand flashes to slap it shut again.

"Not here. Get yourself to this address." He hands me a handwritten card. "Look inside the bag on your own time. You will never go back to your old place. It's off limits. I'll be calling you tonight in two hours. We will discuss the job then. Now get the fuck out."

As soon as my feet hit the pavement, the car begins to quietly roll away into the dark. With the satchel draped over my shoulder, I look at the address written on the card and enter it into my smartphone. My driver shows up in minutes, and I say goodbye to my old neighborhood. The address is across the bay in San Francisco. Apparently, I'm moving into a higher rent district. Things are looking up.

*   *   *

I've seen this man before, a couple of times. First at the university, then at the bloodbath breakfast that got me promoted. It looks as though I'm tethered to this guy. I flip the picture over to see if the Dark Man has written any notes to me. Nothing.

There's a thin stack of paper clipped together that remains in the satchel along with a clip of bullets. There is no gun. I guess the man doesn't trust me enough to hand me a loaded pistol. I can't say I blame him. I wouldn't trust me either.

The papers are filled with writing, and I take the next hour before my call to read through them. It's not so much that there's a lot to read. It's just I feel a need to absorb it all, as if the Dark Man might test me on the contents. Everyone has always underestimated my intellectual abilities and assumed I can't read as well as I should. I have no doubt the Dark Man thinks the same. That said, learning to read was tough. Mom always joked I was the product of a shitty public-school system. I know my problems with learning stemmed not from the system but from never getting to attend a school for more than a month at a time. It wasn't the shitty school's fault; it was my shitty mother. In any case, I was smart enough to teach myself to read well enough to get by and understand what I read, but it still takes me more time to get through something.

I give credit to the Dark Man. He writes concisely and simply. I have no troubles understanding what he wants me to do. No demands. I'm to assassinate this politician. He doesn't go into any reason about why. I probably shouldn't know, but then again, I am an inquisitive cuss and can't help wondering what this man has done that makes him so terrible he needs to die.

Even though I love killing, and have killed numerous times, the sterility of this assignment takes the fun out of the deed. There's no spontaneity this time, no room for me to invent, no room for failure. The plan has been established and outlined in detail by the Dark Man. He will expect it to be carried out without deviation. I can do it, but so can anyone else. I can't help thinking this turns me into nothing more than a tool. That wouldn't be so bad. I used to think of myself as a hammer, but perhaps I'm nothing more than the nail being pounded into something by someone a lot more powerful. I don't like the feeling.

The paper tells me the who, the when, and the where. It ignores the why, and it leaves me guessing on the how. It merely says this will be discussed during our meeting. I suspect the "meeting" refers to the call I'm expecting in a few minutes. I wait. And wait. And wait. There is no call, and it is well beyond the time the Dark Man had set for our discussion. I'm not surprised. He's into driving home the point of who is boss. He'll let me wait until it suits him. Hell, he might even have cameras set up in this new apartment to spy on me. Perhaps he's waiting for me to nod off so he can startle me awake and use my fluster against me. I hate this guy.

I need to crap, so I head down the hallway to the bathroom, looking at the artwork that hangs on the wall as I go. I've never lived in a place with real artwork. That's for people with money and power. Even though I've spent a lifetime stealing money and exercising my power over others, I now realize I was just a pretender. I have never had art.

As soon as my bare ass hits the seat of the pot, my phone rings. Thank goodness I carried it with me. There must be a God in that he has seen fit to let me push out a shit while I'm talking to the Dark Man.

There is no introduction, just a "Busy?"

"Why would I be busy? I have nothing to do but wait for your instruction."

"Good, that is what I want to hear. I take it you made it to the apartment and find it satisfactory?"

"Yes, and yes, but why do you care?"

"Look, I care about all my assets, and you are one of my assets. Not a very important one, but an asset, just the same. You can be replaced at any time, but if you are my asset, I want you to be cared for. Got it?"

"Sure."

"Good." The Dark Man goes quiet. I check the phone to see if I still have the connection. It is good.

"So, are you going to shit or not? Call me back at this number when you're done. Do not make me wait long." He drops off the call.

"What the fuck?" I whisper to myself. The asshole has been watching me. I have no doubt he's been observing me from the time I entered the front door. I turn off the light to finish my duty. I can't crap with someone watching. I've never been able to do it. At least in the dark, I can pretend I can't be seen. The fucker has been watching me. I feel violated. I wonder if the Dark Man is a perv. I'm sure he is. I know he can't be trusted.

CHAPTER 10: Ready, Set...

"I doubt he will notice you, but he is going to have guards that will certainly recognize you. You need to stay out of sight. He's going to be speaking the day after tomorrow at the Moscone Center in the Soma District. It's on the other side of the city, so you're going to need to give yourself some time to get there and set up."

The Dark Man continues through his plan point by point and then starts through it again, as if I'm a moron. My mind is drifting, and I'm tired. I feel it is too late to continue.

"If I bore you, I can stop, but if you screw up this job, it will be the last thing you do. Got it?"

"I'm just tired, that's all. I need some shuteye."

"We'll be done when I'm done."

He drones on even though he must know I'm not getting anything new from his talk. I think he believes the more he talks of the plan, the more plausible it is. Maybe he needs to convince himself, so I lower my head to the table while listening, hoping I don't fall asleep. He doesn't miss a beat. He either doesn't have a camera trained on the kitchen table or he has become so engaged that he's forgotten about spying on me. Then...

"Tau!? What the hell are you doing? I need you alert, man."

I must have dozed off. For how long? I don't know. I do know that I'm in trouble.

"I'll send a car to pick you up at seven tomorrow morning to run you through the logistics. Do not be late, and for God's sake, put on some clean clothes. There are some in the bedroom drawers that should fit you fine." The phone clicks off.

It's already one in the morning, and I need to get some sleep before the Dark Man's cronies show up in six hours. This isn't fair, but I doubt the Dark Man is ever concerned about being "fair." His only concerns are about power and winning.

*   *   *

Apparently, the Dark Man scratched using the same blue sedan from yesterday and traded it for a silver Toyota Prius with an Uber sticker in the window. It's about as nondescript a vehicle as one can get in San Francisco. I'm dressed in tan khakis, topsiders, and an untucked denim shirt. I'm as boring as the car. Together we are invisible.

Unfortunately, the driver has missed the entire concept of fading into the background. He's wearing a cheap blue sports jacket, a white shirt, and stark blue and red striped tie. He sticks out like a sore thumb. I debate calling the Dark Man but decide not to when I realize people will watch the driver. They'll never even notice me. I can hide in plain sight. The Dark Man remains a step ahead of me.

The driver lowers the front passenger window as I reach for the handle. He politely invites me to hop in the back and points to the Uber sticker. "No one is going to notice someone in the back seat, but the front, maybe."

I hop in the back and close my eyes, hoping for some shut eye before we get to the assassination site. The driver doesn't introduce himself and I don't ask. I think I'll just call him Dick. He looks like a dick.

"You bring the bullet clip?" Dick is looking at me in his rearview mirror.

"Nope"

"Strike one. That's okay. I have a spare." He holds up a loaded clip, as if for some reason I needed proof. "There's a present for you in the pocket on the back of my seat."

I reach in the pocket and pull out a flat, plastic, hinged box. Inside is a semi-automatic pistol.

"It's a Glock, nine-millimeter. You ever shoot one?"

"Nope."

"No problem. I'll show you what you'll need to know when we get to where we're going. You shouldn't need it anyway. It's for 'just in case.'"

"Just in case?"

"Yeah, just in case you fuck up. You get to shoot yourself right here." He points to a spot on the side of his head, just in front of his right ear. "You won't feel a thing. At least that's what they tell me."

"Who's 'they?'"

"Does it matter?"

I don't answer. I guess it doesn't.

"When we stop, bring the gun with you, but leave it in the box."

The car turns into a parking garage and pulls abruptly into a reserved slot just inside the toll gate. "So, I guess you aren't concerned about getting towed?"

Dick doesn't bother with an answer. Instead, he shakes his head before climbing out of the driver's seat. He moves around to the rear of the car to open the hatch. He pulls out a black canvas tool bag, a couple pairs of overalls, along with some scuffed-up work shoes. "Here, put this on and change your shoes." He tosses the clothes to me. I pull the overalls on over my clothes. They are loose so they fit fine. The shoes are brand new even though someone has obviously taken some effort to make them look old and worn.

Dick discards his tie and sports coat and pulls on his pair of overalls. His shoes are already scuffed, so he doesn't bother changing them.

"Stick your 'present' in here." He holds open the tool bag to me. "Let's go." And he takes off back to the street with the tool bag in hand. I jog to keep up.

He moves across the street and enters a long building made of silver glass and steel. It's a convention center and is huge inside. I love my name for this guy; it fits him well. The dick slows to a leisurely walk so as not to attract attention.

The place is relatively empty save for a half dozen or so lost-looking attendees of some function or another. They pass by us with blank looks on their face. It's as if the building has sucked the energy out of them. I feel it too. There's nothing in this place that sparks interest. It's just big. The walls are a creamy-gray color with ugly red lines painted on them. The carpet is a plain gray. The monotony is broken with the occasional interruption of steel and glass escalators. This is a place to hold a lot of people, like cattle in a feedlot, nothing more. I hate it and can't wait to get back out into the street.

My driver motions to me and points up the escalator. "This is where the magic will happen."

I have no idea what he's talking about until he unlocks a utility door with a key card hanging from his neck and steps inside. Inside, a wide video monitor hangs on a wall. It's linked to a camera in a large auditorium, at least I think it's an auditorium. It's difficult to make out much from the picture; everything appears to be a grainy gray, except for some bright splotches of light spaced intermittently on the walls.

"You can watch from in here. The picture will be a lot better when the lights are on. I'm surprised the camera picks up anything with as dark as it is in there now. When you see the prick step up to the mic, set it off. We don't need him speaking. Got it?"

"Sure, but why set it off here? Why not from across the street? Why not from Starbucks halfway across town?"

"If he makes it through the blast, you take the Glock and finish him. Then get out or…" He stops and puts his index finger against his head like the barrel of a gun. "…bang. Either way, Aldus Simmons doesn't walk out of here." He pulls the Glock from the bag and slides the clip into it. Instead of replacing the gun back into his bag, he pushes it into the cavity between the TV screen and the wall.

He opens the door again and walks across a huge hallway to double steel doors. "Let's get to work."

Surprisingly, the doors are unlocked … thank you Fire Marshal. A light tug on the handles and they open outward. We slip inside and let the doors snap shut behind us before Dick flips on a small flashlight. I wish I had a light, too. It's pitch black in here except for the occasional illuminated "exit" signs above what must be doors leading out of the room. Outside of the meager beam of light, it's almost impossible to see where we're going. My eyes struggle to adjust to the dark. The little flashlight is focused several yards in front of us, so I can't even see where my feet are landing.

The light stops and I bump into Dick. "Fucking A. Pay attention to where you're going."

"Fuck you. If I had a flashlight, too, I would know where the fuck I was going."

The light goes out. We are enveloped in darkness. "You feel better? We're even now."

The punch is a surprise, and it doubles me over. The wind is knocked from me, and I can't breathe. I fall to the ground, struggling to suck in air. The small flashlight clicks back on. This time illuminating the driver's face. "Just be happy we can't afford to mess up your face before tomorrow. People might remember someone with a broken nose."

Fuck you! I want to yell, but I can't get the words out as I continue gasping. It's probably good I can't talk. I have no doubt he would enjoy kicking me while I lay here. I think this guy pretty much hates me. He's here only because the Dark Man told him to be here. In any case, that light has helped burn that fucker's face into my memory. It'll be there until I kill him.

The light flips away to come to rest on a wooden lectern, already set up on a podium on the stage overlooking the large hall, a hall so large that the small beam does not reach the walls as my new nemesis turns around in an attempt to get his bearings in the room. The light just disappears into the ether. Redirecting the beam back on the lectern, he says, "That's our baby. Get up and let's get to work. I've got to be out of here before the end of the hour and report back to the boss that we're ready."

I roll up to my hands and knees, calming myself to allow the air to fill my lungs again. I stand and follow the prick up onto the stage and watch over his shoulder as he opens his toolbox. He holds the flashlight in his teeth as he pulls on gloves before starting his work. I guess he doesn't trust me with the light. He removes a panel concealing the lectern's built-in lighting system. The exposed cavity is not large but provides plenty of room for a block of Semtex along with the detonator and transmitter. Dick replaces the face panel.

"Time to go." He pulls off his gloves and drops them, along with the screwdriver, into the toolbox. He jumps from the stage to the floor. I choose to use the steps. It's a drop of more than five feet. By the time I'm down, the flashlight glare is already halfway across the room on the way to the exit doors. Thank goodness my eyes have finally adjusted because I need to run to catch up. Dick is smiling as he opens the doors into the lit hall. The light doesn't seem to bother him, but I feel as though I'm blinded.

"So, when should I be back?"

"Shut the fuck up. What are you, stupid or something?" he whispers.

He's right. I need to shut up until we get back to the car. The walls have ears. We can't take a chance on being discovered. I am stupid.

CHAPTER 11: Who the Fuck is Aldus?

The convention center will be busy today. During the ride over, my driver, the same prick who was with me yesterday, goes over the security I'll face this morning when I enter the convention hall. He nods toward the glove compartment. Inside is a large manila envelope.

"You have everything you need in there."

I open the envelope and slide the contents out onto my lap: a security badge on a "Moscone Center Staff" lanyard, a cheap pen, a canvas wallet, and a keycard.

"Today you are 'Bob Hayes.'" My driver smiles as he says this. "You know who Bob Hayes was?"

"No, should I?"

"Hell, yeah. He used to be the fastest man alive, but that was in the sixties. You fuck this up and you're going to need to run faster than him."

"What's with the pen?"

"That's your transmitter. Don't click it until you want the bomb to go off. It has a range of a few hundred feet, so we're safe here, but once you get inside, don't push it until Aldus is at the podium or you'll blow the snot out of somebody else."

Dick pulls up to a curb a full block from the convention center and waits.

I nod in understanding before opening the car door to step onto the walk. I wait for Dick to say something, maybe a good luck, or even a "don't fuck it up." Nothing. I slam the door shut, and he puts the car in gear and leaves me standing.

*   *   *

The room is dark except for the illumination provided by the video monitor. With the lights on in the auditorium across the hall, the cameras see everything clearly. The activity in prep for the political shindig has been going on for hours, and the room transformed from an empty cavern to an exciting stage, showing off the pretty candidates. My target is only one of many speakers, but he is obviously the most important. He will be the second to last speaker this evening and is scheduled to be the longest speech.

I'm surprised when Aldus arrives early to run through a couple items shortly after I set up in my room. It would be easy to take him out as he stands at the microphones for his sound check, but the Dark Man's plan was adamant that the hit needs to occur while the cameras are on. The effect is everything.

Aldus stays in the hall only a short time. Hours later, and I'm still here, rocking back and forth in my chair, staring at a video screen. My phone lies on the table in front of me, its ring silenced. I've left the vibrate on in case the Dark Man or his crony, Dick, needs to contact me. Why? I have no idea, but I can't rule anything out. There are no excuses with the Dark Man. If he wants to get hold of me, I must answer the call. I look around the room, looking for potential hiding places for mics or cameras. I know he can see me; he sees everything. They must be incorporated into the monitor or the PC sitting on the table in front me. I don't see any other places in this room to hide them. This is nothing more than a painted box, a large closet. There is no art, no plants, no fancy lighting, no furniture even, other than the black mesh and plastic chair where I sit, and the plain Formica-covered table in front of me. The room is gray, and the fluorescent ceiling lighting is a sickly blue. Maybe that's where the cameras hide. I spin away from the monitor and lean back in my chair to stare at the ceiling. I don't see anything that looks like a microphone or camera, but it must be there. I extend my middle fingers on both hands and point them generally toward the light fixtures and air vent. Take that, Dark Man.

I should have brought something to drink and eat. I wasn't thinking this morning when I hopped into the car with Dick. Even though I'm hungry and thirsty, I can't take the chance of leaving the room. Even when I need to piss, I decide it's better to just do it in the far corner. I keep my back to the monitor and the ceiling light. I don't know why, but I don't want the Dark Man looking at my prick. My urine splatters against the wall and runs toward my feet. I back up as I piss to keep out of the expanding pool of yellow. It's better to live with the stink for a few hours than to take a chance of leaving my sanctuary. If I leave the room, I run the risk of getting questioned and caught. If I'm caught, I fail in my assignment. I should have crapped before leaving my apartment. I hope I can stave off the urge to shit for a few more hours, but I'm already cramping. I close my eyes for a moment before the action starts, attempting to will the pain away.

The auditorium is hopping as the program begins. I turn on the volume to hear everything. I don't want to be surprised. The first couple of speakers are boring as hell. I can tell they must have a ton of dough; they reek of it. That said, they suck at speech making. I suspect they were invited just because they paid for tonight's show. Maybe they did, but they are putting a damper on the evening.

When Aldus is introduced, the crowd perks up and the noise level ramps. I hold the transmitter in my right hand tightly, so tightly that I'm concerned I'll break it. I force myself to loosen my grip. I'm sweating. I didn't notice the room getting so hot, but it feels like an oven. I fear nerves are overwhelming me. My only solace is knowing that it'll all be over in a few minutes. Aldus will step up behind the lectern, and just as he starts, BOOM! There will be pandemonium, and I'll be able to walk out of here unnoticed. Aldus will be splattered all over his supporters and the stage. It'll make great news.

But Aldus doesn't step behind the lectern. He's wearing a microphone and is walking to the edge of the stage, far away from where he is supposed to be. He's moving to the steps leading down to the floor of the auditorium. I have no idea what to do. By the time I collect myself, he's starting his speech from a central position close to the crowd, well below and far away from the bomb.

My only option is the Glock, but as I open the door leading to the hall, all I see is security personnel and adoring fans crowding the convention center hallway, hoping for a view of their candidate. There is no way to push myself through the throng to get across the hallway, let alone gain access to the auditorium. I could pull the pistol and just open fire. People will run for cover, maybe giving me a shot at making it to the entrance, but I only have one ammo clip. I'll be out of bullets before I get inside. Even if I get to the door and have a few bullets left, they won't get me past the security. I'll be tackled and cuffed before Aldus even knows there's been a threat on his life … or I'll be shot and killed. The latter is probably more likely. I have no doubt the Dark Man has some fail-safe resources here, hiding somewhere, to make sure I'm not captured alive. The moment I'm arrested, I'll be as good as dead. The organization can't afford for me to be captured. There's no chance for success, only death, my death. I let the door close silently, hoping no one noticed it being opened in the first place. I sit back down at my monitor to wait, watching and listening to the candidate, hoping that serendipity will deliver me a solution. Beads of sweat run down my face. My shirt is wet with perspiration. The AC kicks on and chills me to the bone. I know I'm screwed.

As Aldus speaks, I must admit the guy shows a commitment to his cause. He lost his wife only a couple months ago, and yet here he is, stomping for his election. Why Aldus is hated by the Dark Man, I don't have a clue, but he is. I do know that the Dark Man almost assuredly has someone beyond the door of this room, waiting to punish me if I fail. Perhaps it's terror, perhaps imagination, or maybe just an aha feeling, but it hits me like a brick; the Dark Man has someone dispatched to kill me in any case … no loose ends.

He was clear. I was to stop Aldus cold, before he could speak. Now his speech has been going on for what? Twenty minutes or so? I should stop watching and begin running … you know, Bob Hayes-like, because my time alive is defined only by how long it takes for the Dark Man, Dick, or some other crony to slip into the convention center.

My phone vibrates. As it buzzes, it seemingly floats across the table. I ignore it until it stops. It starts again. I must answer. To avoid it again would be to invite my death sentence. "Yeah, what is it?"

"Why have you not acted, Tau? What misunderstanding could there possibly be? You have failed in your responsibility to me and to our organization. What is holding you up? Act now."

"I can't. There isn't a way to make it work."

"I don't want to hear 'can't.' Just get it done. Now."

"But…"

"Push the fucking button and get out of there. I need to hear the boom in the next ten seconds or I will consider you a failure and rogue. There is only one way I deal with failure. Think hard before you piss me off."

The phone goes dead. I want to leave, but I'm caught up in what this guy has to say. He makes sense, and he says it so simply. It's like he's speaking directly to me. Obviously, he isn't a politician, he is a businessman, and he doesn't seem to want the fame. In fact, he would be out of place behind the lectern. He's meant to be among the people. He likes it. He doesn't need money. He has more money than I could spend in a hundred lifetimes. But he is talking change, big time change. It clicks. That's why the Dark Man needs him gone. He is a part of what will be changed.

I need to leave. The Dark Man isn't going to be sending one of his minions after me; they're already here. Hell, they are probably part of the security team gathered outside and are just waiting for the signal to corner me. It'll happen soon.

I grab the Glock, remove the clip, and toss it into the puddle of piss in the corner. I slip the clip into my pocket. I keep the transmitter. I don't want them to set off the bomb. What the fuck am I thinking? They probably have several transmitters in the hall already. I'm so stupid. I push the door open and run. They'll be following me, so I can't stop now, never … not unless I first stop the Dark Man.

Dark Man, you are so dead.

BOOK TWO

SIMON: Hammer Until it Fits

"…too young and too good looking to be trusted by the audience." That's my producer's opinion. Now I'm sitting in this damn salon to get my blond hair darkened, with just a tinge of gray at my temples. In addition, I'm no longer shaving each day. Instead, I retired the razor in deference to electric hair clippers that leave me with just enough stubble each morning to make me look rugged and defiant. At least that is my hope. I'm not sure how it'll come across on the TV. I think I look older, tougher, and maybe wiser than I did a day ago.

I can't recall how many times Mom asked me why I would ever choose to follow my dad into the journalism industry. To be honest, I have no idea. It always seemed like something preordained for the Cartwrights. I'm the third generation of reporters in our family. That said, I doubt my dad would have thought what I do is real reporting. Although I'm not the first of our family to make the move from print to the television screen—Dad did it almost four decades before me—he was different. He was drawn to the dangerous stuff, like a moth to a light, fluttering ever closer until it touches the heated glass bulb and dies. Mom said he knew that eventually he would get burned, but he couldn't stop himself. He jumped at the chance to become a war correspondent. He got a rush from it and thought it was his fast track to fame. I suspect he fooled himself into thinking he would eventually return to the States to a huge job, both in public reach and pay. It was neither. The only fast track he was on was to the grave. Dad was killed in Vietnam doing a story a couple of months before I was born.

Somehow, I still got the reporting bug. It was so seductive as I grew up. I would sit plastered to the TV screen as Mom played tapes of Dad. Even though I never met the guy, I felt as though I grew up with him. I certainly didn't want to let him down if he was up in heaven somewhere looking down at me.

I had my chances to become a war correspondent, just like Dad. There seemed to be perpetual war in the Mideast, and the US public seemed as though they could not get enough of it. Not for me. I preferred doing my reporting in a sports coat and tie rather than a helmet and fatigues.

The closest I got to danger was interviewing a crazed homeless guy sleeping on the sidewalk outside of a downtown shelter. I couldn't get anything coherent out of the guy. As I walked by, he started yelling, not at me, but at some non-existent person apparently standing behind me. He threw a bag of trash at the invisible threat and ran. He scared the shit out of me. I remember slipping into the shelter's lobby to compose myself. I have a persona to manage, and I could not let the camera crew see how flustered I had been by the confrontation. I hate confrontation.

No, for me, I'll pass on the wars. Let me bounce around doing some nice local interest stories until I can ride popularity into some news anchor role.

At least that's how I thought it was going to play out …
until I got caught up in covering a locally popular
businessman running for a US Senate seat. Politics in
California had always been nasty… and expensive … and
dirty, but I never thought of them as dangerous. I jumped at
the chance to follow this wannabe politician around the state
to report on his progress.

Presumably, my objective was to report on both major
candidates for the position, providing insight as to where they
differed and where they aligned on policy, how their messages
were received, and generally, how their campaigns were
faring. If all went well, I would get some serious TV time to
provide my opinions along with the facts I reported. Why
anyone wanted my opinion, I had no idea. I don't know shit
about anything other than reporting and writing. Hence, the
darkening and the graying of the hair to make me look as
though I am some wise, more experienced person. It doesn't
matter that I don't know anything, so long as the viewers think
I do. In any case, the producers feed me what to say. This was
a lesson I'd learned early on. My opinion would only be heard
if, and when, it was in concert with the producer. My pay and
public stature depended on this. As a reminder, the money is
always right.

Today, I will roll out the new look at two events: the first
at an early afternoon rally to supposedly kick off the campaign
for the businessman for his Senate run, the second to cover a
dinner fundraiser for the incumbent. It will be a long day, but
I'm excited. I'll have my face plastered on LA TV this
morning to tell folks a little about the challenger, then at lunch
to show a snippet of the speech along with my (ahem,)
producer's commentary, and then at ten to show the pretty
people attending the fundraiser. My coverage of the dinner
and the kick-off speech will be aired on all our affiliates, and
I've been asked to be available to these stations for live
comment. By the time I get to bed tonight, I'll have had more

airtime today than I've had in the previous week. Exposure, exposure, exposure.

The station has already been kind enough to develop a storyline for me to push. I guess I'm fine with this. I don't know anything about either of the candidates, and I've had so little time to do any research and prepare. I'll take their spin and be thankful. The message from the producer is clear, stay on script and remember, this is just the opportunity I should be willing to kill for. Stray, even a little, and I'll be doing local special interest stories for the morning news until I retire.

CHAPTER 1: Impression

This is a first for me. The state has not seen a competitive run for a Senate seat in more than two decades, long before I got my journalism degree. California voters are either brain dead, incapable of considering anyone new, or the opposition party cannot find a candidate worth salt. In any case, the citizens of the state have managed to return the same two senators to Washington, DC term after term after term. This habitual voting seems almost crazy given that the same people who elect the candidates seem to take great pleasure in complaining about the jobs they are doing.

Personally, I have not established much of an opinion on either of our senators' performance. So long as I'm employed and can visit the beach on the weekends, I'm basically happy.

This election is setting up a little different. First off, the incumbent, Betty Sweinhart, is truly showing her age. Her voice falters and shakes when she is under stress, and her right hand has taken to involuntary shaking when she raises it to wave to the crowds. We all notice she now has significant pauses in her speeches. Some think it is to inject a dramatic flair. I think she's just getting lost in her text. Rumor has it that this will be her last hurrah.

Her likely opponent brings with him a formidable resume that has the political world standing up and taking notice. Aldus Simmons has erupted on the political scene with a bang.

Although his name is not new to anyone who follows business, nobody expected him to walk away from his business success to try public service at this time. At only forty years of age, he already has a couple of major corporate successes under his belt. The first is a social networking effort that he took public four years ago, netting him billions. The next is a cyber-security effort that looks like it might generate financial returns that dwarf his first effort. He has the proverbial Midas touch. It's tough to believe that he might choose to leave his sanguine world of business, trading it in for political cynicism.

So, he is rich, successful, smart, good-looking, and connected. He seems to have it all, excluding the crappy name. Who names their kid "Aldus" anymore?

I admit, I feel the excitement in the air as my crew and I await the arrival of Simmons to the hotel ballroom. I don't recall ever seeing folks line up in Los Angeles to see any politician. Movie actors or musicians, yes, but a senatorial candidate? Heck no … let alone one who is expected to downsize government and chip away at some of the entitlements to which these same fans have become addicted. My producers don't share any of the same infatuation with Mister Simmons. They have provided me with intros to kick off each segment. Each intro makes it abundantly clear that Aldus is intent on impoverishing and maintaining an underclass. It doesn't make sense to me, but who cares. I'm only here to report.

My feed is live when I'm surprised by a hand grabbing me by the shoulder and spinning me around to face a smiling Aldus Simmons. My own camera crew is working fervently to catch the interaction. Apparently, Aldus shunned the planned grand arrival via car and instead chose to exit his ride several blocks away and take a leisurely stroll to the facility. He is so unassuming, nobody notices him as he weaves his way through the crowd toward me and my TV crew. His nonchalance is refreshing, but I find it unnerving. He surprised us all and I am left fumbling for words. He has seized control of our interview.

"So, Simon, I'm so happy to see you this afternoon. I have to say that after seeing you on the news for so long, I was quite excited to finally get a chance to meet you."

He is smiling as he continues without giving me any chance to ask questions. Vaguely, I notice he has taken my hand with its microphone and is speaking directly to our viewers, my viewers. I'm dumbfounded and he knows it. He undoubtedly heard my comments earlier today in which I stuck to a script, positioning him as a rich, entitled guy who was in the race only to enrich himself and his cronies while making a mockery of the process. He knows my station and I have declared war on him, and he has just launched what now appears to be a wildly successful counterattack.

I pull back the microphone and make some meaningless "thank you for your time" comment while moving directly into a canned "back to you," to signify cutting our live feed.

Before I can confront Simmons for his impromptu speech at my expense, he disappears through the doors of the ballroom, his fans funneling in as water behind him. My crew is already gathering their equipment to move inside so as not to miss any of the kickoff. My camera man smiles as he works.

"What's so goddamn funny, Jerry."

Jerry doesn't bother looking up at me as he collapses his tripod. "Nothing, boss. It's just that I don't know when I have ever seen you speechless. You kind of reminded me of my kids' guppies. Their mouths work, but there ain't no noise. Gawd, that was funny."

"It isn't going to be so funny when you're looking for a new job, so let's get inside to our place. And, damnit, don't let me get blindsided again."

"That what you call it? Looked more like a massacre to me, and we were all on the receiving end."

Jerry turns away as he follows the crowd inside. He continues talking, but I don't have a clue what he's saying. He is right, of course; we just got ambushed. He's wrong in saying it was a massacre. It wasn't. In a massacre, everyone dies. In this case, I'm the only casualty. The rest of my coverage today determines if I am a fatality.

*   *   *

Aldus gets credit for being an A-plus speaker. I would have loved having him as a professor back in my school days. Perhaps I would not have fallen asleep as often during lectures. Even though I know I'm supposed to dislike this guy, I find myself caught up in his ideas. Excitement hits me. For the same reason, I've always been an easy touch for salespeople. That's why I drive a hybrid I've hated from the time I drove it off the lot, and I own a time share in a milquetoast resort not more than a twenty-minute drive from my home. I still remember how the sales guy got me hyped-up about the convenience of the amenities the piece-of-shit place offered. I have owned it for three years now and have yet to set foot in the facilities. Similarly, I have no doubt my thrill with Aldus will be a distant memory thirty seconds after Sweinhart opens her mouth to speak later tonight.

That said, I am not hearing evidence of the cronyism I had been led to expect. In fact, the guy seems sincere enough in his desire to get the power brokers out of the system. Who these power brokers are, I don't have a clue, but I gather from his comments that his opponent, Sweinhart, must be intimately aware and connected to this small, exclusive group of loathsome people? Overall, his message is clear: shrink government. He finishes by telling us he doesn't want this job, and he doesn't need this job, but he is right for this job, so vote for him. Here, I think he is full of shit. After his little surprise attack on me outside, I have no doubt he wants this job more than anything. Likewise, he needs this role if for no other reason than to fuel his ego.

There is more to Aldus than he is telling us. I can't tell if the guy is an egomaniac, a crook, or a fool. Hell, why would he put his company's IPO at risk for the sake of a job that pays him peanuts compared to his current role as CEO and, ultimately, could cost him billions in company value? Of course, there is the power. It is the most seductive concept throughout history. Wealth is attractive, but the desire for power is consuming. Wealth is sacrificed, populations killed, and countries destroyed all to enable one to lord over others.

I motion Jerry to cut the video so we can move in close to hopefully snag a few moments with the candidate before he leaves.

"Jerry, we record the next segment, no live feed. Got that?"

The asshole laughs at me. Can you believe that? "You got it, boss. You afraid he'll take you down a peg again?"

I don't bother answering. Instead, I flip him the finger and head off toward Aldus Simmons with Jerry and the rest of the crew in tow.

I can't believe it. Aldus breaks from a conversation as soon as he sees me approach. Instead of leaving, he heads directly toward me with his right hand out. "So, you get everything you want?"

I'm not sure what he means.

"Let me put it another way. Do you have any questions for me, Cartwright?" He smiles and continues, "You looked mighty tongue tied earlier. So, I assume you have some questions for me?"

He waits a second, shakes his head, and begins to turn from me just as I ask, "I didn't hear a thing about how you're going to help the poor and impoverished of our country. Is that why your opponent thinks you're the enemy of the little guy? Why should my viewers ever be interested in you?"

Aldus turns back around to face me and the camera. "Look, find me another candidate that gives a crap about the people they supposedly represent and I will give you a seat on my board. They don't care about you, me, anybody, except, of course, for themselves. Oh, hell, yes, maybe they started out wanting to do the right thing, but today they wouldn't know the right thing if it bit them in the ass. My opponent, Betty, probably makes money every time she votes on a bill. Not me. I don't give a shit about the money."

"Seriously? So, what do you care about? Aren't you really saying that you are just going to cost a hell of a lot more?" I motion for Jerry to cut the tape and spin to walk away.

"Hey, Cartwright."

I turn back around.

"Well parried. Can't wait until next time." Aldus shakes his head and smiles. I'm smiling, too. "By the way, I doubt that Betty gives a shit about the dough anymore. For her, it's always been the power."

CHAPTER 2: Being Seen

I'm still exhilarated from this afternoon. Even Jerry is impressed at my counterattack on Aldus.

"Dude, I'm blown away you pulled that off today. Gawd, you got balls."

"Not at all. We couldn't let him get the best of us twice. By the way, the station heads were thrilled when they got the recording. Thanks for uploading it. I'll bet that gets repeated dozens of times before tonight's news shows are done."

"Fame and glory, bud. Don't go forgetting about us little guys when you get an anchor job."

"Forget who?" I jest. "I'll make sure you guys are going to get gigs that will make you famous. You know, something where you get to wear combat fatigues and dodge bullets. Sound good?"

"Dude, ouch. At least make sure I get to carry a gun. Cameras don't provide much protection. Not on the battlefield or in here." He nods toward the front of the room where Betty Sweinhart is sitting at a table eating dinner with some rich muckety-mucks.

This is a different breed of folks. They have each unloaded five thousand bucks or more for a plate of chicken and some overcooked veggies. My station paid forty thousand to buy a table of eight: for me, my cameraman, and some execs from the station, including my senior producer, along with our CEO. Betty has been gracious enough to bless our table with her presence for a few moments and to press the flesh. She's taken great interest in my producer, Brandon, but quite frankly, I don't think she even noticed me or Jerry. We're only the hired help. If you can't afford the five grand, you better be good at taking pictures, cleaning up the dishes, or serving the wine. Even with Betty taking a seat between my producer and his wife, the wine is the only good thing at the table.

Halfway through dinner, after the main course but before the dessert, the real program begins. First, the state party chairman climbs the steps to take his place behind the microphone. It's our signal that Jerry and I don't get dessert; it's time to go to work. Jerry follows me to the back of the room so we can start recording. The first speech is nothing but fluff and is boring. Although we have no interest in using it, it does give us time to record the audience. We've been provided a seating chart showing the rich and famous, the opinion setters. We'll need to hit a half dozen of these pretty people to demonstrate to the world who is the right candidate.

As the first speech winds down, the crowd stands in applause as Betty makes her way across the stage. I don't know whether people are standing because they love this woman or because they just need to get their blood circulating again after ten minutes of listening to the chairman droning on combined with an increase in serotonin levels from dinner. I don't understand how the event planners can screw this up time and time again. What better way to lower energy levels than complement a meal filled with tryptophan with abundant wine? They may as well provide pillows, too. At least the wait staff are busy filling cups with coffee … probably too little, too late.

In comparison, Sweinhart is great. She starts off with a joke poked at the chairman and then moves seamlessly into an attack on Aldus' launch this morning. "So, you think five thousand is a little rich for chicken? You could have joined my opponent earlier today and had turkey." The crowd makes the obligatory laugh to a very old joke. It will be a good line for tonight's news. The one liner is just the right thing to post on social media.

"Seriously, folks, look to your right and left. You see that individual? That is what this election is about. It is not about you, it's about all of us. Without your support, you let down those less fortunate, the hopeless, the helpless, the voiceless. You have dug into your pockets tonight, not for your own benefit, but for the benefit of all of us, for the benefit of the country. Look around again. The country sees you standing up for right, standing up for what I stand for. You are with me. I can feel it and I will remember it. You are like family to me.

"So, my friend and opponent—yes, I think of him as a friend—says he is about the little guy, but he doesn't even know what a normal person looks like. Would he even recognize you? You represent this state, and you need to provide the leadership to ensure my opponent never gets a toe hold in the minds of people. He is a cancer to our democracy. He would remove the very controls government currently provides, ensuring we are all appropriately taken care of. To his way of thinking, we should return to the time of the acid rain and the Love Canal. I don't want to go there and neither do you.

"I have an agenda I started twenty-four years ago, and we continue to progress forward in support of that agenda. When I started down this path, I was young and inexperienced, but I had a vision of where our government should take us, not the other way around. Government owes taking care of us all, not just a few, the lucky, the well connected. Look around at those at your table and those at the tables around you and you see the leaders who make a change for our betterment every day. You are the privileged and, as such, owe much to the rest of us. You are the wise, so you owe leading us and spreading the message. You are the gifted, so you will be part of the enlightenment. Our progress cannot be allowed to dissolve into the ether just because you fail, you get tired, or you begin to question. No, we press forward because we know that through our governance, we prosper…"

I motion for Jerry to cut the recording. He ignores me at first, until I physically push the camera aside.

"What the heck, Cartwright, this is historical."

"Naw, it's the same speech we'll hear a dozen times more as we follow this campaign. Let's set up outside so we can catch the crowd as they exit. I want to catch some of the Hollywood A-listers."

"You really think they'll be up for a couple questions?"

"Why else would they pay five thousand bucks for a dry chicken breast and cheap wine?"

*   *   *

I hate this part of the job, talking to someone who knows nothing and pretending they know something. My last interviewee is a great example of why the ancient Greeks referred to actors as *hupokritēs*, or hypocrites; they pretend to be something they aren't. This guy has had a successful acting career starring in a comedic drama television series as a social worker working with the skid row homeless community. Now the world thinks he is an expert on poverty and mental health. I'm listening to this guy parrot soundbite after soundbite from Betty's last election run in which she was pushing for a national program to battle homelessness. He must not have heard a word from tonight's speech because she never touched on homelessness. Given the failure of her last foray into this topic, I suspect she never will again. The scary thing is this guy thinks she is addressing the problem … and she is the only one with the answer … and he should know because he has been directly involved in solving the problem for years. It's too bad he's never even spoken to someone living on the street, unless it was to tell the individual to go somewhere else to piss. This guy is clueless to the point of being comical, but since he is an A-lister, I'll include some snippets of him with two or three of the other beautiful people from tonight. This is my attempt at "kissing the ring."

We are getting ready to wrap the interviews up so that we can prepare for my live commentary when I spot Brandon, my producer, weaving and wobbling from one or four glasses of wine. On his arm is Betty. To her credit, she has taken complete control of the situation and has him pointed in my direction. Even though they are still twenty feet or more away, my producer stops to lean against a railing. It's clear he is going no further.

Obviously drunk, he says, "Cartwright, put Senator Sweinhart on during your live feed. Don't worry about a script. Just ask her a couple questions and let her go. It'll be good for the public to get to know her." He closes his eyes and I think he's passed out while standing until he starts up again. "And tell the team we're going to give her some free rein to speak. Free up a couple minutes. It's our exclusive."

"Okay? Senator Sweinhart, you okay with this?"

"Of course. Why would I not be? But just the same, limit your questions to my speech tonight. Understood?"

"Sure, why not. We were just getting ready to go live, so if you don't mind giving us ten minutes or so to upload some of our video, that would be great."

Although I am being pleasant, I'm quietly seething over what my SOB producer has just pulled. The likelihood of this going over well is not good. That said, it means our other interviews will take a backseat. I might be able to get some more distance out of them in the morning.

I call the studio to inform them of the change in plans for tonight's broadcast. I'm not sure who is in more trouble, me or the producer, but if I must bet, the producer may be in the hot seat tomorrow morning.

Jerry has the camera on, and I feel completely inadequate to fire a question or two to this four-term senator. "Senator, tonight you made a significant point of stressing how our government owes us more. Would you like to share a few points where the government needs to exercise more control?"

I can tell from Sweinhart's forehead that she is less than happy with my first question. Although I don't know why, she has taken exception to me sharing her desire to make government's role more significant in our lives.

"Simon, you don't mind if I call you Simon, do you?" Before I can even respond, she barrels on, "Of course, you don't. I think you have misrepresented my vision for the country. It is not that I think government needs to exercise more control over the populace, but it must be prepared to exercise control when we have organizations and businesses that choose to operate in a manner inconsistent with our values. I, for one, think it is a right for us all to receive the best of educations and to have the health care we deserve. Our government owes us that, and I will ensure it delivers. It is a simple message we should all get behind."

"That sounds great, but will teachers still have the right to strike for pay? Are doctors and nurses going to be compelled to provide care?"

"Those are hypothetical questions that have no merit. Of course the teachers' unions will have the right to strike. I have always defended the right to unionize. So I love that my comments stimulated some thought. I will never shy away from the tough issues. Too bad the same thing cannot be said about my opponent. I trust I can count on your support in this election?"

"Of course. Just like last time."

She smiles at me as Jerry says, "Off." The smile disappears instantly. "Look, you prick. How dare you try to push me into a stupid debate on government powers. You better get in line with your boss over there..." She nods her head toward Brandon. "...if you ever want to get ahead in this industry."

She doesn't even give me the chance to apologize before she marches back inside. It's probably a good thing, because I really have no idea why I would be apologizing. That said, I'm sure my producer will tell me in the morning, right after his ass gets chewed out for pulling such a lame brain stunt.

CHAPTER 3: The Cost of Fame

Shit, shit, shit, shit. I can't believe this. Brandon just sits there in his fucking chair, grinning from ear to ear while I get reamed for asking a couple questions the Lady Sweinhart didn't care for. I'm so angry I am having difficulty concentrating on what the CEO from our parent, Meyer Broadcasting, is yelling. I can't believe it. He's yelling and pointing at me as if I am a dog that crapped on the carpet. I don't doubt he would punch me if he were not every bit of sixty years of age and fifty pounds overweight. He's a heart attack waiting to happen. I find myself hoping it happens now.

Even though I'm only getting part of what he is screaming, it's clear he thinks I don't have a clue of what team I am on.

He finally uses up his energy as he falls back into the desk chair. The chair sinks and rebounds slightly under his tonnage. I'm surprised it doesn't collapse.

He continues calmly now, "What the hell were you thinking? I mean it, seriously, what could possibly have motivated you to ask her, live on TV, to explain why she thinks the government needs to control us more? Goddamn, that could frighten away voters like crazy. Are you nuts? Or are you really that stupid?"

"Honest, I had no intention of crossing her up. I had no time to even think of a question. My boss..." I nod toward my producer, "…was having a tough time thinking through the fog of alcohol and he set me up."

That was a mistake, a big mistake. Even though Brandon seemed to enjoy watching me taking the heat, at least he had remained quiet. Now I'd invited him into the ambush to take more bites out of my already bloodied ego.

Brandon jumps in with, "Who the fuck do you think you are? Did you think you were invited to the dinner so you might pretend to be one of the important folks? Are you kidding? You were there for one job, reporting, and it seems that you somehow forgot it. How dare you blame your lack of prep on me! I gave you an opportunity anyone else on the news team would have died for. Well, fuck. You died out there, and you tried damn hard to take us with you."

Brandon leans back in his chair as he links his hands in front of his face to hide his smirk. I see it, but our CEO is oblivious. "Look, Cartwright, I've got a shitload of money riding on this election, and you were the horse I was counting on to deliver. Are you up to it or not?"

"Of course, I'm your guy. What happened last night will not happen again. From now on, I'll provide her my questions ahead of time."

The CEO interrupts me. "Look, I don't want to know how you make her look good. You get it? I need to be able to say my reporting is 'ethical,' so I leave it up to you to define what ethical means. However you play it, it's between you and this jerk." He points his thumb in the direction of Brandon.

"But let's not lose sight of the fact that there are powers that make my life very lucrative. I have no desire to let the money train slow down, and what you did last night certainly could have thrown on the brakes. Now, I talked with Betty's campaign director last night for hours." He paused. "Yes, for fucking hours, but we finally agreed there is a silver lining to your screw up. I think everyone who saw that interview, and by now it probably includes half of the state since that Aldus character couldn't wait to get it on social media ... well, they all probably think you're anything but a supporter of the senator. Certainly, no one is going think you're her lackey. You now get a pass to be considered objective by the voters. You are perfect to push her now. Don't fuck it up."

He is right, of course. If I can make the senator look good, people will believe it. How could they not? Right now, they think I'm not in her camp. I am perfectly positioned. "I can do this. The senator is going to look like the right choice for the state and the country. She is—"

The CEO interrupts me. "That's because she is the right choice. I know it, he knows it..." He points at Brandon. "...she knows, and you better know it."

"What about Aldus Simmons?" Brandon asks.

"What about him? Cartwright, here, covers them both, but you've got to stay in line with the story. He is all about the rich. Doesn't give a shit about the poor sops. Trust me. I've known the guy from his first company. He thought his shit didn't stink. He keeps talking about people being free to make choices. That's easy for him to say with his billions. It's not so easy when you can't get a decent paying job. The government needs to step in, and it has to come from the top."

I haven't a clue as to what his point is, but I won't argue. I just nod in agreement.

"Cartwright, time to get the fuck out of here and get to work. By the way, give the senator's campaign manager a call and fit them in for an interview today. Brandon will figure out when to air it. I want it to be something special.

"And you may as well set up something with that Aldus character. For some reason, his publicist thinks you love the guy. He wants to give you an interview sometime next week."

*   *   *

This is uncomfortable. I feel as though I'm an actor. I am no longer a journalist, just some good-looking guy playing the part. I shot some questions I thought would be good for the interview over to the senator's campaign office for their review and approval. What I got back was a series of replacement questions for me to ask, none of which were related to my original prompts.

On the surface, their questions appear to be reasonable, but they all provide outs for her to duck tough issues while sounding as though she is smart as hell. Smart sells. Intermingled are some softballs that I'm sure they'll use to show the human side of the individual. Smart and sensitive sells even better. These guys get great grades for being manipulative ... and now I get to be a part of it. I get to stand there with a microphone in my hand and read questions I don't even like.

Sweinhart gets to act, too. She gets to pretend that these questions are intended to trip her up. I suspect she'll feign anger at a couple of them to keep my audience thinking that she and I are antagonists. We are antagonists only in that we do not like or respect each other, but who cares? We are both getting what we want from the relation: for me, it is notoriety; for her, it is independent affirmation. I know I'll feel a lot smaller when I look in the mirror tomorrow. I don't think a day's stubble or graying of my hair will help.

We have a small stage set up in the studio for her interview. I love the way we fool the viewer. A little set design consisting of a couple chairs, a coffee table, a couple nondescript books and flowers combined with a digital background is going to make it look as though I'm interviewing the senator in her living room. You might ask why we don't interview her there? Rumor is that she does not want the interruption to her personal life. I think she doesn't want our five-year-old van sitting in front of her mega-million-dollar mansion. Hell, she probably would have had us patted down when we left to make sure we didn't walk off with something. In other words, I'm perfectly happy having the interview occur in the comfort of our own studio.

When the senator finally arrives, she is already half an hour late. There is no apology, no excuse, no acknowledgement of being late. Instead, she acts as though we, meaning I, am holding her up. I stand up from my chair, extending my hand in welcome. She ignores it and sits in her chair.

"I thought there would be a table by my chair for the coffee. Where is it?"

I motion to one of the channel staff. "Do we have an end table or something?"

I'm not sure which cameraman makes the comment, but I hear a low, "What the fuck?"

We all hear it. Just what I need to piss off the senator again.

Thankfully, she laughs off the comment and waves her hand. "Screw it. We'll just use the coffee table. But there's not a chance in hell you are going to catch me reaching for a cup. You need to make sure the camera stays on him…" She points at me. "…if I am grabbing my drink."

While she continues providing her orders to the director, Sweinhart's campaign manager kneels beside me and whispers, "You have our questions, right?"

"Yes."

"So I can count on there being no slip-ups?"

"That is the plan."

"Then sign this." She pushes a non-disclosure agreement into my hand. "It essentially says that anything discussed here today outside of the agreed upon questions is confidential. That includes the crap with the table and whatever else she is demanding. You got it?"

"I think this is something Brandon needs to sign. I can't sign anything legal for the station or the news program."

"Look, this is personal. We don't give a rat's ass about your station. I want to make sure you stay in line. If you don't, there will be hell to pay … and I understand hell is expensive this time of year. You can't afford it. Just sign it and let's get going. We have a busy schedule today and you're holding me up."

I peruse the document quickly, acting like I might understand what the legalese means. I don't. The only thing I do get from looking at the agreement is that if I don't sign it, I get no interview. Plus, I'll likely get canned. I pull a pen from my folder and sign. I think she just castrated me.

CHAPTER 4: Glass Cuts Twice

"**S**hit, I'm killing your segment for the afternoon."

My mind went blank after Brandon's words hit me. He is going on and on about how we can't allow the public to begin feeling sorry about Aldus. I'm tempted to hang up on him, but of course, I can't.

"…you got it? Yeah, that will work great."

I shake myself from my stupor. I can't help it. "What? I don't know why but the signal must have dropped out. Say it again."

"Cartwright, what the fuck? Are you not even paying attention? I said I changed my mind. We'll run live. Have the guys see if they can get some of the blood in your background. Start it off with a basic overview that stresses his wife is dead. We'll take care of a brief bio for her from down here at the station. You are our eyes and ears on the street. We'll ask you live what happened and what you saw. Make it sound respectful but be sure to drop the bombshell … that it looked like Aldus Simmons jumped behind his wife when the glass crashed. He used her as a shield, and she fucking died. This is going to be great. He won't be able to get a vote from his mom after this."

"But, Brandon, that's not what happened."

"How the fuck do you know? You said you were standing outside when it happened. I'm sure the glare of the window is going to make seeing anything tough. Hell, Aldus' team is going to fight your story, but they'll never get ahead of it. Hell, this might push him right out of the race. Betty will give you another interview as thanks. I love it … just love it."

"Brandon, she was sitting on the other side of the table. He couldn't have jumped behind her."

"You don't get it. I don't care. Say what you want, but at the end of your report, people better believe this guy is the chickenshit we all know him to be."

This is a problem. Sure, I can massage my message to make it sound very plausible that Simmons was the reason his wife is still laying in a pool of blood, but he wasn't, and I think he is anything but a chickenshit. After my report, he will be my enemy. I'm not sure who might be more dangerous, him or Sweinhart. Although Sweinhart probably has more experience at getting back at people, somehow I think Aldus Simmons' retribution will be significantly harsher.

No time to be concerned. I have my marching orders and I will be a good soldier.

My team sets up for the shot. I'm tempted to scratch the blood shot, but I think I'll keep it. Aldus is still inside, holding his dead wife in his arms while the emergency team stands by, looking on stupidly. Sure, my viewers are going to feel sorry for him, initially, but once I let it out that he ducked behind her and let her take the brunt of the crashing glass, they will hate him.

And here I thought our drive up from LA in the dark hours before sunrise was going to be a waste. The fact that my team had to face the dangers of a riotous crowd along with real danger when all hell broke loose is great. The image of Aldus and the story of his cowardice might just land me an Edward R. Murrow Award nomination. Especially if I can follow it up later this evening with some suggestion that the meeting potentially had some nefarious aspect related to taking down his opponent. Some will think he got just what he deserved.

Of course, I have no doubt the meeting did have something to do with defeating Betty. It just didn't have a nasty vein. My notes show the meeting was really nothing more than a planning meeting to review the effectiveness of his messaging before heading off to a couple of important "meet the public" events today. Well, I guess those just fell from his agenda.

On the phone, I hear, "Live in five, four, three…"

*   *   *

The drive home is quiet. My team knows exactly what I have done. I can't tell if they're ashamed of me or themselves for being part of my journalistic terrorist attack. You know, I'm not too proud of what I did today either. How can I be. I have torpedoed a run for office. I have slandered an innocent man at a time when he was ill prepared to defend himself. I fool myself into thinking that this is the price of fame in my business, but I cannot believe my dad or granddad would ever have stooped to what I did today.

The moonless night is dark. Inside of our van, it seems even darker, the only light coming from the green glow of the speedometer telling the driver he is cruising well above the posted speed limit. It is silent except for the noise of our tires humming against the asphalt of the Five as we roll home. I'm thankful I don't have to see the faces of my crew. I suspect they are just as happy to not have to look at mine. I'm concerned they will turn in their badges and quit as soon as we get back to the studio, but who is kidding who? They are just as hungry for fame and success as I am. The only difference is that they have cover: me. If things go bad, I take the fall. They can just pretend they were following orders. Or that they thought I was telling the truth.

Jerry is the first one to break the silence. "Simon, what the heck was that all about? Why the hatchet job?"

I don't know whether I'm better off to lie or come clean. I lie. "I don't know what you're talking about."

"Shut the fuck up, man. You know exactly what I mean. You couldn't see what happened inside when the window broke. None of us could. There was way too much glare. Besides, you were talking to me for a quick sound and video check. You wanted to make sure the mic picked you up okay even with the crowd revving up. You weren't even looking in the right direction until the window shattered."

"I think you are remembering the situation wrong. I know damn well what I saw."

The rest of the team stays quiet and ignores Jerry and me. It's as if we don't exist.

"You are fucking amazing, dude. I got you on camera with your back to the window when it all went down. I even have that lectern thing, or whatever you call it, being tossed through the window. I got the guy throwing it, too. You want to see it?" He pushes the camera's view finder toward me, but I refuse to take the camera into my hands. He shakes his head. "It's amazing, but we can't give it to the cops now without hanging us all out to dry. Why'd you make up that piece of shit story?"

What do you do when you are caught in a lie? In my case, you double down. I guess I'm not so different from the politicians I cover. "Look, I don't know what you think you see on the video, but it is not right. Plus, remember, you don't own the video, the station does. Give it to Brandon and let him deal with it."

"Damnit, Simon, you got to do what's right. We all do."

I can see his eyes glistening from the oncoming headlights. I don't respond. Jerry puts the camera back into its bag, turns away from me, folds his arms across his chest, and stares out the window into the darkness of night. It's the last time we'll talk. I just don't know it yet.

CHAPTER 5: Consequences

Jerry does not utter a word as our van turns into the station's parking lot. It's late and we're all tired. I can attribute the silence to fatigue, but we all know that our relation and trust in one another changed today. At least the rest of the crew has managed to rise above the issue, recognizing it as just a function of doing business. They murmur the typical "goodnight" and "see you in the a.m." and the sort of meaningless salutation that really means I am bushed and there is no need to respond. It's the type of comment I have become used to my entire professional life. They sound cordial enough but reflect no true friendship or interest in one another.

Jerry was the one I could normally count on to break the monotony by asking if I wanted to grab a beer or something before heading home. He's probably the closest thing I've ever had to a friend at work. He didn't even bother with the obligatory "goodnight." Instead, he's already on his way to his car before I pull my satchel from the seat beside me. By the time I'm out of the van, he's already started up his car. That's okay. I don't feel like drinking a beer tonight. I could use something significantly stronger.

The station door opens, letting the bright illumination inside cut through the darkness of our parking lot. I never could understand why we didn't get some lighting out here. It's a surprise someone hasn't been attacked in the dark.

Brandon steps out. He's just a silhouette, but I can tell it's him as soon as he opens his mouth.

"Sounds like you guys had an interesting trip today. You can take tomorrow off. You deserve it." He pauses. "Except you, Cartwright. We're going to need you in the studio to comment on what happened today. You are going to be famous. And swing on into my office after you dump your stuff. We need to talk tonight. No ifs, ands, or buts."

"Brandon, are you kidding? I'm completely spent. I just want to dive into a glass of Jack Daniels. Can't we put off your reaming of me until the morning?"

Even though I can't make out his face, I know Brandon is smiling. "No reaming tonight, buddy. Be in my office in ten." I barely make out his last words since he's already on his way back inside. He lets the heavy fire door slam behind him. In the silence of night, it sounds like a gun firing.

I have no desire to meet with the prick tonight. I consider blowing him off and just loading myself into my Lexus and heading to my apartment. Even at this late hour, traffic is still going to make it hard for me to get home within an hour. I need to grab some shut eye before tomorrow's time on TV. I can't be looking strung out.

I toy with leaving, but who am I kidding. I'll never stand up to Brandon. "Fuck." I toss my bag into the passenger seat, lock the doors and head inside.

*　　*　　*

Brandon is talking on the phone as I enter his office. He holds his hand up, palm facing me, as if to suggest "give me a moment" and "be quiet." This is a typical Brandon welcome. At this late hour, I wonder if he has someone on the line or if this is his way of acting important and driving home that his time is precious, implying mine isn't. I turn as if to leave and hear him say, "Hold on a sec," and then to me, "Cartwright, this is only going to take a moment. Just sit down."

If anything, I am compliant. It is not until I sit that I notice Brandon and I are not alone. In the corner of the office sits a man with his arms crossed over his chest and his legs extended out in front of him. His head is extended back to rest against the wall. I can't tell if he's awake. His eyes are hidden behind dark sunglasses.

On the surface, he appears to be a caricature of a private detective from some old TV show: clean shaven, short hair with silvered sideburns, cheap gray suit, worn leather dress shoes, a bulge under his arm that I assume is a pistol. The only thing he's missing to make the picture complete is a felt fedora. I can't help but stare at the guy while I wait for Brandon to hang up the phone.

"Got a problem?" he says without moving.

"Huh?"

"You got a problem with me? Perhaps you don't like me being in here for your meeting with your producer?"

"No, of course not. As long as Brandon is okay with it, I am, too."

"Good." He pulls the glasses down below his eyes, peering at me. "So, tell me, what happened today?"

"I think I should wait for Brandon." I notice now that Brandon has put down the phone and is now intently looking at me.

"Your boss doesn't care. Isn't that right, Brandon?" He doesn't wait for a reply. He plows on, "In fact, I don't think Brandon gives a fuck what happened today as long as it made Aldus look bad. Right? So, tell me. What happened today?"

I look toward Brandon. I catch his eyes just before they dart to a piece of paper on his desk, as if it has caught his attention and is now the most important thing in the world. Without looking at me, he says, "Go ahead and tell him. Pretend I'm not here."

I jump into describing how the day went, and the man cuts me off.

"Look, you dumb fuck. I already know what happened up in San Fran. You think I'm stupid or something? It's been all over the news. How could I not know? I want to know what happened between you and your crew afterwards."

"Nothing." He's removed his glasses completely now and his blue eyes feel as though they are boring into me. "Seriously, nothing."

He waits a moment longer before continuing his questioning. "I have information that says your cameraman is not too happy. I want to know about that."

"Not much to say. He doesn't agree with what I reported at the scene today."

"Is there a reason he should not agree with what you saw?"

I look to Brandon, but he continues ignoring me. As a person, Brandon is a piece of shit. As a producer, he is worth even less. "Brandon, I think we need to get an attorney in here."

The man stops me. "There aren't going to be any attorneys involved with this. I am not looking to charge you with anything. If I wanted to, I could have had you behind bars before your butt ever got back into the van. All I want to know is if there is a reason for him to not agree with you?"

"I don't know what you're getting at, but he says the video seems to tell a different story from what I saw, but with glare and all, who knows. All I can tell you is what I saw."

"If I look at the video, will I agree with you or him?"

I straighten myself up in the chair and lean into the man to make myself look surer of myself than I feel. "That doesn't matter because you are never going to see the video. It's the property of the station, and video gets fucked up all the time. I don't even know if the video still exists since we decided not to use it."

"Mister Producer, may I have the video if I ask nicely?"

Brandon shows me once again he is the prick I always thought him to be. "Sure. Cartwright, hand it over."

"But I don't have it. Jerry still has it in the camera. You're going to have to wait until tomorrow. I mean the day after tomorrow. You already gave the crew the day off."

"Well, that is a problem. Maybe I will need to wake Jerry up at home." He looks to my producer. "Any problem with that?"

"Whatever you want, Gedeon. It's your call."

I can't believe what I'm hearing. "Brandon, who is this Gideon character and why would you give him my video?"

The man answers for Brandon. "First off, it is Gedeon, not Gideon. Sounds like a small thing, but pronounce it correctly, would you. And it is not your recording. You made it perfectly clear when we started, it is the property of the station. You have ownership of, well, nothing here."

He pulls out his phone and, without punching in a number, says, "You know where it is. Get it.

"Gentlemen, this has been a wonderful evening. Simon Cartwright, I think I will remember you. Nice job trying to stand up to me. Just remember, there is a big difference between trying and doing. In my world, you either succeed or fail. You get no brownie points for making the effort, but, hey, you showed a little spunk. Maybe your boss is right, you do have a bright future. Just remember that future might be over in a flash if you cross me again.

"Brandon, good night." He stands up and walks by me to the door. He pushes it open and leaves without saying anything more.

"What the heck was that all about, Brandon? Am I in trouble?"

"Not now. I think you need to go home. Don't stop anywhere along the way, and don't call Jerry. I want you here by eight so we can get you prepped for your interviews. Tomorrow, you will be answering the questions, not asking them, and you need to answer them right."

"What about Jerry?"

"What about him?"

"You're not seriously going to let Gedeon roust him tonight for the video file, are you?"

"Look, you need to know, Gedeon is a big wig for us at the corporate level. He was brought in as a special consultant to address questionable business and reporting practices. He's going to cover your butt on this, but make sure you know he is doing it for the company, not you. He couldn't possibly care less about you except for the fact that you went off the reservation today and exposed us. You aren't in trouble because you enabled an attack against Aldus, but you are on his radar screen now. That might not be a good thing."

"Okay, fine, but what about Jerry?"

"Jerry who? Go home, Simon."

CHAPTER 6: I am Boss?

I t sucks having to deal with a new cameraman on every assignment. Ever since Jerry left the organization, we've been shorthanded, calling out cameramen from the studio to fill the void he left by just choosing not to show up at work. He won't even return my phone calls. I know he was upset with what I did a couple of weeks ago, but I never thought it would motivate him to quit. Granted, the job sucked, but it was one of those sucky jobs you love to have. It gave us something to complain about. Now, he has moved on. I hope it is something he really loves.

For me, I feel like a sports athlete that has been optioned to another team. I'm on my way up to an affiliated station in the bay area. It makes a lot of sense in that most of what I'll be covering for the election will be centered either in San Francisco or Sacramento, plus my reporting crew in LA is in a state of flux until the station gets us a permanent replacement for Jerry. It's good to be out of that turmoil for a while.

My new loaner team—I guess that is what they are—is anything but friendly. I don't fit in with them. Part of it is a natural competitiveness between northern and southern California, but I think this is more deep-seated. It's like the Irish and the Brits, I think, and the San Francisco team is the Irish. They won't be happy until I'm pushed out. Sure, they are professional, but I'm convinced they do everything in their power to make me look bad. My work takes twice as long as it should because I inevitably need to reshoot video on every assignment. I even need to check the video feeds they send in to ensure the video I want makes it to the viewer. I dread live interviews because I know the crew will screw it up by ensuring something awkward shows up in the background, or the audio drops out, or we go live before I expect. This team sucks.

Today, we're heading out to provide all-day coverage of the two major senatorial candidates. In the afternoon, we'll be with Aldus for a major rally. In the evening, we're going to repeat the effort with Senator Sweinhart. As a note, we refer to Aldus by his first name and Betty Sweinhart as Senator. It is the unwritten policy to make sure everyone views Betty as the only real senatorial talent in the election. The way we address the candidates is intended to reinforce the message.

My team is particularly quiet on the trip to the convention center for our first assignment of the day.

"Okay, guys, what's up? What do you have planned to fuck me over today?" I wait for an answer. None comes.

"Seriously, what gives? You going to flip off my microphone if I get Aldus for a few moments? You going to interrupt the feed so the station stops our live transmissions? What?"

"Nothing, Cartwright. We're playing it straight today. The word is out that we're done if we mess around today. You can count on us. Don't worry. No more funny stuff."

"Really?"

"Really."

"So, come clean, why the change of heart? You could have, should have, been fired days ago for the shit you've pulled."

"That's the point; nobody noticed because the problems were covered up at the station. Now somebody knows and cares. They apparently care a lot. We're playing it straight from now on."

"Good, so let's go over the plan then for Aldus' rally. He is a prick who's trying to buy his way to Washington, DC. I want two cameras going. One on him continuously, and a second spanning the crowd and his henchman. I want something, anything, that makes a joke of this. Get him picking his nose, get someone falling asleep while he talks. Use the parabolic mic to catch him saying something, anything, he thinks is private. I'm going to take him down. Now that you're onboard with the agenda, we actually might be able to do something."

For the first time in the last couple of weeks, I think I might be able to get something good. If these jerks let me down today, I might need to get Brandon to call in Gedeon. He'd scare the shit out of these guys.

I text Aldus' campaign manager to see if I can steal a couple minutes from him before his speech to get some comments. It's my chance to get him rattled. If I wait until after, I'll be lumped in with a half dozen half-wit reporter wannabes from San Francisco. One would think the money from Silicon Valley would be sufficient to attract real reporting talent to the city; it doesn't. These hacks are only a couple of steps ahead of the Ozarks. They are a world away from LA or New York. I am so spoiled.

I get a text back suggesting the interview sounds great and they'll be ready for my team at noon if we don't mind the noise of the final preparations for the rally. They are already at the Moscone Center, so I just need to tell the head of security once I arrive and they'll send someone down to discuss the ground rules.

Ground rules? Everyone has their ground rules, but I no longer feel compelled to live within them. Sure, I'll agree, but once the live interview starts, they're going to be screwed. I guess they think that ignoring the ground rules is a big deal because I'll risk pissing away any future access to the candidate, that I'll effectively be locked out of doing my job. What a joke. They are whores for exposure. They need me as much as I need them, and I'm not concerned they'll freeze me out.

In any case, the San Fran news crew is shocked I locked up an interview during the twenty minutes it took us to drive from the studio to the convention center. In their world, producers act as though setting up an interview of this magnitude requires them to move heaven and earth. I smile. I let them think my notoriety is beginning to catch on and is opening doors. Little does my temporary crew know, the Simmons campaign has been demanding a live interview from my producer in LA since my story suggesting Aldus used his wife as a shield from a falling shower of glass. Even though the story has calmed over the past three weeks, the Simmons' campaign wants Aldus to have a chance to set the record straight. They even found another video supporting their position. It's too bad they don't get it. Bad news travels so much faster and further than good news. They will be fighting perception right up to the election.

Between the obvious support from somewhere within the four walls of the San Francisco station and my newfound fame, I expect my problems with this crew are a thing of the past.

*   *   *

"What the fuck?" The driver lays on the horn, adding to the craziness we see before us. For the last two blocks, ReAl protestors in the street have held the van to a crawling pace. I have no idea what this group's objectives are, but at least they are consistent with us in their hate for Aldus. They have shown up at every event he's had planned. Now that we have the Moscone Center in our sight, they have, unfortunately, forced us to a standstill. The driver pushes on the horn again, but the people are unwilling to move. It's not that there are so many that one would consider it a crowd, but they are still blocking all access to the Moscone.

"You guys are going to need to hoof it. I'll meet you inside once I find a way through these jerks." The driver throws the van into park and hops out to help us unload our gear.

It's only a couple of blocks to the entrance, so this should be okay. We'll get set up later than expected for the interview, but I suspect the campaign manager will still be thrilled to get Aldus on the air. Maybe she'll have second thoughts in a couple of hours.

I stop my cameraman just as he's about to set off to the entrance. "Take some video here." I point at an angle in front of the van that makes the crowd look larger than it is. This will be great for our feed during the rally. It'll provide a contrast of inside versus outside. It'll be the battle between the "haves" and the "have nots." Even though the protestors look as though they are part of the "haves" club, I'll position them as the downtrodden. The viewer believes whatever I say. So today, as the protestors run around with their thousand-dollar phones, their two-hundred-dollar shoes, and their designer clothes, the country will think of them as the "have nots" fighting the guy who made them poor. I should become a novelist because I have plenty of experience making up stories.

After shooting for a couple of minutes, it's off to the Moscone. Aldus' campaign manager meets me at the door. "Where have you been? We agreed you would meet us more than a half hour ago?"

"So, you want to cancel the interview?"

"Not on your life, but we need to talk about what I want you to ask as we walk."

"Don't bother. I already have my questions."

"Look, you misled everybody with your bullshit story about seeing Aldus duck behind his wife like a coward. You lied. You know it, I know it. After today, everybody is going to know you lied unless you do as I say."

"You seem to be awful demanding for someone who was begging me for an interview."

"You're right. Because before I didn't have any video of you not even looking in the right direction when the window smashed. You lied and we can prove it. I'm offering you a chance to duck the admission of guilt by asking my questions. You don't want to play it our way, we release the video before the rally. Your career will be fucked."

My mind is racing. There is no way I can let a video out that proves me a liar. In the same vein, if this is a bluff, I can't let on that I did not see what I reported. "First off, you couldn't possibly have a video that shows what you say … unless you fabricated it. But let me be fair about this. Let me see your questions."

She hands me her list. The questions are innocuous. They are not what I expected. No issues here. "I'm okay with these, but I want to ask a couple of my own, too. You okay with that … as long as I promise to ask yours, too?"

"But you've got to ask ours first. I know how you act; you'll get yours in and then you'll pull the plug on the interview before we get our message out. So, ours go first and we have a deal."

That was easy. They are still going to lose because I get to make comments throughout the rally, and Brandon is observing from our video feed so he can set me up with what to say. Aldus is going to suffer. My feed is going to be provided to affiliates not just in California, but nationally, due to the social importance being assigned to this election.

The public has moved from seeing Aldus as a successful businessman with a small government message to one in which he is a coward intent on hurting the little guy. They believe his motivation is to take away all government assistance for the poor.

His opponent has skated by with almost no serious examination. She is floating above the fray as the only candidate interested in social equality. What that means, I'm still not sure, but it is great as a catchall. Aldus talks about lowering the cost of government. Betty states his policy will hurt the pay from good jobs paid for by the government. It will take away pay from the poor and relegate them to poverty. It is social inequality. The message is clear: everything Aldus stands for is against social equality. I'm going to pin him to the wall on why he thinks taking away government-enabled jobs is good.

"You got a deal, but…" I say.

"But what? When do we go on?"

"The interview isn't going live."

"You prick, you know damn well that's what we demand. We want our story getting out, not the story you're going to make up with editing." She is fuming, then she smiles. "No problem, as long as you let us shoot it with our own people, too. Fuck us over and it goes out to everyone."

I pull out my phone to touch base with Brandon on the request. I'm surprised when he says, "Go for it." I nod to the campaign manager.

"So, when do you want Aldus?"

I look to my cameraman to see if he is ready. He gives me the thumbs up. "Ten minutes. We don't have much time, so tell your candidate to be quick. He starts pontificating, I pull the plug." Without waiting for her response, I jump to, "We'll set up next to the stage, so have your video crew and Aldus ready in five."

I walk over to the stage and pull out a couple of chairs to prep for the interview. "Guys, if I shake my head, pull the plug on their camera." I smile. "Just kidding." But I'm not.

The cameraman checks his lighting and sound and is ready to go when a couple of cameras show up from the campaign. One is going to stay focused on Aldus and me, while the other is going to keep us all, including my crew, in view during the entire interview. They don't trust us. Smart of them.

"So, Cartwright, let's get started." It's Aldus, and his crew is already recording. He's surprised me again.

"Mister Simmons, it's good to see you again. First off, let me provide my sincerest condolences on the loss of your wife. I know it must be heart wrenching."

"You have no idea how heart wrenching it was and still is. And you spreading a complete lie about what happened makes it even worse. You should be ashamed, but that would require you to hold truth as a value. I'm not sure you do."

"It's a shame you feel that way. I only want to report the truth, and in that spirit, I have agreed to let your team provide me with a couple of questions to kick off the interview. So, to get started. You've made a point of stressing how government needs to get smaller and that you want to create legislation that will trim hundreds of thousands of jobs, many of them from here in California. How can you justify hurting regular people by taking away their jobs?"

This first question has nothing to do with either of the questions they had provided to me, but I don't care. This is the question Brandon insisted I ask first. I have no idea how Aldus is going to respond, but I half expect him to call me an ass and walk off or pound me into the floor with his fists. Either way, I win.

He surprises me with, "Excellent question. My policies would never take good jobs from people, but it will change what those jobs are and who hires the individuals."

I interject, "But your policies—"

He stops me cold. "You asked the question, not me. Now quit interrupting and let me answer it. Today, your goonies have wasted money building useless personal projects while needed infrastructure goes wanting. Your system allows bureaucrats to consume huge portions of our tax dollars while underpaying our workers. Your bullshit ends up turning a buck into fifty cents on good days. On bad days, it turns it into a dime, all the while filling the pockets of those well connected to government. Well, I am not going to let that happen anymore. I'm the only candidate who gives a hoot about the taxpayer. I cannot and will not be bought off." He stops for a moment. "And I'm the only one who isn't buying their way into this job with money. Unfortunately, people from your side are making me buy the job with blood.

"By the way, we gave you a couple questions. When are you planning to ask them? I have a little side bet that you're too chicken to let me have a crack at them." He smiles into my camera. "The first question was 'Why am I taking on Betty for the US Senate seat?' I think it is straight forward. She's a crook and needs to be pushed out of office. As a private citizen, if I did what she does daily, I would go to jail. But it's not just her, it's the whole lot of them. They vote on things that will enrich themselves. Sure, they pretend their vote is in the interest of the taxpayer, but would they vote the same way if they didn't own the land where a dam was to be built? Or stock in a company that is going to benefit from government subsidies? You've got to question how dolts who could not make it in business can enter government and, suddenly, become rich and powerful. I'm sick of it. I'm committed to you the people, not my own pocketbook.

"You got that? Oh, and by the way, you lied about my wife and her murder. I would have given my life for her. The video shows it. Yes, the video shows it, but I know you'll never let it air. We're done here." And he steps up onto the stage and people start clapping.

I'm left alone, looking not into the camera but staring up at the man as he approaches the podium.

CHAPTER 7: The Gedeon Connection

Not a good day, and it had started out so promising, but it was all an illusion. Now the van is tomblike. It is dark, hot, and quiet, so quiet. Our interview with Aldus set the tone for the day. I was on my heels from that point on. He got the better of me, and it bothered me. I could not help but think about how I let it get out of control. We already sent the interview feed back to the studio, and now I have to come to grips with it not airing in the manner I'd hoped for, meaning, my lie from three weeks ago will probably be exploding across the news about this same time tomorrow evening. I'll be done as a reporter.

We pull into the station's underground parking garage. I hate this place. It lacks all appropriate lighting and ventilation. I'm surprised it meets with health code standards. It's eerie hearing the echo of my own footfall as I step down from the van onto the water-stained concrete. Maybe it is not water stained. It smells like piss. In a town with as many homeless as we see in San Francisco, it's inevitable these poor souls find a way into underground parking to protect themselves from the elements. I'd do it, too. But for now, I don't feel any sympathy for them. I'm only concerned for myself.

A man waits in the shadow of a support pillar. I would not have noticed him except for the glow of his cigarette and smell of the smoke. Smoke and piss, it almost makes me want to vomit. I suspect the man is homeless and nod to the rest of the crew to avoid him. You never know how crazy these folks are. It's best to get inside and call security. Let them deal with him.

"You guys head on up. I want to talk with Cartwright alone."

I know the voice. Its Brandon's guest, the corporate consultant. "Gedeon?"

"I am so glad you remember me. That way we don't need to waste time getting to know each other. You probably have gathered that I work with this station, too. Or it might be more correct to say they work with me. I ask them to do things and they do them. I do not expect, nor do I get, pushback. My clients get what they want, and the station managers get nice fat paychecks. By the way, you are going to see a nice bonus in your next pay. Just a little something to remind you who you work for. What we are going to talk about now is what I expect from you." He stops and looks me up and down.

"So," I begin to ask.

"Shut the fuck up. I'm thinking. I'll tell you when you can speak."

He pauses again. I'm very uncomfortable, waiting in silence. I want to say something, anything, to break the silence.

"We got a tape this evening from the breakfast where Missus Simmons bled out, very messy business." He laughs and I must have looked perplexed. "Messy blood and messy situation, get it? Funny thing, you weren't even looking in the right direction to see the action. It's a pity this video survived. I thought we stopped it the night we met, the night your friend Jerry tried to swim to Catalina Island. Yeah, I don't think he made it, especially with the bullet hole in his head. So maybe now you are getting the point. Do what I say, you get rich and famous. Cross me and you get to go swimming. Now that isn't so hard to understand. Is it?"

He doesn't wait for me to answer. "It's rhetorical, Cartwright, of course it isn't tough to understand. Now I do have a question I want you to answer, and I want you to think hard before you do. How in the hell could you let Aldus get the better of you again?"

We moved to the office suites on the upper floor of the station. Gedeon has invited a couple of his associates to join us. He doesn't ask if their attendance is okay with me, nor does he bother to introduce them. They are dressed like their boss—I assume Gedeon is their boss: cheap suits, scuffed leather shoes, white shirts, and nondescript ties. All they need is pocket protectors and they could double as my accountant. Well, not exactly. They are both carrying pistols under their coats. I can see the bulge of the holster. One wears a blue suit, one a gray. The guy in blue is of normal height and weight, just a little smaller than me. The guy in gray is imposing. He is big. He has me by at least five inches and fifty pounds.

I guess Gedeon was okay with how I answered his question because I'm still alive and dry, although I wet my pants a little when his two goons sit next to me. I am certain I'm about to die.

We are watching the video Jerry shot several weeks ago. It's good. It clearly shows the individual breaking the glass. In fact, I can see his face as he turns to run. I don't recognize the man, but the resolution is exceptional. I suspect it is more than sufficient to land the guy in jail for a long time.

Blue suit is talking. I think the gray suit is here just to intimidate me. "Looks like your friend made a copy we didn't get, a mistake that will not happen again. The Simmons' campaign got their hands on it and forwarded copies to half a dozen stations in town and to the police department. Our friends at the department have agreed to deep six this. They agree with us that the quality is just not good enough to find the perpetrator, as have the stations. Well, all but one, but we're not concerned. We are pulling together experts to attest to the video being a fake. We are taking care of you."

Gedeon interrupts with, "But you need to step up to the plate and reciprocate a little. When your producer gives you something to say, just say it verbatim. This is not a contest where you are trying to outshine your peers for ratings. You are all going to be famous … just as long as you say the lines as they are written. Think of yourself as an actor in a Shakespearian play. You think you can do better than Shakespeare? No, you cannot. Stick to the lines. The power is in everybody hearing the same thing over and over. We are feeding people what they want to hear. Don't confuse them.

"You screwed up with Aldus by letting him call the shots. You don't need to be nice to him. You don't owe him anything. Trust me, he is bad for our country, bad for our institutions, bad for my people. Cut him off whenever he gets going. I don't care if you need to grab the microphone out of his sweaty hands, you do it, then accuse him of something bad. Call him a liar, a pedophile, a fascist, whatever. It doesn't matter. People will believe you."

Blue Suit starts again. "Tomorrow, you are going on national TV to discuss the faked video. You are big time now. Here are the questions and the answers. Think of this as a midterm exam, but there is no reason for you to mess this up because it is open book. Make it look good, so do some prep and practice tonight. The message you push out tomorrow is 'Aldus is trying to change history to fit his narrative and I am not going to let him get away with it.' Everyone on TV is prepped to repeat this mantra all day. You have to say that line in every interview, exactly as I just stated. You got it?"

I nod.

We go through some basic logistics for tomorrow and Gedeon leaves, followed by the two suits. I'm alone in the office as I read through the questions and answers. I feel as though I have stepped out of my role as a journalist and entered the high-risk vocation of character assassin.

I give the questions a cursory once over. They imply that I am the de facto expert when it comes to Aldus Simmons, something that could not be further from the truth. My answers support the presumption of my expertise. I even note they include comments like "in my research," and "my investigation," and "unnamed sources suggest." What the fuck are they talking about? I haven't put any effort into investigating Aldus. I haven't got a clue why he really entered the race. I can't even recall the name of the companies he created. My producers know I spend more time brushing my hair than I do on hardcore research. To be frank, politics bore me to tears. Even though I'll be commenting on Simmons' policies, this is the first time I've read what those policies are. Thank goodness Gedeon's team has loaded me appropriately.

I'm concerned the answers seem to contradict much of what I've heard Simmons say in his speeches. Not a surprise; he wouldn't be the first politician who says things in public that have nothing to do with what he really believes. It just doesn't seem right, but who am I to argue with the experts.

The office phone rings. Without thinking, I answer it before considering what I will say. This isn't my office. I don't know whose office this is. I just say, "Hello."

"Cartwright?" It's Brandon.

"Yes, what's up?"

"I'm glad I caught you before you took off. You got what you're going to say tomorrow?"

"Sure, the script was hand delivered by some guys that scared the bejusus out of me."

"Me, too. You have any issues with what you are to say?"

"No, should I?"

"I did."

The phone remains quiet. I'm waiting for him to make sense of what he just said.

He continues, "Did you hear me?"

"Yes, of course. What issues?"

"Look, you are accusing the guy of doctoring a recording that might have helped find his wife's killer. It's a crime to knowingly tamper with evidence. You're going to accuse him of a crime, and it's eventually going to force you to testify. You ready for that?"

"Screw that, Brandon. No way. I could end up with a perjury charge. I'm not going to jail just because Gedeon has it in for Aldus."

"That's what I want to talk with you about. You're in this now for good. There is no way out unless you want to take same path Jerry took. I'm not kidding. You don't answer the questions exactly the way they are written, you are going down … and Gedeon says I get to go with you. So don't screw it up."

I hear the fear in Brandon's voice. He has me scared, too. I can't believe he continues to fuck me over even here in San Francisco. "Okay. I understand."

"What does that mean? Are you going to do what Gedeon wants or not?"

"I'll do it. I have no choice."

CHAPTER 8: Sinking Man

This is crazy. There are at least a half dozen stations here to cover my interview live. My little lie is spinning out of control, and I doubt Brandon will be able to help even if he wants to. I know Gedeon can help, but he won't. He has no desire to. His only objective is to take down Aldus Simmons. I'm afraid I might have already been written off as collateral damage.

After a brief introduction, the anchor from our affiliated San Francisco station begins firing his questions. This is his time for national notoriety. He thinks this interview is only a steppingstone for him. He doesn't give a shit about me. I suspect he has his marching directions to stay with the script, too. It's easy for him. He's not the guy lying. He's just an enabler. "Simon, this tape's taken us all by surprise. What do you make of it?"

"Is there any question? We have a candidate hemorrhaging in the polls and he's trying anything to look better, even doctoring video to make it look as though he isn't the coward he is. I have covered this guy and his campaign for months and he has yet to demonstrate even a scintilla of ethics or leadership. In my opinion, he should have stayed in the private industry where lying is apparently okay."

"You bring up lying. I understand you have uncovered case after case in which Simmons has misled the public.

Would you provide us a little update from your investigations?"

I love it. "Investigations" as in plural. I hold up a sheet of paper to the camera for emphasis and then launch into a series of accusations for which I have no background, no evidence, no knowledge, but I sound as though I do. My advantage: I am in friendly company. I have no need to document or support my charges. I feel like God. I say it, therefore it must be true.

Truth has nothing to do with today's interview. My accusations will spread like a California wildfire. Money and support will run from Aldus to avoid being burned. Betty could get caught snorting cocaine on video and it still wouldn't hurt her now. I have delivered the Senate seat to her for another term.

"So, the Simmons' campaign has accused you of withholding this video from the officials due to the unfavorable light it sheds on you, that you could not have possibly seen the window shattering. Frankly, I see their point. Why are you so intent on attacking Simmons?"

This is not in the script, at least in my script. Who knows what Gedeon gave to this prick? I try to stay focused so as not to let my eyes waver. I feel the heat rising in my face. The camera will see me turning red with anger, telling the viewers I have been caught in a lie. "Why would I make any of this up? I see what I see. I report exactly what I find, and I have always remained objective. Personally, I would have loved having a vigorous debate between these two candidates, but it isn't likely going to happen now."

"Perhaps it still can. We have a commitment from the Simmons camp to address your accusations in person, live today. This is going to be exciting. For our viewers, we will be showing this exclusively tonight at ten. We have contacted the Sweinhart camp for comment and will be including those as a preamble. I assume I can count on having you participate, too?"

The prick doesn't know what he is getting into. He thinks this is an LA versus San Fran thing and it isn't, not by a long shot. Someone is going to die over this. I just don't know who that someone is.

As soon as the camera cuts, my phone vibrates. The caller number is blocked; I assume it is Gedeon or one of his henchmen.

I start, "It wasn't my fault. You guys set me up."

"Shut up and listen." It is Gedeon. "Somebody set you up for sure, but it wasn't me. Aldus got you again?"

"Not me. This one is on you guys. You can't lay this on me. You need to get control of your players. What am I supposed to do now? I don't have a fucking clue if there is any truth behind the accusations you fed me. For all I know, they are made up out of the ether. I don't want to be anywhere close to the camera when Aldus starts tearing into them."

"You will be at the studio tonight. You are going to be there early, and you are going to be visible, very visible. Am I clear?"

"You can't be serious? You're destroying my career."

"Is that what you think?" He laughs. "You have no career without me. You can ride this with me, or perhaps I should be setting you up for a short swim in the bay. Look, with me you are going to be successful beyond your dreams. You can trust me."

"Trust you? You have me getting in deeper and deeper in this mess. I can't—"

"Correction!" He is yelling now. "You have gotten yourself deeper into trouble! Do not attempt to absolve yourself from responsibility. Your insane need for fame, for recognition, created this problem. I don't give a rat's ass about fame. I'm doing this for the good of the world and there is nothing that will get in the way of me fulfilling my responsibility. Be at the studio by seven." My phone goes dead.

This is not going to be good. I have no doubt someone will die tonight. I wonder who that will be if it isn't me.

*   *   *

The News at Six is just wrapping up as I wait to enter the studio. I've taken Gedeon's advice to heart and I'm entering from the main entrance to make sure the receptionist and lobby camera have me in full view. I think his exact words were "very visible," so here I am, Gedeon. I know you are watching me from some dark shadow, you sick fuck.

"Can I go on in? They need to get me ready for the interview with Aldus Simmons."

"Yes, I'm aware, Simon." She doesn't even look up from her monitor to say hello. I take this as a bad sign.

"You can't go in yet. They will be done with Senator Sweinhart soon and then I am to escort you into Studio Two."

"You don't need to escort me. I work here."

"Look, that corporate bigwig—"

"You mean Gedeon?"

"Yeah, I think that's his name. He made it very clear that I'm not to leave you alone until I deliver you to him in Studio Two. You sure you still work here?" Now she is smiling.

What a bitch. She thinks this is funny. I'll bet she would love seeing an LA reporter get shafted in San Fran.

"If I need to take a piss, are you going to come in the bathroom with me?"

She doesn't answer. She pretends to be intently interested in her computer screen.

Her phone rings. She picks it up but doesn't say anything; she is listening.

"Time to go." She sets the phone back in its cradle.

She leads, I follow, as we head through a darkened corridor to the studio. Sweinhart and a couple of her aides exit the studio as we enter.

"Simon, so good to see you. I thank you for your support and hope I can count on your vote." She gives me a quick wink as she turns down the corridor toward the rear exit of the building. Be "very visible" was not in her directions.

Inside, I see the blue suit, except tonight he has shed his suit for a designer black tee shirt and black slacks. His beaten shoes have been replaced with black Gucci loafers. He has shed the pedestrian accountant look for Hollywood producer. Gedeon is absent, as is the news anchor who tripped me up earlier.

"Cartwright, it looks like we may have wasted your time tonight. Aldus' campaign manager says she didn't know anything about confronting you live. They would love to, but they already have commitments for tonight."

"Okay, but where's that prick who started all this in the first place?"

"You're right here." He smiles. "Oh, you mean that other prick? He seems to be running late. He was MIA for the News at Six. Between you and me, he's going to be fired if he is lucky. He forgot to stick to the script. Oh well?" He holds his hands up to imply he has nothing to do with the situation.

"So, it's time for you to get into some make-up and prep for the Ten O'clock News. You are sitting in as the interim anchor. I have put out the story that the old one just up and quit, no heads-up or anything. You're right; he was a prick. Think of this as an audition."

I notice that he mentioned him in the past tense. Blue suit is smiling like crazy now. I think he is truly enjoying this. I'm not sure he is happy for me, but I know he's thrilled that someone who would not follow directions has become fish food tonight.

CHAPTER 9: Get What You Want

I speak to Brandon more now than I did when he was my producer in LA. We obviously did not like each other then, so I have no idea why he insists on calling me daily now that I'm working out of San Francisco.

"Cartwright, we gotta talk. I have an offer from a national news program, but it has a catch. I need to bring you, too. You got that? National exposure every day. No more schmucking around covering local stuff. No more being the little local guy trying to compete for time with important people. Now you can do what you really want. You can cover politics full time."

"Whoa, I never wanted to cover politics. You forced me into that. It almost got me killed. I've been staying low for the past couple of weeks, and I'm pretty okay with that."

"Bullshit, and you know it. Look, your contract is in your email. Take a look and get back to me ASAP. These guys are serious about the offer, but there is no negotiation, and there will not be a second chance. Fuck this one up and you're done."

"And what happens to you if I decline?"

"I'm not worried. I've done what I was told to do, and this is my reward. I get to take you along. I don't forget my friends."

To myself I ask, *So when did we become friends?* but I am cool. "Let me take a quick look and get back to you."

"Okay, thirty minutes? I'll give you a call?"

"Sure." I'm opening his email as I hang up.

I am literally shaking as I read Brandon's email. He is right. This is the opportunity of a lifetime. A national media giant wants me for a daily TV political news and commentary program. The program airs twice a day: drive time and late evening. Plus, it is syndicated via audio streaming services. This is the big time. The money is huge to me, maybe not great for established hosts, but it's more than I ever hoped to earn.

It's funny, the position is not as a reporter, but a commentator. I will have access to a staff who will research and write the commentary for me. Brandon will remain my producer, but assignments will come directly from something referred to as the Leadership Committee. The contract is for five days per week, but specifically provides for the agreement to be extended to both weekend days with a commensurate pro rata increase in pay. The contract is only for one year, with three one-year options that can be exercised at the pleasure of the company. I guess at this type of pay, who cares if they take up the options?

There are pages upon pages of details, exclusions, and limitations that I should read through, but who is kidding who? I am signing.

My phone rings. I don't even look at the number. I just answer, "I'm signing."

"That is good to hear." The voice is not Brandon's. It's Gedeon. "Then you are off to DC tonight. You start tomorrow. You can thank me now. I think you will agree I have not screwed up your career?"

"Thanks." What else can I say? If this guy has landed this for me, I am his for good.

"What about Brandon?"

"What about him. He left for DC yesterday. He is getting introduced to the Committee tonight. Reply to "all" with your acceptance. I'm on the distribution already, and I will send you your plane tickets. Welcome aboard."

He drops off before I can ask any further questions.

My phone rings again. It's Brandon. I answer Brandon's question before he asks it. "I'm signing. I already told Gedeon."

"He called you?"

"Yeah, I just hung up before you called. I thought it was you. I wouldn't have answered if I'd known it was him. He gives me the creeps."

"You probably shouldn't talk about him like that."

"Why not? He is scary."

"I'm just saying, he hears a lot, and you don't want to say anything that might … upset him."

I pause before answering. "Okay, you got me there. He is taking care of me, and I owe him a lot. I don't want him getting upset because of some stupid comment I make."

"That's better. You need to send back the contract so we can get started."

"Just did. You and Gedeon should be seeing my acceptance coming through your email in a moment or two. By the way, when did you get your offer?"

I hear a "bing" over the phone. "Just now." He laughs. "I am to keep you in line. If you didn't accept, they didn't need me. Depending on your answer, I was either going to grab a couple stiff ones and head back to LA or buy myself a wonderful steak dinner before meeting this Leadership Committee. I'll tell you tomorrow if the steak was good."

The line goes dead. I have no idea how much Brandon is getting paid, but I don't care. I may not be rich, but I am on my way. I type up a note to the Executive Producer at my station. "I quit, effective immediately. Regards, Simon Cartwright."

I hope my dad would be proud of me. I'm finally going to be doing some real journalism work. People are going to be hearing my opinions every night all across the nation. He would have loved to have had this opportunity.

CHAPTER 10: Who Wants to Be King

The call wakes me from sleep. My alarm hasn't gone off yet. It is still dark outside. "Hello, and I hope someone died because there can't be another reason to be waking me at this time of night."

"My car is waiting for you outside the lobby." It's Gedeon. "Be downstairs in fifteen minutes. You and I are going to have breakfast together."

Shit, I don't recall reading anywhere in the contract that this prick gets to bother me whenever he wants. I've just spent the better part of five hours on my flight from LA to DC reading his emails and talking with him through my PC. How can there possibly be more to talk about that can't wait until the sun comes up. He's already made it abundantly clear my continued employment is centered on my ability to take direction. The Leadership Committee is making the same point clear to Brandon.

When I agreed to take the job, I thought I was being hired because I was smart and insightful. Now I understand I will operate under the exact same rules as LA and San Francisco. It's just now I get to have a bigger audience and a lot fatter wallet. I guess I can live with that. To some extent it is a relief. I don't need to ferret out my own information. The staff will do it for me. My job is not to F-up the delivery and look good while doing it. This is right up my alley.

I do owe Dad an apology. I don't think he'd be proud of me for this, but he would understand. Journalism has changed so much with news being twenty-four-seven. It is no longer okay to be a good or even a great reporter. Today, it is about ratings. It's about spoon feeding the public exactly what they want to hear. Keep them tuning in day after day. It's about making them feel smart and informed. Information is power, and power is seductive. It's about giving them something unique to share around the coffee machine at work. It isn't about sharing the truth. In fact, the truth has little to do with what we communicate. Sure, it has to sound true, but that's as far as it goes. I fully expect each of the members of the "Leadership Committee" would informally agree with my understanding, at least after a few glasses of scotch. Formally, however, they will swear upon death their only objective is truth. They will hide behind plausible deniability to avoid ever saying they directed me to lie. Their reviews will go something like this: "So, you have sources that support your investigation?" "Of course, they are unnamed." "Well, good then." And that will be the end if the story fits their narrative.

I hop in and out of the shower to wash the sleep from me. I don't even take time for the water to heat up. Fifteen minutes ticks away fast and I have no idea what the consequences will be for being late. I do not want to find out my first day on the job.

My only saving grace is that I laid out my clothes for today last night before going to bed. It's a habit I started years ago to avoid waking up to find out I had nothing clean to wear.

I'm out of the hotel room in just under twelve minutes and wait at the elevator. Thank goodness it's still in the wee hours of the morning. I'm not competing for priority on the lift. It shows up in less than a minute and I am falling the twelve stories to the lobby. I make it out of the lobby to the curb with thirty seconds to spare. A black sedan slides up next to me and the driver lowers his window. "Hop in the back."

The door pops open without my help and I lower myself into the empty back seat.

"Should I expect you every day at this time?" I intend the comment as a joke, but the driver does not see any humor in it.

"If the boss wants me here at three every morning, you bet you can expect me. The only problem with that is you won't be staying here. You have signed a lease on a townhouse all the way up in Glenmont, so you'll be taking the Pink Line into town every day. I hope you like to commute."

"Actually, I'm thinking about getting a car. I hope I can drive in."

The driver looks at me in his rearview mirror. "Yeah? Tell me how that goes."

I suspect I will be taking the rail into town.

The rest of the ride is quiet. No commentary from my pilot and no questions from me. I don't know why, but I develop an almost instant disdain for the guy. I think the feeling is mutual.

The drive is long, and I don't even have an idea of the direction we are traveling until I notice a slight lightening of the sky as dawn approaches. I think we've been driving south for almost two hours before taking an exit that says Richmond, Virginia. Within minutes, the car stops in a Walmart parking lot and my driver points to another dark, unassuming sedan. "He's waiting for you. Have fun." He has the car moving again before I even shut the door.

The rear car door opens, but no interior light kicks on; the interior remains dark. From the shadowy inside, I hear, "Get in." It's Gedeon, so I comply. No reason to piss off the boss.

The door closes without my help. Fucking creepy. It makes me feel like a prisoner, and there is no escaping now.

Gedeon starts. "You know you did not need to send your resignation letter. I already knew you were jumping to a new job."

"It wasn't to you. It was to my old producer."

"What producer? He no longer works for the firm. Seems like the previous owner got some consulting help to decide who should stay and who should be fired. The producer showed up on the second list. It is a shame."

"All because of the bullshit question from the anchor?"

"Hell yes, because of the bullshit question. Look, I run a tight ship. If the producer can't or won't control his team, I don't want him. The organization can't have crazy-ass ideas and positions getting to the public. That goes for me, too. That is why I make no room for exceptions. They tried to fuck me over when they knew the consequences.

"Now it's time to discuss what is expected of you, but first let us grab some breakfast. There's a place just down the street that makes some great biscuits and gravy."

For the next two hours, Gedeon beats into me what he expects of me. He only stops to pound cup after cup of black coffee. His biscuits and gravy go untouched. The grease has congealed to make the meal inedible. Although I love breakfast, I have no appetite, so I fall into the habit of matching Gedeon cup for cup. The caffeine has me wired and I can't help fiddling with my silverware while Gedeon speaks.

"Damn, Cartwright, stop fidgeting. If you can't control something as basic as your hands, how can you deliver our message? You must be in control of everything you do, or people will not believe you. Believability is why we are paying you the big bucks."

He is right, of course. I clasp my hands in front of me and I laser my eyes to Gedeon. I can and will control my actions. I will become an actor.

"That's better."

*   *   *

My first reporting centers on the need to limit free speech to ensure the safety of the people. I find it ironic that a newscaster would propose that expressing one's thoughts is problematic. The logic is compelling, though. It goes like this: people who spread untrue information are enemies to everyone. They damage the free speech rights of all of us by undermining the expectation of truth. As such, false speech is not guaranteed by right. In fact, it chips away at our rights, therefore anything that is false must be stopped. We need brave leaders who are willing to fight the fight for all of us.

Of course, in this message, it will be made clear that we—and by that I mean I—will never state anything as true until we research it extensively. My co-patriots on the show will be sharing the exact same message as it relates to them. The personal commitment makes us all sound like independent, free thinkers, although, ironically, our actual language will be one hundred percent consistent. Repetition of message is critical to making sure we carve a place in our listeners' minds for acceptance. To some, we might look like a propaganda machine, not a news agency. For the money they are paying me, I'm okay with that.

As commentators, we benefit from stories and data coming directly from the Leadership Committee, and the Committee would never state untruths. They are blessed with massive research resources and can be trusted to only push out stories that have been vetted through multiple sources. I have no reason to doubt them. So far, they have been almost prophetic. Everything they say is going to happen, happens.

I am proud to be a part of this select community blessed with feedback from the Leadership Committee. I'm in the know and have the unique opportunity to share my knowledge broadly. My reporting is a patriotic responsibility. Likewise, I now see the importance of taking down certain politicians. First on the list is Aldus Simmons.

Aldus' lies center on the destruction of our government institutions, even though these are the same institutions required to protect the normal guy from the greed and corruption slithering though our business institutions. It figures that someone like an Aldus would push to shrink the power of government. His success means the big guy wins at the expense of us little guys. The government is the only thing left to provide us the safety we need.

I knew he needed to be stopped, I just didn't know why. Now I do. If I were the king of this country, I would have him rot in jail. Free speech should never apply to him.

I now understand why we've been pushing Betty Sweinhart. She is a leading member of the Senate pushing for the passing of an omnibus bill that defines what is free speech, and creating specific agencies to determine when individuals violate our free speech rights by spreading opinions that cannot be effectively supported. The legislation is being referred to as the 'Let Freedom Speak' bill and will redefine how aggressively the country can go after seditionists. The bill establishes criminal penalties for violation and effectively strengthens certain freedom of speech rights for many by ensuring they no longer must hear the lies of other people. I think it clarifies and protects our First Amendment. At least, that is what the Leadership Committee has told me I should think.

Aldus states the bill undermines the rights of all. Lies again. This is exactly what needs to be stopped.

My story is a masterpiece at outlining how politicians like Aldus are undermining our rights and how it is critical to stop these pariahs to our society. I show excerpts from his speeches in which he calls for a reduction on government intervention and control even though they are the very backbone of our civil society. It also shows others in the industry blatantly lying about such topics as employee pay levels, unfair tax laws, and cronyism in government. I suggest we invite Aldus Simmons onto the show to address our concerns, but the invitation is politely declined. Truthfully, the invitation went to my producer, who declined to pass it on to the Simmons' campaign. Technically, I did not lie. I finish by stating, "Without the government defining right and wrong, we collapse. People like Aldus Simmons are calling for the very collapse of our country."

Within minutes of my story airing and our brief live discussion, the station is flooded with support. It is amazing how great people think you are when you say something that supports what they already believe. I love this.

Of course, I don't have a clue if the "Let Freedom Speak" bill will do what I say it does. Quite frankly, no one else on the show knows either. We've never seen the bill. In fact, I'd never heard of it prior to a couple hours ago. What I do know is that we have created a movement to limit free speech tonight. From now on, when a good, chosen politician is questioned, there will be winners and losers. My side will include the winners. I guess we define the winners. We may not be the king, but we are the king maker. After one day, I am drunk with power, real power.

CHAPTER 11: God Isn't Here

My segment of tonight's show centers on a change to the Insurrection Act to better define and expand its powers. It is being touted as the "Let America Speak" reform bill. In this legislation, a permanent National Police Force will be created specifically to enforce the requirements of the law. This policing body will be granted the ability to use deadly force upon the orders of the Secretary of Homeland Security. We love this. At least I've been told to love it, since it is specifically being touted as the only way to protect our rights under the Let Freedom Speak Bill. We are postulating that the first target of the revised insurrection legislation will be the industry leaders who provide funds to oust the very elected officials fighting for our safety. The bill will enable the government to protect our way of life by sending these misguided individuals to reform programs, or if they fight back, to kill them. We are facing the same anarchists that fight our ability to keep us safe. Thank God the media has become the purveyors of safety. It is about time someone has stepped into this role.

I step off the set to see Gedeon waiting for me. "We got him."

"Got who?"

"Aldus."

"I know. I think tonight we pretty much stuck a stick in his dying campaign."

"No, I mean we really, finally got him. He's dead."

I am speechless for a moment. "God, what happened?"

He laughs. "God wishes he could do what I do. Let us just say his car had an appointment with a concrete lane divider in San Diego. The car must have been going a hundred miles per hour and was sliced in half before exploding into flame. Such a pity we'll never know what really happened. Everything was pretty much incinerated. Our team was the first on the scene to see if anyone survived. It's a shame to see such destruction. At least the lane divider survived. I love this job.

"Anyway, you need to go back on to tell the world, but you have to act shocked."

There is no reason to act. I am shocked. I accept the paper and take my place back on set along with the rest of the crew. I am to read the announcement of Aldus' death, and the rest of the team is to look sad while they await their scripts to be transferred to the teleprompter. My job is to stall while scripts are being feverishly generated by the Leadership Committee.

"I have just been informed of some very sad news that will be rocking the political landscape tonight. Aldus Simmons was killed not more than ten minutes ago when the car he was driving collided with the concrete center median on Interstate 15 in San Diego, California. We understand the car was traveling at an excessive and unsafe speed, but it is unknown whether drugs or alcohol were involved. You will all recall that Simmons' campaign for the US Senate began to unravel several months ago with the untimely death of his wife. Although we at "The US Tonight" and its leadership expressed significant differences with Aldus and his policies, we recognize that even dissenting opinions are critical for the health of our democracy. As advocates for the underprivileged, we are disheartened that voters will no longer be able to have their voices heard. Please join us for a moment of silence." I want to continue with 'while our writers push out the next line of crap for you to digest,' but I don't.

I step off the set while my colleagues proceed with their assignments. Gedeon is glaring at me. He whispers, "Get the hell back up there. You still have things to say. We are running you guys for another hour to take advantage of your ratings."

"You killed him, didn't you? Man, that is fucking murder. I never signed up for this."

"So, you think the anchor in San Fran was an accident? What about his producer? What about your fucking cameraman? You are a murderer as much as if you pulled the trigger. March your ass back up there before I begin to question whether you are the right guy for this. I know you don't want to be the wrong guy."

Did I ever say I was brave? I'm not. Did I ever imply I was heroic? I doubt it. I do as Gedeon demands and silently creep back into my seat on the set. The viewers never know I stepped away. I can tell from the faces on the rest of the cast, they are relieved when I return. Everyone on the set is aware of what just occurred, but nobody can say anything to suggest this was anything but a terrible accident. If the viewer gets the impression Aldus killed himself, or was drunk, or was on drugs, great. We are under no obligation to speculate on what really happened to Aldus. Accidents happen.

The truth is, Gedeon never truly admitted he had anything to do with Aldus Simmons' death. It would be wrong for me to accuse him without evidence, and it would be stupid of me to look for that evidence.

The next hour seems to fly by. We have our commentary fed to us individually and we are sightreading live to millions of viewers, viewers that believe everything we say. They think of us as infallible purveyors of truth. After a night like this, we even begin to believe what we say. It is such a convoluted logic: we want to say the truth; therefore, if we say it, it must be true. Funny thing is, I don't know if I have said anything truthful since being in this job. I probably wouldn't recognize the truth. No, there is no "probably" about it. I know I would not recognize the truth. I say whatever the Committee wants me to say. I had taken comfort in knowing the Committee was only concerned with the country's safety. After tonight, I'm not so sure.

"You are off." The camera operators step out from their viewfinders. The overhead fluorescent lights flip on so we can now see the rest of the crew in the dreary, dead light.

To my right, my cast member whispers, "So, what do you think? Any chance Aldus Simmons' death was an accident?"

Another member jumps in with, "Not a snowball's chance in hell. Somebody killed the guy, but I'm not sorry. He was a prick. You've all seen the same stuff as me from the Committee. Hell, he should have been locked up long ago, and he would have been if the 'Let America Speak' bill was passed instead of being bounced around in Congress. It's funny, the bill Aldus was fighting against probably would have saved his sorry life. True, he would be sitting in a reform camp somewhere, but that sure as heck beats a zippered black vinyl bag."

The first cast member continues, "I can't believe what I'm hearing. You sound happy the guy is dead? What is wrong with you? Now we won't have him to pick on every night. I'm going to miss the guy." She is laughing now as if this has been some great joke.

I want to puke. I've covered the guy several times, and even though he pisses me off almost every time, I've never seen him do or say the things we accuse him of nightly. Perhaps I never pushed him hard enough to get him to slip up, but I think it's more likely that he wasn't who we said he was. I'm having doubts as I make for the exit from the studio.

"Nice job," Gedeon says while blocking the doorway, "but for some reason I get the sense your heart wasn't in it tonight. Perhaps you and I should discuss Aldus. Do I need to remind you of the bad things he was up to since his campaign kicked off?"

"No." I try to ignore him and slip around him. His hand slaps on the door, holding it shut.

"My question is rhetorical. You and I are going to have a chat. Right now."

He grabs my sports coat by the shoulder pad and pulls me through the door to the elevator. "I think we can find some quiet space up on the fourth floor. Let me show you the way."

It is late, so the elevator ride is quiet, and I hear only the whirr of the cable as the cab rises. We pass the fourth floor and stop at the fifth. "Gotcha, didn't I. I never was planning on the fourth. We have company waiting for us here."

The door slides open, and we are greeted by two guys I've seen before: Blue Suit and Gray Suit. I think they are wearing the same outfits they had on back in San Francisco, albeit they might have switched colors. In any case, I didn't like them then and I really don't like them tonight. Instantly, I am fearful. Sensing my reluctance, Gedeon walks me out of the lift.

"Simon, Simon, Simon, there is no reason to be apprehensive. You are among friends tonight. These gentlemen are only here to make sure you don't trip and fall. We can't have you getting hurt now, can we?

"Let's head into the conference room. We have some special people waiting for us. They have wanted to meet you for some time. I think you would agree it's about time you got to know a little more about why we brought you onto the show."

Blue Suit and Gray Suit follow us to the door, and Gedeon opens it and leads me in. I follow. His two goons stay outside. I wish I could stay with them.

Inside, there are several people. Some I recognize, some not. There are only two I know: my producer and the CEO from my old station's parent company.

The CEO begins talking before I can even sit down. "Cartwright, I never thought we'd be seeing you make it this far. God, after your fiasco with Sweinhart—what was that four, five months ago? —I thought you'd have moved on to some tiny little fuck-up station, pitching plant-sitting, donut-making or some other sort of local nonsense. And look at you now. You get to speak to millions every night. You are quoted by those same millions every morning at their office coffee maker. And you know why?" He waits and waits, eating up the drama. He smiles. "Because we…" He takes his hand and slowly motions to the rest of the people in the room. "…have made you into some type of God.

"And you want to know why? It's because Aldus either loved you or hated you. I could never figure him out. But now the son-of-a-bitch is dead, kaput, ashes. Tell me why we need you now."

I have no idea what to say. I feel as though I'm in a very high-stakes interview in which failure doesn't just mean not getting the job, but never, ever getting any job again. I look around at the faces to get a take at the individuals in the room, to see if there is any hint as to what they want to hear. Brandon sits at the far corner of the large conference table. He is avoiding eye contact with me.

"I feel as though I can make anyone like me or hate me. I think Aldus trusted me. It wasn't like he could trust me to help him. Just the opposite. He knew I would shaft him at every opportunity. I think he got a kick out of trying to best me. It became a game. A game he was bound to lose, but he felt he had to play just the same.

"I can do that with anyone you pick to screw over." I stop. I look to see if I overplayed my hand by suggesting the CEO and his group were picking winners and losers.

The CEO is smiling now. "Damn, if you don't just tickle the shit out of me. You haven't a clue, but you talk as if you still have some value to us. I doubt you do, of course, but I think we are going to have to find you another foil to give it a try. How do you feel about Sweinhart?"

"I thought she was one of your chosen politicians?"

"Oh, she is, as long as she delivers the 'Let Freedom Speak' bill per our requirements. You see, she delivers, she remains on the team. She doesn't? Well, let's just say we don't have any issue with trading players. You get my drift?

"In any case, she doesn't need our help with the election anymore. Gedeon has made sure of that. Some of us were getting concerned that prick Aldus was going to pull out a win. Gedeon, we are forever grateful to you for taking care of this problem." He nods to Gedeon, and Gedeon returns the gesture.

"Back to Betty. We do question her ability to deliver the legislation we need. Seems like she has lost some of her ability to lead over the years. Maybe she is just coasting now. Unfortunately, coasting is not what we have paid for. Maybe she has begun to believe she is as wonderful as you guys on 'The US Tonight' say she is. She is neither wonderful nor smart; she is just a tool for the time. In other words, she is just damn lucky.

"So, you think you can fight some of her battles for her with her foes on the hill? For some reason, there are some real pricks up there who don't want Homeland Security to have their own big-time police force." He looks around, smiles, then laughs. "Whatever could be their problem with it?"

"Sir, look, just point me in a direction and tell me what to say. I can pull millions in the direction you want. They trust me."

"Trust you? Fuck you, son. They don't trust you at all. They trust themselves, and you are telling them something they already believe. And we…" He waves his hands at several individuals around the table. "…tell them what to believe. You just patronize them and make them feel good. They are too stupid to know they aren't anything but puppets and we're the puppeteer."

"Maybe so, but they do trust me, so I am too good of a tool to waste, don't you think?"

"Okay, okay." He looks toward my producer. "Brandon, you know your marching orders. Get Cartwright ready for act two. It starts tomorrow morning."

Brandon stands and walks up to me and nods toward the door, signaling me to follow him. He makes no noise as we leave.

Blue Suit and Gray Suit remain at their posts by the conference room door as we enter the elevator. I begin to talk, but Brandon raises his finger to his lips to communicate "silence."

We exit on the second floor to a shadowy hallway illuminated only by the required fire lighting. I follow-him into a vacated office and he closes the door behind us. He puts his hand up in the air, waiting for a high five. I slap his hand and he is beaming with a smile. He is screaming, but in a volume no more than a whisper. "Good job getting through that! I thought we were goners."

I get the message we need to stay quiet, so I adopt speaking in the same whispered tone. "What do you mean?"

"I mean, with Aldus gone, they didn't think they needed you or us anymore. I think we were to be fired tonight. You saved our asses in there." He holds up his hand for another high-five.

I return it again. I have no idea as to why some adult men get a charge out of something so juvenile, but he seems to need it, so I won't take the simple pleasure from him tonight. He is elated, more so than makes any sense to me.

CHAPTER 12: No Place to Hide

This is crazy. Since Aldus' accident, I am getting an endless series of requests from folks in Congress to be on my show. Yes, it is my show now. Sure, it's still called "The US Tonight," but it now has the "with Simon Cartwright" tagged on. I don't think the rest of the cast cares too much that my role has been elevated. At least they don't show any animosity. In fact, I think they are relieved to know that if we fail to get "Let Freedom Speak" through, it's my ass on the line. Failure means I will likely be cleaning the bathrooms for them.

I think the Congressmen and women are looking for a platform to tell the world why they think "Let America Speak" is bad. Seriously, how can something that ensures we Americans are safe and protected be bad for anyone? I would love to get one of these useless pieces of shit on live to grill them, but my producer nixes that every time. He just rolls his eyes and says, "No effing way."

I know he thinks we are better off limiting these anarchists' ability to communicate broadly. It might be tough to argue that point, but I would love to let these jerks' own words point out the need for the legislation. Can you imagine the ludicrous logic they would need to push: that we need to tear down government, that they should have the freedom to trash the government? They are a twisted set of individuals. It's a good thing their numbers are finally dwindling as the election approaches. I think our reporting has put a significant dent in their fundraising, so some have traded in their fight against "Let America Speak" for re-election.

"Brandon, we can't duck these guys forever."

"Of course we can."

"But why should we? We can make them look like fools for fighting this. We can win the battle in just a few minutes. Our antagonists would never know what hit them. And Gedeon would love us. He would chalk up another victory and move on to the next battle. You and I would get bonuses and we could afford to move a half hour closer to work." For the first time since we started this argument, I got his attention.

He started, "Look, the Committee has been pretty damn adamant about this. They don't want someone coming in and mucking with the heads of our viewers. We need them to pressure their reps to push for this law. It is critical to providing a way to protect our basic government and its power. Without this, it will be undermined."

"Sure, sure, I get it, but don't you think that'll come out in an interview … and in front of millions? There'll be no place to hide."

"Simon, I get it, but the Committee doesn't."

"Or maybe they don't want to get it. Maybe they've gotten scared, conservative, chicken. Hell, they're running from the fight. I won't."

"You won't? What the hell does that mean? You planning on booking a senator or rep on your own? It isn't going to happen."

"I'm not booking them; you are."

*   *   *

I know this is stupid. I'm risking my job by inviting this prickish senator from Colorado, Senator Delmonico, onto the show for a short interview. Delmonico hates the measure and jumps at the chance to make comments. The Committee thinks the interviewee is going to be Betty Sweinhart speaking on behalf of the law, but she knows nothing of it. Our camera crew knows nothing about Betty. As far as they know, they are to give Delmonico a microphone and an earpiece and limit him to two minutes. After two minutes, the camera goes dark even if it is mid-sentence.

Brandon is pacing in the studio. I know he's going to give away our surprise. As with every show, I start out with a brief monologue expressing my, I mean the Committee's opinion, and then we jump into the meat of the show. Tonight, my monologue is centered on "Let America Speak" with a brief lead-in as to who people think will be Betty. I am counting on the executive producer not paying too much attention to the interview. He's gone through the motions with Sweinhart before. Even though she has slipped in the last couple of years, she can be counted on to stick to the script. She's a pro.

I finish my intro and move on to the senator.

"Senator, you have expressed huge misgivings on 'Let America Speak.' How dare you defend a position that leaves us normal people exposed to those who would destroy our very way of life?" Out of the corner of my eye, I see the executive producer do a double take at the monitors in the control room. "What have you to say to the individual who counts on the support from our government while you tear away at the very fabric that keeps this poor soul from tumbling into the abyss?"

"Simon, you miss the point completely. You put this law into effect, there is NO fabric of government. Instead, the fabric is replaced with steel bars and punishment for those who speak their mind. And heaven help you if you ever get on the wrong side of that government. You would get to join us. You would disappear. It's what happens to—" My earpiece goes dead as do the monitors. We are off the air.

It is silent on the set until I hear the door of the control room bounce off the wall as our executive producer races out. The rest of my cast gets up as if to run.

The exec yells, "Sit the fuck back down. Everyone except you, Simon. You are so fucked." I have never heard the man yell, let alone swear. His face is so red it is almost violet … and contorted. Veins are popping out on his forehead. He grabs me and yanks me from my seat, throwing me to the floor.

I am not a small guy, but seriously, he has thrown me down with a strength I am sure even he never knew he possessed. Maybe his heart will give out before he beats the shit out of me. Instead, he kicks me once, twice in the head, before turning on Brandon.

"Where in the fuck did you get the idea that Delmonico could ever be a good idea?"

Brandon points at me.

"Are you fucking kidding? You got one job and only one job, keep Cartwright on a leash, a tight leash, and you let him call the shots. I told you he was a fuck-up. Now you ruined it for everyone."

The exec points to the rest of my cast. "Sit the fuck back down. I told you to sit the fuck down. We are skipping to the next chapter for tonight. Who is going to take fucking Simon's lines?" He waits while nobody raises their hand. "You." He points to his anointed one and then into the control room. "Get the script redone as we go. No more Simon. Simon, you got a couple choices: one, wait for your friend Gedeon, or two, get out of here now." He is finally getting himself composed, or perhaps he's just run out of energy. He falls on his butt to the floor with his hands over his face. "I said get the fuck out of here, now."

I do not need to hear him warn me again. I hit the exit door, running. I trust Brandon is right behind me. I hop in the driver's seat and start my car. Brandon pounds on the passenger window for me to unlock the door. I don't have time, or more accurately, I will not make the time to let him in. I speed away, leaving him in the parking lot, flipping me off with both hands. I see him in my rearview mirror, running after me as I turn the corner. A black sedan passes behind my car going the opposite direction as I complete my turn. I suspect it's going to turn into the parking lot. I pray they don't notice Brandon.

BOOK THREE

GEDEON: Hammer Home the Point

I t had been such a productive day for me, at least until I got here. I arrived at the office of the Secretary of Homeland Security at nine fifty-five for my ten o'clock appointment twenty minutes ago. My schedule has ground to a halt, and I am not happy. The rumor is that Secretary Harvey loves to make people wait. It feeds his ample ego, but it screws over everybody else. That said, I have no doubt had I been even a minute late to this long-calendared meeting, the secretary's assistant would have reminded me I was late and therefore would need to reschedule. This is the secretary's way of driving home who is boss. It is a childish game and serves no purpose other than to piss me off, and I am one nobody should want to piss off. Titles mean nothing to me, only real power, and power is something of which I possess in abundant supply.

I feign a yawn, stretch out my arms, glance at my watch, and rise from my seat. Special Agent Gedeon Rose is on the move. I approach the closed door to Secretary Harvey's office. When the assistant reminds me I need to wait until being requested by the big guy, I politely suggest the assistant go "fuck yourself" and open the door to catch the secretary on a phone call.

"Excuse me a moment," he says, then directly to me, "What is your problem? Get the hell out. I'll call you when I want you."

"Funny thing, sir, is that I think you should want to talk with me now." I sit down and kick my feet up on Harvey's desk.

The secretary pushes his chair back from his desk to stand. Harvey is a big man and at one time he cut a formidable physique, but that was perhaps fifteen years and thousands of glasses of scotch and cigars ago. Now he is just a tall, fat man. He no longer represents any physical threat, even though he has me by five inches and more than a hundred pounds. I refuse to move even as the secretary makes his obvious attempt to threaten, although I admit, a smile is beginning to form on my lips. Harvey has no idea what to make of me.

"Old man, you ought to sit your ass back in your chair before I'm compelled to get up from this comfortable seat and show you who is truly the boss around here. You sorry-ass fuck. You let me sit out there for twenty minutes. That's hardly customer oriented. I pay my taxes. I'm a customer, and you will do well to remember that. In fact, I am a very important customer, probably the most important you will ever meet. You can't treat your most important visitor…" I pause to let the fact that I am his MOST important visitor to sink in. "…in such a sorry manner if you desire to have a long, healthy, and happy life. Not that I would normally brag about myself, but for you, I think it appropriate to clarify our relation. My happiness will be essential to your success in the future. You should remember that and never leave me waiting again."

The secretary slowly lowers himself back into his chair. "So, you're the agent I was expecting to meet with? Special Agent Rose, isn't it? It was suggested to me that you lacked decorum and I might need to provide you some latitude for your direct communication style, but now I see it is not direct; it's just rude.

"Do you think you can come in here and address me like this and expect to keep your job? I could have you removed and placed in jail for threatening me. In fact, I think your handlers made a big mistake even sending you here. I think it best that you get your goddamn shoes off my desk and leave my office now. You might want to consider drafting up a resignation letter, because if I don't have one by the end of day, I'm going to transfer your sorry ass to some hell hole."

I still do not move, but I respond calmly, "Let me make this clear. I will address you however I see fit. I will have you note that I was even being kind enough to refer to you as sir. I don't call anyone sir. Obviously, you don't deserve my respect and it won't happen again. In private, when we are alone and you speak to me, I expect you to call me sir, no ifs, ands, or buts. I know I deserve it. By the way, I have no handlers. As far as you know, I have no bosses. Consider me an independent contractor."

"You are trying my patience. Get the—"

"You didn't say 'sir' first." I throw my feet from the top of the desk and in the same motion launch myself across the massive work surface at the secretary. I grab the fat man by his tie and pull his head toward me. "You should say something like 'Sir, I am sorry' before I pound your face into this beautiful walnut desk you hide behind."

"I will do no—"

Before Harvey can complete his sentence, I drive his face into the desk surface hard enough to break bone. I hear his nose pop.

"You are going to need something to stop that bleeding. Broken noses suck. They hurt like hell. Now, I am going to sit here while you head into your private bathroom and clean yourself up. I trust that when you return, you might have a better attitude."

Secretary Harvey is already waddling to the door of his lavatory as I call after him, "And do feel free to contact my 'handlers' to complain. I'm sure they will get a hoot out of it."

CHAPTER 1: Friends?

It's been months since Secretary Harvey joined the fold. Though the relation seemed to have gotten off to a rough start, things improved substantially once the secretary realized how effective I can be at delivering results. If he needs additional funding, I have connections with certain representatives who guarantee the appropriations happen. That is an easy one. Making sure Harvey isn't surprised by awkward questions when testifying on the Hill is a little tougher, but members of the Homeland Security Committee have finally become more compliant. Now, for Harvey, testifying is a pleasant experience, and his naysayers remain quiet. If he needs time on someone's important calendar, miraculously, I make sure the appropriate schedules are cleared.

Of course, I'm not here to run interference for the Secretary of the Department of Homeland Security. I've done these things to remind him I have the power to make things happen. I report to a higher authority. He doesn't need to know who. Initially, he made the mistake of thinking the resources in his organization were his to control and direct as he saw fit. He kicked off an investigation of me. What a joke. The effort was scrapped even before it started. I used this as an opportunity to reteach him who was the boss. It's too bad it cost him a granddaughter. I think Harvey will be a model partner from now on. I use the term 'partner' loosely. He is anything but a partner. He is my servant. I just haven't told him what he needs to do.

To use a sports analogy, Harvey was traded to another team, my team. He was not asked if he wanted to be traded, and quite frankly, he didn't have much choice in the matter. Of course, he gets it that there is value in being part of a winning team, and his new team is much more powerful than his previous one. The part he doesn't get is that he has been demoted from star to support player. It's only because he can be useful that I don't relegate him to bench warmer. I am the star, but nobody other than me and my friends knows it. Everyone else thinks Secretary Harvey is still calling the shots, including Harvey himself. Truly, we don't need him; we just want access to his position of authority. Because of this, Harvey should consider himself lucky. We let him survive. He gets a gift that he neither earned nor deserved. Personally, I find him tedious and hope he screws up again.

Today, Harvey will show his worth as my servant. He just doesn't know it yet.

As is my habit, I enter Harvey's office without waiting or knocking. His administrative assistant no longer attempts to delay me. He understands I am one to be reckoned with. I think he is perfectly happy to pretend I don't exist. That is probably a smart thing to do.

Harvey is on the phone as I enter. He sees me and stops talking, but leaves the phone glued to his ear. I whisper, "Harvey, hang up the goddamn phone." There is no reason to take the chance of someone overhearing us.

Harvey starts muttering again into the phone until he sees the irritation beginning to show in my face. He places the receiver silently in the cradle, hanging up on whoever he has been talking to. I couldn't care less who it is. He yells out of his open office door to his assistant, "Ryan, set up a new time for me to finish that call. Make up some excuse for why I hopped off." Then to me, "Mr. Rose, what can I do for you today?"

I push the door shut. "We have an assignment for you. You are going to want to take notes because I don't want to have to go over it again. Understand?" I wait and wait until he finally gets it and pulls out a notepad and pen. I wonder how this man got this far in his career. He seems doltish.

"Now that's more like it. So glad to see you understand I do not make suggestions. We have a challenge, and I think you might help to address it."

"Sure, anything."

I can't help smiling. The bastard is broken and now he is mine. It never ceases to amaze me how effective it is to whack someone's kid or grandkid; that is, as long as they have more. When we kill the only one, it seems not to be so effective. The target has nothing more to lose. In Harvey's case, he has five more grandchildren. I have confidence he'll never cross me again.

"I'm sure you are familiar with an organization called ReAl."

"Of course, they are a quasi-terrorist org. They are beginning to spin out of control. I think we need—"

"I don't recall asking you what you think we need to do."

"Understood. So, what do you want from Homeland Security?"

"First off, you are to meet with Senator Sweinhart to push some legislation." I pull a thick envelope from my breast pocket and toss it onto Harvey's desk. "It's an outline of what I need from her. Betty will be very keen on taking this input and turning it into something I can use, but this needs to happen quickly. You need to push."

Harvey opens the envelope and reads my notes. "There is no fucking way this is going to pass. You may as well quit while you're ahead. By the way, Betty hates the Administration."

"On this, she'll kiss your butt, that is, if she has any desire to continue on as a senator. This is her ticket to money and power for years. And in the end, isn't that all any of you really want?"

"Look, I left a pretty good job for this, and I take exception to—"

"Save your speech for the cameras. In here, it's just you and me, so drop it. Sure, you had money, but here you get power and fame. Hell, you get on TV almost every night, and for you the recognition is like a drug. I get it, so stop. Sweinhart rides this legislation to another term. Her hubby gets a sweetheart deal for one of his companies. You get to stay in this cushy office another day. Sounds like everybody wins."

"So, Gedeon, what do you get?"

"I get some very happy partners. And I always keep them smiling. By the way, Sweinhart thinks her alliance with us puts her on the fast track to something like a World Senator. She's senile and insane, but I play on that insanity. Don't fuck this up. If she thinks I'm pushing toward a world government, so be it. In the end, you just toss her husband a contract or two and I get what I want."

"This is still never going to pass. There is no way this can be constitutional. Hell, it shits on almost every right we have."

"Just be happy you are on the right side of it. It is going to pass. Our wonderful senators and reps are going to hold their noses and say hallelujah. Nobody is going to speak out against the 'Let America Speak' bill. Kind of catchy, isn't it?"

"You are crazy. Nobody cares what you call it. It does everything but let America speak. This opens up the potential to put folks away just because they don't agree with you."

"Say amen. You are getting the religion. This guarantees you get to speak, so long as you don't rock the boat. Nobody has the right to rock the boat."

"The courts are going to stop this in its tracks."

"Maybe, but I doubt it. Let me worry about that. You just need to figure out how to keep good old Betty moving. She has no energy, and I can't afford the program to stall out before the elections. For you, you have a second job. You need to figure out how to get the new 'Freedom Force' up and running. Got that? It is going to replace ReAl, but ReAl doesn't know it."

"Huh, I thought you wanted to stop ReAl, not replace it."

"Now why would I want to lose what ReAl brings to the table. It has real power; it just doesn't have formal power. The Freedom Force is going to harness and legitimize it. God, I love that name. I came up with it myself. To be effective, I'm thinking it needs to be something like twenty-five thousand strong, so I need at least that many. Plus, these are armed folks, so training is imperative."

"I don't get it. What you need? I thought this was part of Homeland Security?"

"Of course it is, but I get to define the Force and, trust me, it will be so powerful that we are never questioned."

CHAPTER 2: What's the Deal?

Sweinhart is a pro at selling her support. It has made her one of the richest and most powerful people in the Senate. I find it repulsive that she is too chicken to put it out on the table that her support of Let America Speak is for sale, and it is going to cost my clients a lot of money. Even though everyone knows she has made a career out of selling her vote, she is smart about it. Personally, she won't touch the dollars, but her hubby will rake it in, just as he has on so many other government contracts. He and his cronies have established half a dozen firms explicitly to bid for government business. In each case, ownership is complicated by a series of limited liability corporations that split up portions of his businesses. Once you weave through the BS, he may not explicitly show up as an owner, but he controls them all, and his wife's influence helps ensure they get favorable consideration due to their extensive experience and expertise. Johns' firms have yet to find a "Necessary Experience" they didn't possess. It is a Congressional joke, albeit not a very funny one, that the next contribution one of his firms brings to a contract will be their first real contribution. The value add of a Johns company is always some ambiguously defined consulting deliverable or some management of a yet to be determined organization. The point is obvious: the fees are huge, the work product not so much.

Sweinhart and her hubby have turned the US Congress into a formidable money machine. Let America Speak is just another opportunity for family money and power. I can't wait to see what Betty comes up with for her husband this time. I am resigned that she will make us pay for a bunch of shit we don't want, don't need, and will never be delivered.

"I think I love this," Betty says. "It's about time someone stops the craziness that gets in my way. Of course, I presume you concur that my Mister Johns will be a huge asset to the cause." Betty Sweinhart is fishing for money. Mister Johns is her husband of more than three decades. Rumor has it she kept her maiden name when they got married to make their relationship less obvious. When she talks of him, she makes it sound as though they are nothing more than business acquaintances. Personally, I think she kept her name because 'Johns' just sounded too pedestrian for her.

I sit quietly in the corner of Harvey's office while Betty continues to prattle on about Mister Johns. "That's my beau. You know how this works. I want mine involved to ensure everything is copacetic. He's the only guy I trust in this godforsaken town. And he only trusts me, so I will need to provide the terms. You just need to give me an idea of how he can participate, and we can create the right kind of Request for Proposal. You know, one that only he can fulfill. So, what shall he do for you, Harvey?"

Secretary Harvey hasn't quite gotten into the swing of things. "Senator, this sounds a little like a shakedown."

His comment puts Betty on the defense. "Damn it, Harvey, if you screw this up for me."

Time for me to change the game. "Betty, I think what Secretary Harvey means is that your country has been blessed by the work your husband has provided, and certainly structuring an RFP with your input would be greatly helpful."

"Who are you?" It's almost as if she didn't notice I was in the room even though I was sitting here quietly when she entered. It's as if I was invisible. That's okay, being invisible is critical to my success. I'm not surprised. Betty only notices those she thinks are important to her. I never want to be noticed until it's in my best interest. I pride myself on being able to disappear into the background. It is in my best interest now that Betty never overlooks me again.

"Some refer to me as "Special Agent Gedeon, but to you, just call me 'sir' and forget I was ever here. I think I can help iron some things out for us all without having to suffer this little dance you seem so intent on having. Betty, you and your husband are whores. Always have been and always will be. I would just as soon have a hernia than work with you, but my clients seem to think you and the good Secretary Harvey can be assets to me. So, whether you like it or not, you are now working for me. The good thing: I could not possibly hold you in any less esteem just because you want something out of this. Harvey here wants fame, you want power, and your husband wants the bucks. I guess you want the money, too. Well, you'll be happy to know there is plenty to go around. Just don't fuck with me."

I wait for a response and get nothing other than blank stares from Betty and Harvey. It's likely nobody has ever been so direct with them. Or maybe they are so stupid they think no one knew what was going on. Personally, I will bet on the latter. In fact, I'm counting on it.

"This little thing, 'Let America Speak,' is very important to my clients and, therefore, it is very important to me. Your husband is going to get the opportunity to define the entire structure of the re-education system along with the required resource map."

"But my Mister Johns does not normally provide that type of support."

"No shit. Of course he doesn't. He doesn't do anything other than create ever more complex business structures to hide behind. Betty, do you really think my clients would leave anything of importance up to him? He wouldn't even know where to start. I have the completed product he will submit to Harvey. All Johns needs to do is, well, nothing. He gets to look good and collect his fees. I don't give a fuck what you two do with the money."

Secretary Harvey interrupts me. "Gedeon, it doesn't work that way. I don't get to define what is required in the proposal, and I certainly don't get to decide who gets the contract."

"Gawd, Harvey, how long have you been Secretary? This is already taken care of. You think there aren't ways around your government's internal controls? They suck. This is a done deal once the legislation passes."

I take a poke at Sweinhart. "You got that, Betty? Once it passes, what are you doing about getting it through Congress?"

"It's not my fault that it is stalled in committee."

"Are you kidding? My clients have been adamant that you were the one to deliver the goods and now you can't? That is unacceptable. You know what 'unacceptable' means?" Not waiting for her to respond, I answer my own question. "It means you are so fucked if you don't get it un-stalled. Am I clear?"

Betty still thinks she's the boss as she raises her eyes to glare at me. "I don't have the time to babysit it. You do realize, of course, that I am engaged in a pretty tough election race."

"That's BS. I'm the one making sure your campaign gets what it needs to beat what's his name?" I wave my hand. "Oh yeah, Aldus Simmons. The idea you struggle to beat the guy just shows how ineffectual you've become. I should never have listened to my clients to bring you into the fold. If you want out now, just say it."

"And if I do back out?"

I fall silent. She knows the answer. I will not allow loose ends. I never have. She is going to stay in.

"Look, I'm taking care of Aldus. You take care of 'Let America Speak.' Harvey, you have a copy of the RFP and the response. It would be very good of you to become familiar with it. This whole effort is going to land in Homeland Security. It's going to make you famous. And Betty, you should enjoy this. Maybe you are going to chair the subcommittee providing oversight."

Betty responds, "Hell no. Personally, I want to be as far away from this as possible when it implodes, but I do want to be the last person standing to pick up the pieces. Have you read the legislation?"

I smile. Sure, I've read it. I defined it. My team wrote it. I doubt she's read it. She doesn't have any idea what it really says or means.

She continues, "If this doesn't fall apart, maybe I can ride this to President Sweinhart, or maybe the head of the UN. They never have been too concerned about limiting rights." Maybe she has read it and gets it. She smiles. I can almost see the gears turning in her pea-size brain. She thinks this will be something that will place her squarely in the history books when she retires. It probably will, but not in the way she expects.

CHAPTER 3: Excuses?

I don't have time for this anymore. The Sweinhart campaign seems to lose inertia whenever I rely on her resources to push forward. Her entire organization is like a boat taking on water and I am constantly being called on to bail it out. It is tedious and pulls me away from preparing Homeland Security for its ultimate role in this world. I no longer take the time to fly out to the coast to meet with Betty or her team. I find these meetings useless and wasteful. Today we meet via video conference. I have always hated video conferencing. I find them less than effective, but how much less effective can they be? I'm convinced a change is required to get Betty's attention. She has no sense of urgency. That will change in a few minutes.

The meeting is already started, but as usual, Betty is late. On my monitor, I see nothing but three empty seats in a darkened room. I used to think Betty's perpetual tardiness was her way of telling me she was boss (it certainly was for Secretary Harvey), but now I chalk it up to just piss-poor time management, something I find even worse than disrespect. I have no doubt she will enter the meeting in a few minutes with some stupid excuse that she thinks will make everything all right. Maybe in the past, but no longer. Today, Betty goes back to school. Her first lesson is likely going to be tough for her.

I hear them before I see them. Color flashes on my screen as someone turns on the lights in the conference room more than two thousand miles away. First to show on the screen is a young woman—probably fresh out of school with her poly-sci degree—hugging a large binder to her chest with one hand. In the other, she holds a Starbucks cup. She is talking with someone outside of the camera's view. I can't make out what they are discussing, but I don't think it has much to do with our topic for today. I hear laughing. She takes the first seat right of center.

I assume the next person showing up in the picture is significantly older, and she waves to me as she takes a seat to the left of center. I met this person briefly on my last trip to the west coast. She is Betty's campaign manager. I found her competent, but hardly dynamic. Watching her getting situated drives home the problem with Betty's campaign in general: it operates at an unhurried, almost leisurely, pace. This team doesn't get why they call it an election race. I have yet to see Betty show up when her campaign manager begins speaking.

"Mister Rose, it's good to see you again. Can you hear me?" She plows on without waiting for a response. "I apologize that we're a little late. You know how campaigns go. We got held up in traffic. Betty is going to be here in just a moment. She had to make a brief pit stop."

I have yet to acknowledge her. I wonder if she thinks I can't hear them or if I just don't give a crap. The latter is the case. I want to speak to Betty. Her two compatriots just complicate the communication. I'm sure Betty thinks I will be gentle in my message if her staff members are present. I won't be.

I lean back in my chair and lace my hands behind my head. I have no intent to engage with these underlings. I have a beef with their boss, not them. Her campaign manager appears to have gotten the message. Her eyes continue to dart to someplace outside of the video view in hopes Betty will be entering their conference room sooner rather than later. The young woman has opened her precious binder and is pretending to be engrossed in the content of the pages. I know this is a farce. She can't bring herself to face me. Through the speakers, I hear a door open and close, and smiles appear on the faces of the two women. Betty must have finally decided to show up.

"Gedeon, so sorry to be late," she starts even before taking the center seat. "I assume Shelly has already brought you up to speed as to why we are late?"

I cannot suffer small talk and jump into the conversation I want to have. "You okay with those two being in attendance?"

"Sure, you know Shelly, my campaign manager, and this is Rhonda. We just snagged her out of Georgetown."

"Ladies, thank you for your willingness to attend this meeting, but no, I am not okay with your attending. You are dismissed."

I can see Betty preparing to debate me on this, but she gives up before even opening her mouth. "It looks like Gedeon might want to discuss some private matters, so why don't you both hang in my office and we can debrief after I'm done." The two women gather up their materials, including the coffee cup, and exit the picture.

"Betty, tell me when you are alone."

"I'm alone now, and you are a rude prick."

"Thanks. I am also your boss and savior. Don't forget it. So, just to get us off to a fresh start, I want an apology for calling me a prick."

"Are you kidding?"

"Of course, but apologize anyway. I will wait for, let's say, thirty seconds, and if I don't have that apology, you get a lesson." Her face tells me she is going to need the lesson. "Fuck it. There's no reason to wait."

I pull out my cell so she can see it clearly on the video feed. I send a text and Betty gets a call on her phone. "Senator Sweinhart?"

"Yes, who is this?"

"Never mind who this is. I just want you to know that we are sitting together with your husband, having a nice lunch. Perhaps you would like to say hello?"

"Screw you." She hangs up the call and glares at me. "Gedeon, who do you think you are messing with? I am a US Senator, for God's sake."

How can she still think I give a crap about her being a senator? "I'm waiting for your apology?"

"Fuck you. Fuck you. I'm sorry, okay? Just let him go."

"Now, doesn't that make you feel better? I think my associates are going to keep Mister Johns at lunch until we get through this call. I want to make sure you understand exactly where I am coming from. Apparently, I haven't been clear enough in our previous meetings. And to be clear, I do not like you calling me Gedeon. I am fine with 'sir' or 'Mister Rose,' but if you call me Gedeon again, it costs Johns a finger. Got it?"

She nods but doesn't show much commitment. Nor does she seem to grasp that a nod is hardly what I demand.

"No, seriously, do you understand?"

"I understand perfectly, Mister Rose."

"Very good. Mister Johns will be so happy. Now get me a bill."

* * *

Why do I enjoy firing people? I don't know, but I always have. It is thrilling to see the crushing emotion when one comes to the recognition that tomorrow their whole life collapses. They no longer have time to save away some money, to consider options. Their world comes to a standstill, a boat with no rudder, no sail. I love it. I love it even more when it comes with tears. Yes, I might be a little sick, but it makes me feel even more powerful than killing someone. Killing is easy. When a person dies, their troubles are gone. When I fire a person, their troubles are just beginning. It's like killing their soul while letting the body survive.

When I fire Betty's campaign manager, I get none of the pleasure I was expecting. It's as if she'd hoped to get dismissed from the position. Feeling trapped, she didn't know how to quit, and I freed her. She gets release. I get to pick up her mess, and she takes away my joy of ruining her life. She has stolen something from me. Obviously, she needed to go. She could not control Betty or her staff. The campaign was rudderless.

I'm angry that Betty is incapable of doing what needs to be done. She pretends to be a leader, but truthfully, she is not. She requires someone like me pushing. She is incapable of creating motion on her own. Of course, she lacks the intelligence and bravery to be effective even if she could lead. I suspect this is exactly why my clients picked her for this specific role. Anyone else would ask too many questions, push back on Let America Speak, or perhaps develop a conscience. Betty is not at risk on any of these fronts.

That said, she has excuses for all her failures. Apparently, none of them have anything to do with the fact that she is lazy or stupid, two of her most prevalent attributes. When she broke into the Senate, she was at least a great speaker and presented the voter a better-than-average vision for the future. Today? Not so much. She mumbles and loses her place in speeches and … let's just say, time and numerous cosmetic surgeries have not been kind to her face. In my mind, her looks are repulsive. I suspect her Mister Johns would dump her in a moment if not for the wealth her position brings to him. On his own, his capability is devoid of talent and his business skills are best described as pedestrian. He is probably best suited for some mid-level management position in a large multi-national, a job that could hide his performance weaknesses.

Soon enough, our relations with Sweinhart and Johns will no longer be required. I have no doubt that this couple has no idea they are soon to be expendable. I have joked that we are all expendable in the new world order, but of course that can't be true. People like me are what the order is built upon, and we are few.

My objective is simple: have Let America Speak become law. Betty is only a tool to accomplish this objective. The pragmatist in me acknowledges that if she fails to win her reelection bid, she cannot be useful. I will get her reelected. I have no desire, nor time, to develop another resource. My clients have created the force that's allowed me to get her campaign moving again. This force, ReAl, has the stated goal of Reform All, whatever that means. Their very existence being used to keep Sweinhart in office is ironic in that she will push through legislation that all but outlaws organizations like ReAl. ReAl has a finite life with us, as does Betty. Eventually, they must all be discarded.

CHAPTER 4: Hello, Gedeon

I am tethered to my phone, but anymore, aren't we all. Without it in our hand or pocket, we feel naked. For most, it is not a requirement, but just as a pacifier or blanket provides comfort to the baby, the smartphone is succor to the adult. In my case, the phone I keep in my breast pocket is probably as important as anything I own. It never leaves my side, just in case my clients desire to get hold of me at any time. At first it bothered me that they expected me to be accessible twenty-four hours a day, but I take pride in the presumption that I will always be there for them. They need me and they trust me. I'm one of their primary resources for getting things done. I am their conduit into the US government.

When the phone rings, I answer it. I don't even consider letting it push over to voice mail. That would shock their confidence in me, something I cannot afford.

Being available one hundred percent of the time has changed my life. I no longer have my normal scotch and cigar after dinner. The cigar is fine, but I must keep my mind clear, so alcohol consumption has been scratched from my daily regimen. I don't sleep the way regular, healthy people do. I grab bits of sleep—a couple hours at a time—and I wake continuously in fear I have missed a call. Mornings, I count on my coffee and cocaine to throw off the blankets of fatigue. They both accompany me throughout the day. And who needs a love life? I haven't had one of those since my wife died six years ago. Breast cancer took away two lives the day my Anna passed; my heart succumbed the same day as hers. Sure, it goes on pumping blood, but I no longer experience pure joy, at least not like most people. Instead, joy has been replaced by a perverted thrill when I control others. The power is exhilarating.

The phone rings and I have it to my ear before it can ring a second time. I know who is on the other end. "Hello, Gedeon here."

"We are disappointed that we have not seen Let America Speak show up in the Senate agenda for a vote. Do you have an ETA?"

"Not yet, but I expect Senator Sweinhart is now appropriately motivated to get this out of committee."

"Why did it take you so long to provide this so-called motivation? You do realize we have a schedule to keep?"

I feel the blood rising to my face and find it difficult to control my temper. Sweinhart is their choice, not mine. That said, I do not have a better solution. I respond, hoping my anger does not come through on the call. "Of course. I failed to grasp how age and success has impacted her. She used to be slow and methodical. Now she is just slow, but I found something that finally has her energized."

"Is not her commitment to us enough to drive her to action? Does she understand the consequences of failure?"

"She does now. So does her husband." At this, I can't help but smile. I keep his right pinky finger in my freezer. I no longer need to worry about motivation.

My smile disappears when my client continues. "Perhaps you waited too long before providing the additional incentive. Can you be counted on to deliver this legislation? Should we consider alternatives?"

The threat, though subtle, is clear. Forget Sweinhart, my client is no longer happy with me. "Gedeon, we think it is best you provide Secretary Harvey an introduction to the Committee."

"What about Sweinhart?"

"What about her?"

"Would you like me to set up an introduction, too?"

"Whatever for? She does her job, then cut her loose. She gets what she wants; we get what we need. We certainly have no desire to waste our time with her."

"So why Harvey?"

"Gedeon, Gedeon, are you questioning us? If I did not know better, I would think you are concerned that you are being pushed out of your position."

"It never crossed my mind," I lie.

"Good, but stupid, too. We are all in danger of being pushed aside if we do not deliver. Remember that. But to put you at ease, we merely want to reinforce some things with Secretary Harvey. He needs to understand his long-term role. I think it would be good for you to hear it directly from the Committee, too."

*   *   *

The car ride is unbearably quiet. I haven't told Harvey anything about our short car trip other than we are meeting with the Committee. In truth, I have not a clue what the Committee is planning for the day. Rarely do I experience anxiety, but today I am gripped by it. I can see the stress in Harvey's face, too. He is wiping beads of sweat from his brow even though the air conditioner is keeping the interior at a cool seventy degrees. He is quiet and stares blindly ahead into the back of the driver's seat, only occasionally turning to the side to glimpse the traffic and buildings we pass. He avoids looking at me as I gaze at him, noticing his every move, every twitch, every breath. I am playing a game of control and I am winning.

Harvey speaks without looking at me. "Mister Rose, what is it about me you are finding so interesting this morning?"

"Nothing, really. I'm wondering whether you are prepared to meet my people."

"And why wouldn't I be prepared? Is there something ominous about them that should raise my concern?"

"Of course there is, and you know it. It's why you haven't said more than a couple of sentences in the past hour. It's why you are breathing faster than normal. It's why sweat bleeds through your shirt. It's why you are continuously scraping under your fingernails as if to clean away some fictional dirt. It's why you are wondering if this will be your last car ride. They are a scary group of people, but this isn't likely going to be your last meeting. Think of this as a chance for them to get to know you."

"And me them?"

"I don't think so. I'm not sure I even know them."

"Why are you coming along?"

"I suspect that whatever they will be telling you, they also want me to hear. They want to make sure I keep you on the straight and narrow, and they want to define what exactly that means. Actually, I think they want to make sure you don't run."

"I'm not about to run. Never have, never will."

"That bravado sounds nice. Just remember it when you piss yourself."

"Fuck you, Gedeon."

"And you, too. By the way, straighten up and smile. We're here."

The car slows to pull into the deteriorating parking lot of a boarded-up building that looks to have been a coffee shop in better days, although it hasn't seen a paying customer in years. I'm not surprised at the location. My clients have a penchant for holding these meetings in shitholes. Not that they will be here. They'll be thousands of miles away, calling in from one or several video links. I think they get a kick out of making these meetings as uncomfortable as possible for me. Now I see it is nothing personal. They are not rolling out the red carpet for Harvey, either.

Harvey is obviously flustered when a filthy, homeless-looking fellow opens his door for him. "Welcome."

Harvey doesn't budge.

I prod a little. "Harvey, time to get out. We have a meeting we can't be late to." He looks back at me questioningly. I get it. He thinks this is the end. "Look, Harvey, the only way this ends badly is if you don't get the fuck out of the car and follow this gentleman inside."

I open my door to exit, but the disheveled man stops me. "Stay put awhile, Gedeon. The Committee wants a few words with the Secretary first. Alone."

I close my door. Harvey mouths silently to me, '*What the hell?*'

I shrug my shoulders as if to say, *I don't know,* and Harvey is pulled from the car. The greeter is stronger than he looks and apparently in no mood for delay. Harvey is escorted to what appears to be nothing more than a hole knocked through the exterior wall of the building, and they both disappear inside. I'm left outside with my driver to wait. At least I think he is my driver. At this point, I'm not sure if he is under orders from me or the Committee. I will not push it for fear of it being the latter.

From the driver's seat, "You want some music?"

"I don't think so. I'd prefer to sit quietly and wait until they come get me."

"No, seriously, you're going to love this," he says, and turns on the dash video display. Before I can object, I hear voices. They have already completed their introductions, or as much introduction as anyone gets from the Committee, which is not much. In fact, I can't recall ever hearing any member of the Committee speak, other than the person I have come to know as the Spokesman. I assume they are participating via a closed network video conference. They will only be visible as heavily blurred bodies. They have always been unfocused in previous meetings. It is clear they are intent on keeping their true identities unknown. The video is focused strictly on Harvey as he sits alone, surrounded by darkness.

I give Harvey credit, he seems unintimidated, or at least unimpressed, and has attempted to take control. "Thank you for inviting me here. It is always good to know who one works with."

"Let me correct you, you do not work with us. I may be wrong to even suggest you work for us. We work through you. I think it might be appropriate to describe you as nothing more than a conduit for action in support of a larger purpose, a purpose that, if you are successful, someday you might appreciate and even participate in. But for now, be happy with being the conduit, an empty pipe that does little more than protect, and not screw things up. I trust you knew this already. Gedeon rarely fails to impress upon our assets their place in our community. Let us say he is particularly good at hammering home the hierarchy.

"So, let us start again. My friends and I have become known as the Committee. I hate that name; we are more than a committee. Committees typically do not accomplish anything of value. They merely pass on group think ideas to others to act upon. Those committees exist for no other purpose than to provide cover for individual ineptitude and ignorance. They enable the members to avoid personal responsibility. Think of us as a family. We argue and debate, but, ultimately, we operate as one on all things. We are individually and jointly accountable for our actions. We always have been and always will be.

"We must operate in secrecy, not because of some malevolent objectives, but out of a humble benevolence to mankind. Think of us as serving a larger purpose that perhaps the majority is not capable of understanding. We deal with a flawed society, a society that lost its way and is in need of a strong guiding hand, even though it fights the guidance at every step, much like a rebellious adolescent. We desire to be magnanimous but cannot afford to be so if we desire people to move in the right direction."

"And I assume you define the right direction?" I am shocked that Harvey has interrupted a Committee member.

There is silence. I'm not sure if the feed is still functioning. Harvey is sitting perfectly still, ramrod straight. I think I see his eyes darting from side to side, but it is the only movement I can detect, and even that might be nothing more than an illusion created by the low-light level. There continues to be silence until…

A new voice, one I am familiar with. This is the Spokesman. "Secretary Harvey, you have children, true?"

Harvey's confidence is crushed. He bends toward the camera and the invisible creature behind it. "Please, don't harm them. I don't want a battle with you."

"That is not the point, Mister Secretary. You are mistaken that we desire to threaten your progeny. That is a favorite tactic of Gedeon Rose, but not of ours. If we felt any lack of alignment with you, you would simply disappear. Our point is that when your children were little, they were incapable of understanding much more than basic directives: eat your dinner, go to bed, wash your hands, and that sort of thing. You told them what to do and enforced your rules. It was important to maintain it was you who made the rules. We doubt you even discussed long-term aspects as to why your rules were important to the child. Likewise, we are not here to discuss our long-term direction with you. You would not understand in any case. Perhaps someday, but not now. We are here today to discuss your role in the post Let America Speak United States. What you do will set expectations around the world. We are afraid any reticence on your part will provide avenues for citizens to become obstinate. Much like dealing with headstrong children refusing to go to bed at night, there can be no leniency. Leniency leads to questioning of authority and ultimate anarchy. We do not want that, do we?"

"Of course not. So, what is it you want from me?"

"In a moment. Gedeon, please join us."

CHAPTER 5: Nailed Together

A nother simple wood chair sits next to Harvey. I'm asked to take the seat. It is surprising to see that the Committee is here in person. They are sitting maybe twenty feet in front of us. Spot lighting illuminates Harvey and me from behind and above the Committee members. They are nothing more than silhouettes. I assume this is consistent with what Harvey experienced before I was ushered in.

"Mister Rose, it is so nice to see you again. We trust you have made progress with the good senator and Let America Speak?"

It unnerves me that I can't tell which shadow is speaking. That the shadow desires to speak from the plural personal pronoun is even more unsettling. It's as if individual members of the Committee do not exist. They exist only as a larger organism. They are devoid of personal identity. I think that is how they desire to be seen and recognized. In this way they appear larger and more threatening.

I respond, "Senator Sweinhart has embraced her responsibility. The legislation will be voted on by both the House and the Senate today. I have no concerns about it passing."

"And what if there is a surprise with the vote?"

"There won't be."

"How can you be so sure?"

"Countermeasures are in place and members who had been considered questionable are now well aware of these measures. There will be overwhelming support for the bill."

"And to what do we owe the good Senator's change in velocity in pushing this through? We seem to recall she was not making much progress even with the obvious benefits that were to accrue to her and her husband."

"She was incapable of focusing on the legislation and her election campaign. I merely removed one of the items. She no longer needs to concern herself with the election. She also now better understands my capabilities and level of motivation. There will be no more delays."

"We expect not. Secretary Harvey, this brings us back to what we need from you."

*   *   *

Harvey has taken to fidgeting during the drive home, moving reflexively between twirling his sideburn hair between his thumb and index finger, rubbing eyebrows, and picking his teeth with his fingernails. He has not spoken a word since entering the car. His eyes appear focused on the back of the driver's seat, but I suspect they may as well be sightless. I do not think they are registering anything. After the drive started, I asked him if he knew now what was expected of him. He failed to acknowledge me. I don't believe he heard me. If he did, I'm certain he would have responded. He knows he needs to listen to me. He's lost in a world of thought that has just been invaded by demons.

Until several hours ago, I suspect Harvey thought he would escape his responsibilities, that this was somewhat like a game: no real consequences. It was like so many other things he deals with daily, things that sound critical, but ultimately fade away once the people who initially raised the issue realize that changing policy takes effort. Nobody in DC really wants things to change; it is just a façade put up to excite voters and to provide the illusion of progress. Harvey now understands what we are to achieve is not illusion. We are to change the world.

There are many Harveys in our toolbox, but there are few Gedeons, and I think Harvey now understands that. I represent the power of the Committee for him. Punishment for failure is meted out as I see fit. The Committee trusts me. The Committee holds me accountable to them, and Harvey knows he is accountable to me. He will only let me down once. There will be no second chances in the future. There is no more time.

"Gedeon, what happens if Mister Johns fails to deliver on his contracts for the Re-education System?"

I roll my eyes at this question. Harvey still fails to get it. "He is not going to deliver any Re-education System. I would never trust him with that."

"But he will have the contracts. He needs to deliver. I am not going down the shitter because he fails."

"And you won't. Johns and Sweinhart will be history soon. They were only necessary to deliver Let America Speak, and that should be done this afternoon. Sure, you're going to be signing off on his superb progress, and the US Government is going to write some large checks to various Johns companies, but at the end of the day, he is being paid to stay out of our way. The development of the camps is already in progress, scattered across several states. Smile. You are bringing good jobs to normal, red-blooded Americans who are going to love you."

"Where are you getting the money to develop these camps?"

"That is an area where Johns helps. His companies front the funds. Of course, with the understanding they will be rewarded handsomely on the backend. Those checks you are approving go to him, then some come back to us. Think of him as nothing more than grease to keep things moving."

"Shit, he's funding you before Sweinhart has the bill passed? That is crazy. What is Johns thinking? If she fails, this whole thing could go up in flames."

"If it does, it comes out of the pockets of Sweinhart and Johns. Why the fuck should I care? Plus, if she fails, money will be the least of their concerns."

"How so?"

"Look, we already have her as good as reelected. That was not going to happen without me. She sold her soul long ago, and she knew the bill would eventually need to be paid, one way or another. I think you understand, correct?"

"You can't be serious. What are you suggesting? That you would kill her? She is a US Senator, for God's sake. Are you insane?"

"You would be wise to temper your comments. I am not crazy, but I am serious, deathly so. If anyone knows, you should."

Harvey falls silent. I think I like him better this way. Every time he opens his mouth, I'm reminded that he isn't one of us. He is caught in my web, but continuously struggles to get free. I know he will be a problem. The only thing that keeps him ensnarled is his love for his family. If he finds a way to protect them from me, I have no doubt he will sacrifice himself to stop me. My team watches his family twenty-four seven. They will never be out of my reach. Harvey needs to know this and believe it. I will never let him forget.

The Committee made it perfectly clear to Harvey his role. To some extent, it also told him my marching orders. He is not to get in my way. I know Harvey isn't happy with what he heard, but he should have been thrilled. Hell, he's going to have more power than he ever dreamed about to fulfill on his responsibilities. I am the hammer ensuring that what he wants done gets done. I will run his education camps and ensure they are populated. 'Ensure they are populated.' That is exactly how the Committee spokesman put it. I'm glad to do this, and Harvey gets to keep his hands clean. That is fine with me. I have no issues with doing the dirty work. In fact, I can't think of anything more rewarding than extricating societal problems and sending them to boot camps to inculcate them to our way of thinking. No longer will individuals be allowed to stymie our progress with their hapless demands for freedom. Their freedom threatens safety. I will make them safe, even if it kills them. I love the irony. Harvey still gazes sightlessly out the side window of our car. He does not turn to face me even when I chuckle for no apparent reason, at least one that he would understand.

Tomorrow, we start our work together on Let America Speak. The legislation gives Secretary Harvey massive power, even to the point that he will bypass the government's normal procurement and contracting processes. Essentially, he unilaterally gets to pick Johns and pay him without any oversight. Johns gets rich, and I get my own twenty-first century detainment camps.

Harvey thinks he will define how I will identify the individuals who require re-education, but he is mistaken. I will make sure he understands that completely when we return to his office. Perhaps he will need some re-education. Re-education is not jail, as some suggest. It is merely a place where the individual learns to be a productive citizen. My camps will never be considered imprisonment. There are laws that protect criminals. We are not dealing with criminals, only those that we determine are dangerous because of their cancerous lies and their railing against the government. They are mental deviants. We will refer to them as Corruptors of Society, or C.O.S.'s. Of course, they will not be allowed to leave the camps, but they can leave their barracks as they desire. They are not incarcerated. The C.O.S. will have no contact with others outside of camp. It is because of their mental deficiencies that the state must remove their rights. The Committee is counting on me, and I am glad.

"Mister Rose, who is the Committee?"

It is a question I was not expecting. "What do you mean?"

"You know exactly what I'm asking."

"They are the ones who drive society forward in spite of itself. Let us just say that our country is drifting, and it is necessary for them to impart a little direction."

"You don't know, do you?"

He is right, of course, but I am reluctant to admit it. I have done their bidding for years, but I still don't know them. My meetings have always been like today, a faceless individual speaking on behalf of shadow people, their true identities always hidden. But I have no reason to question them. They have always delivered. I am rich beyond my dreams. People fear me. I am free to act as I see fit … if the Committee's objectives are met. I have never failed them.

"Gedeon?"

"Harvey, they do not want to be known. Don't you get it? They only want what is good for the USA, hell, for the world. If anyone knew their identities, they would not be free to act. It would spoil everything."

"So, if they are so good, why hide?"

"Why didn't you ask them when you had the chance?"

Harvey says nothing and turns his head back to the side window. He thinks our conversation is finished, but it is not. "Chicken?" I ask.

"No more than you."

Ouch, that hurt, but he is right. There will be no more conversation in the car. I sit back and smile. I'm okay with not knowing. Sometimes it is best not to know.

CHAPTER 6: A Bent Nail

This is becoming tiresome. For some reason, Harvey wants to go over the invoices from Johns' companies. I have no time for this. I don't have a clue why in the fuck Harvey pulls me into this shit day after day. Either the charges are consistent with our agreement, or they are not.

"He is screwing us over. The charges are out of line."

"So, do something about it."

"Sure, like what? Tell him to pound sand and take it to the media?"

"Harvey, Johns is deep in this. It's simple. If he says anything, he goes down. So does Sweinhart. It is not going to be an issue."

"And if he talks anyway? Are you prepared for that? What would the Committee say?"

"Fuck you. He is never going to talk."

"What does the Committee do with you if he does?"

* * *

Johns is sweating. I love it. It is just him and me in Secretary Harvey's office, waiting for Harvey to enter, only Harvey is not going to attend this meeting. Johns does not know it. Johns is early to the meeting. His wife will be late. She always is. I plan on our meeting being short, but then again, there are always surprises. I'm prepared for surprises, but it will still impact my schedule, and that will piss me off. I hate having my schedule fucked with.

There is no small talk, just us two silent men. He is rocking back and forth in his chair, perhaps no more than a few millimeters, but I notice the nervous habit. The only noise is his breathing, interrupted by the occasional quiet cough or sniffle. I find him grotesque.

I have been glaring at him since he entered. He avoids looking at me by pretending to read his email on his smartphone. He has been staring at the same screen for ten minutes. It is an act. I'm okay with this. I've established who is the alpha in the room and it is not Johns.

The door opens and startles Johns. He drops his phone, stealing a glance my way as he reaches to the floor to pick it up. Betty Sweinhart sweeps into the office as if she owns the place, until she sees her husband and me. She expects Harvey, not me. She hides her surprise well, but I sense that she knows this is not going to be a pleasant discussion.

"Gedeon, what a nice surprise to see you here. Where is Secretary Harvey?"

Johns is now standing, phone in hand. "Honey, I wasn't aware you were attending too. It appears Secretary Harvey has been delayed. Maybe we need to reschedule." Then to me, he says, "It looks as though we've all been stood up."

"Not really. Everyone needing to be at this meeting is here. Betty, why don't you take my chair." I stand up to relinquish my seat, then surprise them both by taking Secretary Harvey's position behind the desk.

"You folks comfy? If you are not, tough shit. I don't expect this to take too long. But please move your chairs next to each other so I don't have to swivel my head back and forth to look at you. Plus, I want to see both your faces as we talk." I pause. "So, which of you gets to go to re-education camp?"

Their faces are blank with shock, but Sweinhart quickly recovers and goes on the attack. It is just as I expected. Johns is nothing; Sweinhart can be vicious. "Who do you think you are talking to, you little—"

My laughter silences her. "I'm talking to two pricks who think they are more important than they are. I'm talking to two imbeciles who think they can threaten our cause. You are not important, and your threats cannot be forgiven. I now know you can't ever be trusted again. Which of you shitheads thought it a great idea to shake down Harvey for more money? How stupid." I stop, waiting to see who snitches on who. Neither talk. I should consider that one small point of redemption, at least they are not rats.

"Johns, what have you done?" Betty turns on her husband.

"You know damned well what we were doing." He turns to me. "It was her idea. I never violate contracts. A deal is a deal and I stick by them."

"But Johns, aren't you the one who's been charging more than we agreed? Wasn't it you who suggested you might need to go to the press? Wasn't it you who went to the Justice Department to try to cut a deal?"

I think Betty is genuinely shocked at this last point. "What have you done? Were you planning to set me up, too?"

Johns ignores her. "How do you know I went to the FBI?"

"Good, you admit it. At least we don't need to discuss this any further. Tell me, do you have any further surprises?"

"No, but Gedeon, I, I mean we, deserve more for this. You never told us the magnitude of these camps. We need to be fairly compensated."

"I never told you? Are you kidding? Have neither of you read Let America Speak? Did you think this was all rhetoric, that the creation of a small army to enforce the law was a joke? Did you think your wife's opponent in her campaign died in a car accident? We are invested in bringing safety to this country. We are invested in stamping out ideas that do not agree with us. I thought you were part of the 'we.' Apparently, you're not.

"I could respect asking for more money if I had asked you to do more, but I have not. I have not asked you to do anything other than provide a little upfront funding to get this project moving early. I did not even need your money. I only used it to get you hooked, to get you involved, to get you thinking you were important to the mission. You were not then, and you are not now. Your wife was, but I don't even need her anymore. You have overplayed your hand and now you must pay."

Johns is reeling. I think he might pass out. Betty speaks, "Let me speak to Harvey, Gedeon. I can fix this."

"Betty, you can't fix anything. You could not even manage your own reelection campaign. You knew about this, didn't you?"

She is quiet. Her lips are moving, but nothing is coming out of them. Tears are beginning to flow. God, I hate crying. I reach over the desk and slap her. Well, maybe not a slap; my hand was clinched in a fist. Her head jerks to the side and recoils before she drops from her chair to the floor. Johns does not even get up to check on her. He is whimpering. He is not a man, but then I realized that when he first came in. He is a puppet who's been coddled and rewarded for stealing from society. He acts as though he is something important, something big, but he is not. He is a pretender, always has been, he just can't admit it. He borrowed and stole what little strength he managed to show from his wife. Real power never whimpers.

Because I can, I punch Johns and push him to the floor. He neither tries to defend himself nor fights back. It's like punishing bread dough; it merely absorbs the kneading fist. It is no fun. If there is no fight, there can be no winner. I need to win.

I leave him on the floor and exit the office while dialing my phone. "Pick Johns up in Harvey's office. Make sure he gets an all-expense paid visit to the re-education camp in Baltimore. I'm through with him. And take Senator Sweinhart to my office. I'll be waiting." I hang up and nod to Harvey, who sits patiently on his assistant's desk. What a great boss, sitting his butt down where his right-hand man no doubt eats his lunch most days. "Harvey, you might want to take a break so my friends can clean up inside. I think I left a bit of a mess."

CHAPTER 7: Loose Ends

"**M**ister Harvey?"

"Yes. May I ask who this is and how you got this number?" This is Secretary Harvey's personal cell number, a number that is only available to his family members.

"You and I met several days ago at a less than luxurious facility south of Washington, DC. I hope the facility did not leave you under the impression the Committee is wanting. We find it most beneficial to maintain a low profile and that particularly decrepit building appeared most reasonable under the short notice. I will never grasp why you Americans insist on buildings that are almost disposable, buildings built with sticks rather than stone. It is as if you think anything older than forty or fifty years is outdated, without value, and needs to be destroyed to provide room for something new. So wasteful, yet I appreciate the culture of continuous renewal.

"In any case, I think you now know who I am—"

"You are the Spokesman."

"Ahem, yes, and do not interrupt me. To your second question, it does not matter how I received this number. Just know that we always know how to find you. In fact, if I might boast a little, our ability to find just about anybody we desire is one of our many formidable strengths. It would be very unwise for one to underestimate our reach. Perhaps the only thing that outstrips our capabilities is our dedication. You see, we have been on a mission for some time to address the terrible inequities of society, as we see them, and we are positioned now to rectify things. I think that is a good way to put it. In other words, you should assume that your communication is monitored. You will have no secrets from us."

"I don't recall ever giving up my privacy when I signed up to help you."

"Come now, Mister Harvey, you never said you required privacy. Of course, had you requested it, that request would have been denied. Operatives have wrestled with this concept forever, but they all eventually capitulate. Just know that our ability to hear is the only thing guaranteeing the safety of us all. At one time we had to rely on spies, but now, for the most part, people gladly surrender their secrecy for a moment of perceived notoriety or acceptance. Is not technology wonderful?

"But enough of small talk. I understand you were incapable of controlling a Mister Johns. Is that true?"

"I was not aware I was responsible for controlling the bastard."

"You think the Committee has vested so much power in you to have it wasted? How could we not expect you to deal with him appropriately?"

"Look, your Gedeon is the muscle. I brought it to his attention, and he dealt with it."

"Yes, you are correct. We will discuss Gedeon later. Pray tell, how did he deal with it?"

"I'm sure you already know. Why the game? If you wanted me to do something different, just tell me and I'll fix it the next time something like this comes up."

"That is precisely the point. We cannot allow something like this to ever come up again. You are expected to apply pressure to ensure that tasks always move in the correct direction. You allowed Johns too much rope, so to speak, and he took advantage of it."

"Tried to take advantage of it. We stopped him."

"Never correct me. He did take advantage of you, and so did his wife. The fact that he is still with us shows how much we have slipped."

"He's in re-education. He won't be a problem again."

"So naïve. He will always be a problem waiting to happen. We just do not know when. He is a loose end. Gedeon knows this is not acceptable. We never condone loose ends. Secretary Harvey, how should Gedeon have addressed this issue?"

"Are you suggesting he should have had him eliminated?"

"I was unaware you were so pure. There is no need to be euphemistic on my behalf. Yes, he should have been eliminated, killed, murdered, however you desire to put it. Under no circumstance should Johns or Senator Sweinhart still be breathing. Is that clear enough?"

"I guess so. So, what do you want me to do about it now? You know I checked my contacts, and I am plumb out of assassins I can call. Maybe you have a list of killers that you can recommend, but of course, I only want five-star rated folks. I wouldn't want the killing to be sloppy, you know. And, most important, they must be discrete. You know, no loose ends."

"Sarcasm is a very good way of getting on the Committee's bad side. That would not be healthy. As you should know, the Committee is not to be lied to, mocked, or resisted. However, I recognize you are still relatively new to us. I will provide you some forgiveness this time, but note, I have limited patience. The Committee has less.

"To be clear, Sweinhart and Johns are beyond punishment. We punish children because we want them to change, to learn, to respect. We are seeking redemption. I do not care to redeem either of them any longer. They have had their chances and they fumbled. They are no longer on the team, and they will not be allowed to be on anybody else's team. Punishment is wasted on them. The Committee is already putting the resource in place to address the problem. He will be contacting you tomorrow for your direction."

"Whoa, I can't be getting involved in your murders. My God, I'm the Secretary of Homeland Security. There are laws against murder, and if I don't obey them, who will?"

"Pious words, but just words. If it is a law you are concerned with, remember, you are guilty of much worse. I would think you should be thanking me for the opportunity to repair what you have broken. I am not referring to the fact that Johns and Sweinhart are alive. I am talking trust. Can you be trusted with important tasks? The fact that Johns felt he could extort you makes me question whether you are strong enough to do what needs to be done. He certainly did not think you were. We have no need for weakness. We expect loyalty, but we respect strength. The Committee has no concern for your laws, neither should you."

Harvey is speechless. The conversation has shifted the world beneath him, leaving him without balance. He sees his years of public service and steady career advancement being destroyed. He is being asked, no, commanded to violate every principle that has guided his life. He never wanted this. His only desire was to increase his power so he might better protect his fellow citizens. The incessant cries to limit government power thwarted him at every step. He aligned with the Let America Speak so he might finally ensure the peoples' safety. Now it was crashing down on him. He had turned down a path that led to a bad place. He didn't know where, but he knew it was bad. But to stop or turn off this path now meant he must sacrifice himself.

"Okay, who is this man, and what type of direction are you expecting me to provide?"

"That is better. It is not so hard once you realize you are merely being part of the winning team. There is no purpose to being on the losing side, especially if you know the alternative cause is doomed."

*   *   *

Harvey's driver pushes the brake pedal hard, causing the car to screech to a stop without warning.

"What the hell? Did you hit something?"

The driver makes no comment. Instead, he unlocks the vehicle's doors to let a large, very large, black man enter the rear door on the driver's side, opposite the Secretary. The car sinks noticeably to the left when the big man drops onto the seat. He closes the door, and the car begins moving again.

"I'm B," the man begins without being prompted. "Dude, I understand you have a problem. I'm here to fix it. That's what I do."

"B?"

"Yeah, you gotta problem with it?" B turns to face Harvey. "Where do I do it?"

"What are you talking about? Do what?"

"Look, I go where I'm told, and I was told to be waiting back there and a car would stop for me to get in. I got in. Now, don't you go messing this up. Who the fuck am I to off, and where do I do it?"

"Are you talking about Johns or Sweinhart?"

"Which one's the lady? I'm here to off the lady. Someone else is taking care of the guy."

"Then its Sweinhart. She is to meet me for lunch tomorrow at The Darby Grill. You can take care of her as she leaves. It should be about one or one thirty."

"No fucking way, dude. I am not here to get myself killed. I gotta do this secret-like, with some finesse. You get her to show up there when the place opens for breakfast. You don't need to be there 'cause she ain't gonna make it either. I just need her catching her car ride to meet you before the sun comes up. Make it happen tomorrow."

"What if she can't make it then? She has a busy schedule."

"Man, I thought you were someone important. You know, you say jump, they say how high, type of important. Make it fucking happen or I might be having this conversation tomorrow with someone else."

B yells at the driver, "Dude, stop the fucking car up there at the corner so I can get out." Then, turning back to Harvey, he says, "It stinks in here, smells like pussy. You don't want me telling our boss that you is a pussy, do you?" He opens the door and is gone.

CHAPTER 8: Loose Ends Too

"Gedeon, Gedeon, Gedeon, what must I do with you?"

I hate it when the Committee Spokesman calls without warning. What did I do wrong? I don't know, but I certainly don't need the patronizing tone. I will not take the bait and remain quiet. After several seconds, it seems like minutes, the voice says, "The car, now. You take the passenger seat."

It's always the same, black town car, shaded windows, one-way view divider separating the front seats from the rear, the Spokesman's voice, and a long unscheduled drive … always unscheduled, as if I don't have anything that needs to get done. Of course, the Spokesman does not give a shit about my schedule. In his world, he is the only one who counts. I guess I would act the same way if the roles were reversed. Maybe some day. I toy briefly with the idea of getting one of my agents to hop in a car to follow, but that is nothing more than a fantasy. I have no idea who the Spokesman might have his tentacles wrapped around, and this guy has lots of tentacles. Calling anybody might be signing my own death warrant. I'll be smart and bide my time. Eventually, the Committee will see my real value and promote me. Eventually, the Spokesman will work for me, too. He just doesn't realize it. I suspect he already fears me. I hope not, though. Fear leads to awareness and distrust. I want him to trust me and ignore me. My coup will be a surprise.

The car waits where it always does, two blocks from my office building. I think he loves making me walk, regardless of the weather, and the weather in this town always sucks: too cold and wet in the winter, too hot and muggy in the summer. Perhaps saying it always sucks is not fair. May and September are passable, but every other month is pure shit. I can't wait to leave.

I climb into the front passenger seat.

From the car speaker, a faceless voice says, "Gedeon, tell me why Johns is still alive?"

"Who told you he was alive?"

"Let us just say a source informed me you had him sent to one of our re-education camps. Is that not true?"

"Well, it is true I had him sent to one of MY re-education camps, but I doubt he made it there. From what I understand, he was taken on a more scenic route, one that included a boat ride down the Potomac. He fell out of the boat and got caught up in the propellers, messy sight. We haven't told anyone given that we never expected to see him again anyway, and I don't need Senator Sweinhart making a stink about it."

"That is good to hear. Johns was a loose end. Now tell me why Sweinhart is still alive?"

This question shocks me. I wasn't expecting a push to eliminate Sweinhart. She was never going to be a problem to us again. There was no reason to kill her. "What good comes from killing her? She's done her duty by delivering the bill and she's scared to death of ever crossing us again."

"Scared to death now. Wasn't she adequately frightened when her husband lost a finger?"

"She was." I don't like where this is going.

"Yes, was. Past tense. Apparently, she lost the fear somewhere along the way, did she not?"

"But she won't backslide now."

"And that is because?"

"Because she loses Johns if she fucks up again."

"Foolish, Gedeon, she has already lost him. She knows damn well he is never coming back. She may be lazy and senile, but she is not completely stupid. She has nothing more to lose other than her power, but even that is fleeting. She knows we can never trust her with more power. From here, it is all downhill. She has nothing to lose. How could you have missed this?"

He is right. I have violated my own rules for control. I have taken everything from her. There is nothing else I can use to motivate her. She might even be able to cop a plea and avoid being charged for any crimes for her actions. Hell, some might even try to make her out as a hero if she turns against the Committee. She is a liability and I missed it. She is a loose end. Even though I can't see him, I know the Spokesman is smiling at me from the backseat.

"I'll take care of Sweinhart."

"And how do you propose to do that?"

"The way I always have. You know you can count on me."

"Too late, Gedeon. We have put in place alternative plans to address this problem. You may assume your failure has deeply damaged the trust I and the Committee had in you. You will stay in your current role, but, unfortunately, your problem with Sweinhart has become our problem. I am not happy."

The speaker falls silent. The meeting is done. I feel the foundation of my power has been shaken. Not crushed, but certainly damaged. Regardless of the Spokesman's direction, I must move quickly to terminate Sweinhart to prove my worth to the Committee. I can't allow the Spokesman to take that away from me.

*   *   *

"Mister B, I trust you are already moving to address the unfortunate situation with Senator Sweinhart?"

"Of course."

"And when can I expect this charge to be completed?"

"Tomorrow morning before sunrise. She's not going to be a problem ever again."

"May I tell the Committee?"

"Have I ever let you down?"

"Mister B, you have been a tremendous asset to us. I have no doubt in you. I do have doubts about Mister Harvey."

B thought a moment about this last comment. "Okay, don't commit to tomorrow morning, but if Harvey fails in his part, he thinks he will be the next target."

"Good." The Spokesman laughs. It is something B has never heard from him before. "But before you take on Harvey, if he fails, I need you to deal with Gedeon Rose. He has managed to place us all at risk with his irresponsibility. I want him eliminated."

This is something B had not contemplated. Gedeon has been like a God within the GAL community and now he has become a target. "What did Gedeon do? I thought he was your guy."

"That is not for you to ask. You are valuable for two reasons: you never fail, and you never ask questions. It is best that way. It is why we pay you well. Are you not happy with your remuneration?"

"Sure, sure. I didn't mean any disrespect. I will take care of it, but I need some time to figure out how."

"Gedeon will be called to a meeting with the Committee. You are going to greet him. I want this done discretely, no leaks. By the way, with Sweinhart, make sure her body shows up somewhere public. I want our people to know there will be no forgiveness for crossing us."

CHAPTER 9: No Loose Ends

It's been a wild ride for B, from lowly headbanger to rich assassin in six months. He loves his job. Each assignment provides a rush. He would gladly kill for free, and he has in the past, but this is so much better: an almost unlimited expense account, cool guns, fancy clothes, and respect. He is the Assassin; it sounds so much more dignified than killer. He has become a ghost who is feared for a very good reason. If you see him, you are already dead. He has a direct line to the Spokesman, and no one has that, at least as far as he knows.

His calm and silence in the passenger seat belies his excitement. He always gets charged up before he takes out a target. The driver won't look at him when he stops to let him in the car. He's scared. That's good. It's better not to know what he looks like. If he did, B would need to eliminate him, too, a lesson he learned from Gedeon: no loose ends. The driver keeps his eyes forward the entire trip to the senator's home.

The door opens and Betty Sweinhart climbs into the back. B turns his body to face her while pushing the silenced twenty-two through the gap between the two front bucket seats. Thwip, thwip, one round to the chest, one to the space between her eyes just above her nose. This would be the senator's last car ride.

The driver pulls the car out into the silent, darkened lane and drives. He will drive until B tells him to stop. He doesn't need to go far, only to the end of Sweinhart's street. At the stop sign, B motions for the driver to cut the engine. He does and B gets out, but not until he places two rounds in the driver. B takes a moment to enjoy his results. Four bullets, two surprised faces. The car will be left in the middle of the road with the target and her driver. It'll be a great story for the news today, just as the Spokesman wanted. Another success for B.

He walks down the street to a brand new dark blue sedan, unlocks the door, and takes his time to fold his large body into the driver's seat. He drives away just like any of the other thousands of faceless folks heading off to work this morning. He is a ghost.

Now it's time to prepare for Gedeon.

*   *   *

News messages about Sweinhart's death flood Secretary Harvey's phone. It is not yet eight in the morning, though the Secretary has already been in the office for hours. He does not know why, but he felt he needed an alibi so no one would suspect him of being complicit with the senator's murder.

Rumors are flying, speculating about why she was murdered. They vary from foreign spies to the FBI to drug lords. None hint at the real reason for the assassination—a group hell bent on world domination and control that felt compelled to silence her. The media is sick; they are giddy. It has allowed them to fill an otherwise boring news day with something exciting. This is a gift for them. The story will keep them speculating for weeks, or at least until another story pushes it from the headlines. Eventually, her death will disappear from memories, a fatality of the peoples' desire for an endless supply of tragic stories—a populace that has the attention span of a two-year-old always looking for something new.

Though the media will quickly relegate this to old news, suitable only for conspiracy theorists, it will forever serve as a warning to those who knew of the Committee. It certainly serves its purpose for Gedeon and his gang, and has left Harvey unable to focus. He sits at his desk, holding his mobile phone, frozen. He has done his job like a good soldier but cannot help contemplating when the Committee and B will come for him.

His phone rings, shocking him out of his stupor.

*   *   *

"Harvey." I know he's on the line, but so far, he has refused to acknowledge me. "Harvey, answer me, you goddamn prick. Have you heard the news? Betty is dead, murdered." Still no answer. "Harvey, I am headed to your office and you sure as hell better be there when I arrive." I hang up.

Harvey is out on the limb and whether he knows it or not, it is only a matter of time before that limb is severed from the tree. I know he's involved with the senator's death. How? I'm not sure, but I am certain of it. It is better not to speak of this on the phone. In fact, we can't speak of this in his office, either. If I hear what goes on in his office, I have no doubt the Committee is listening too. It is best he did not talk to me on the phone.

When I get to his office, his administrative assistant is gone ... odd, and his door is open. From inside, I hear Harvey. He sounds as though he has been drinking even though the sun has barely risen above the trees.

"Mister Gedeon, what the hell brings you into my neck of the woods this bright and early morn. Come on in and have a drink with me."

Harvey has never struck me as much of a drinker, but he has a half-empty bottle of bourbon sitting on his desk. He opens a side drawer and pulls out another short glass to complement the one he has been using. "Look, I'm not going to ask you to drink from the bottle, just wouldn't be polite. It wouldn't be polite for you to decline my offer either." He looks at me as though I am a bug he intends to crush. He is angry. He should be less angry, and more fearful.

"Fuck you, Harvey. I am not about to drink with you or anyone else. Pull yourself together, man. What has gotten into you?"

"You know damn well. Do I—"

"Not here. Let's go for a walk and get some fresh air into you. I guarantee it'll be good for you. Might make you feel a little better, too."

He looks at me as if this is the first time we have met. I am glad his assistant is AWOL because this guy is acting unhinged. He at least understands me, and he gets up from behind his desk. He leaves the bottle and the glasses where they are to follow me out of the office, slamming the door behind him.

On the way to the steps, I hear him muttering to himself. I can't understand all of what he is saying, but I get the drift. He wants me dead and out of his life.

Once outside, Harvey changes immediately. "Gedeon, those bastards made me help take out Senator Sweinhart. I am so fucked now. I can never get out of this, can I?"

"You should cool the language. Remember, I'm one of 'those bastards' you refer to."

"Are you sure?"

"Of course. What makes you say something so stupid?"

"Well, first off, why'd they come to me to have Sweinhart killed? I think what was involved is much more aligned with your skills than they are with mine."

"Yes, but now you are truly invested in the cause, no backing out." This is bullshit. I don't want to admit it, but Harvey has a point. Using him sent me a message that they are pissed with me. I should have eliminated Johns and Sweinhart long ago. They are driving home the point.

"Now I'm invested? Fuck, Gedeon, how many times have you reminded me how invested I've been? It cost me a granddaughter. They didn't need to do this for me. This was for you. You screwed up somewhere, didn't you? You got a hit out on you now?"

"There is no way the Committee takes me out. I'm too important for their mission's success. I know too much and I'll be impossible to replace."

"You know too much, sure. Doesn't that make you a loose end, as you like to say?"

"Shove it, Harvey. You're pissed because you finally got your hands dirty. By the way, how did you get up the nerve to kill her?"

"God, I didn't kill her. I just got her to agree to a car ride this morning. I don't even know how she died other than it was a murder, and both her and her driver were found dead just a block from her home. The guy who did it was some big black guy who calls himself B. Kind of a silly name, but I wasn't going to say anything. The guy was huge, and he looked like he did this type of thing for fun."

"He does."

"Does what?"

"He does this for fun. I know B. He is very important to the Committee and me. He gets paid well, but I've always thought he would be glad to do our bidding for nothing. I'm surprised you are alive, given you've actually seen the guy."

"You think I'm on the list to be killed?"

"Why would you be? You're being a good soldier. It's all that is asked of you. No reason to waste their time with you, plus you are still motivated … I mean, you got lots of grandkids." I'm being honest. I think he is safe. I'm not so sure about myself. I will be prepared for B.

CHAPTER 10: A B Sees Me

I dial the number for the Spokesman. There is no answer other than an invitation to leave a message. This is bullshit. He never fails to pick up, and leaving a message is a joke. He knows I'm attempting to reach him, but he is ignoring me. This is a bad sign. I know the prick has my office bugged, too, so I decide to call his bluff. To the walls in my office, I say, "If I don't hear from you in the next minute, I get on the horn with the DC police department and share what I know about Senator Sweinhart and where to find her hubby's body."

I wait … and wait. At fifty-five seconds, I pull my phone to prepare to dial. The phone rings. "Gedeon, Gedeon, Gedeon, I am so sorry to have missed your phone calls. As you might imagine, I have been quite busy with all sorts of individuals this morning. It seems Senator Sweinhart's death has created quite a stir in our community. Apparently, her death was not in vain. It served to steer our team along its common goal. I wish that I would have done this earlier, but then again, before now, she was not my responsibility."

"I get it. As I said, it will not happen again. It was a lapse of judgement."

"Yes, it was."

"I understand you have brought an old friend of mine into the equation."

"And who might that be?"

"A gentleman who goes by the name B."

"Bee?"

"Don't play me for a fool. You know exactly who I'm talking about. I won't stand for it. I want to meet with the Committee to clear my name. I have no desire to let you screw things up for me with them."

"Why that sounds wonderful, Mister Rose. Might I suggest we set up a meeting with them when they convene next? I think they have a face-to-face meeting scheduled for March there in Washington, DC. Does that sound good with your calendar?"

"Seriously, you are a trying individual. I need to meet with them now. So set something up in the next couple of days or…"

"Or what?"

"Nothing, just set it up."

"You are a humorous individual. I have been enjoying myself at your expense. I apologize. I, too, think it best you meet with the Committee. After your years of service, I have no doubt they will be interested in hearing your testimony; however, please note, they are not happy. You will be expected to pay some type of penance, I am sure."

"Penance? I don't understand."

"I am sure you don't, but I think you concur it is not good for the Committee to allow failure or lapses of judgement. That said, I am sure the payment will be relatively painless. They have no desire to lose the commitment of such a wonderful soldier."

Soldier? I am not a soldier. I am a general!

*   *   *

I am shocked the Committee is meeting with me at the same location they used when I brought them Harvey. This is sloppy and lazy, but what else should I expect from the Spokesman. His arrogance lends itself to poor decision-making, but not changing locations is beyond risky. I debate turning down the meeting for this very reason. Of course, the risk is all mine. The Committee will be calling in via multiple video links. I doubt any will be physically present. They rarely are. The video links are a joke. They never show themselves. They will be obscured in some way so that I'll never know who they are. They maintain their anonymity in the dark while watching their subjects squirm under bright lights. I will be the subject later today.

I am here early, four hours early. The sky is still dark, with the only light being that reflected from the moon. This blighted area has not seen functioning streetlights for years. There is a white blanket of frost on the ground that helps to amplify the moonlight. I smell the ice in the air. I have only a thermos of hot coffee and my coat to keep me warm as I wait. Wait for what? I am not sure. Maybe this is a trap. Maybe B is already here, waiting inside, or perhaps in one of the neighboring buildings, staring out at me from one of the sightless windows. I'm afraid my penance will be painless, but only because B is very good at killing. I won't feel a thing. Maybe I'm becoming paranoid. I'm shivering, probably as much out of fear as the frigid cold.

Then I see him. He is unmistakable. He exits the building through the same large hole roughly cut out of an exterior wall that we used with Harvey. I see his breath in the cold. He lights up a cigarette. I do not recall B being a smoker, but I haven't heard from him for several months. Killing changes a man. I'm sure he is not the same man ReAl recruited last summer. He draws deeply on his cigarette, holds it before exhaling the smoke into a dense cloud surrounding his head. Although I can't be sure, I feel he is looking at me, staring at me. Possibly, he's just asking himself why a new sedan would be parked half a block away on a deserted street in a shitty section of town. I'm not very discreet, but then again, I am not trying to be. It is too dark still and I am too far away for him to recognize me. More importantly, I am too far away for him to take a shot at me if he is intent on killing me. With the lit cigarette in his right hand, he raises his face in acknowledgement and gives me an informal salute. He drops the cigarette to the ground, steps on it, and reenters the building through the same hole from which he had just come.

Adrenaline hits me. I know I need to leave. Why? I do not know. I just know I am not safe here. I can feel my heart rate increase. I know if I don't leave right now, I will never leave, at least alive. I push the ignition button and the car shudders and coughs to life. It is very cold. Where to go? I don't care. I suspect I still have a four-hour head start. Even if B tells the Spokesman I was here and left, he will not be able to imagine that I would not return in time for the appointed meeting. It is unfathomable to the Spokesman that I might disregard a Committee order. And I would not. I just doubt this meeting is with the Committee. I think it is an appointment with B and the Spokesman. Hell, I'm not sure even the Spokesman is here. He normally doesn't desire to get so close to the real dirty work. In one respect, the Spokesman was honest. If I am a target of B, the penance will be painless. Even so, it is a price I am not prepared to pay.

CHAPTER 11: Owing B

Sometimes luck helps. It is still early enough to avoid the bulk of the rush hour traffic back to my home. I no longer get the term "rush hour." The city has not had a rush hour for decades. Now, rush hour encompasses the entire day except for a couple of one-hour periods: one mid-morning and one in mid-afternoon, when the highway traffic occasionally gets to flow at something approaching the posted speed limit. To avoid the worst of the traffic, one needs to head for work well before the rising sun provides even a hint of light pushing back the night. My ride back to Washington, DC is in the dark. The morning sun will not break over the horizon for an hour or so. By that time, I will be comfortably in my home office preparing for my escape.

I never expected to need to escape, but I've still prepared for the unlikely event. It comes with the territory. You know, being a special agent and all. The 'and all' really does not have anything to do with being an agent of Homeland Security. I always knew there was a chance our cause would fail, and I would need to run. Now I'm running, not because I think the cause will fail, but because the cause has decided it no longer needs me. During the ride, my mindset has shifted from purely escape to one of escape and fight. I will make the Spokesman sorry for fighting me. I will replace him. I will be the right hand of the Committee as they lead.

I decide to avoid the parking garage below my condominium complex. I should expect that the Committee observes me through the apartment camera system. It is one of the disadvantages of my apartment's modern surveillance system: the video feeds can be hacked into and observed from anywhere. I must assume the Spokesman and his goons are watching for my car, hoping they might trap me once I drive into my garage, essentially a jail of concrete. Most of the cars would have already left for the day, so I would be exposed, out in the open, with only a few pillars to provide cover. That would make their job too easy. I must make them work. Best to park on the street a block or so from home. I'll drive around the block a few times looking for Committee resources. They should be easy enough to spot. They used to work for me and are probably using their government-issued vehicles. They are too cheap to use their private vehicles. Plus, they would never take a chance on getting their car harmed, and it would be a safe bet they are not going to get out of today without some damage if they intend to take me on.

I turn off the main crossroad onto my street for a first pass around the block. There is no reason to proceed any further. The Committee is not even attempting to be discrete. Two dark blue sedans are parked in the street in front of my complex. Even in the brief instant my headlights hit them, I can tell they have not been outside long. They have no frost glued to their side windows or their roofs. They spent the night in some cushy government parking garage, not in front of my home. I turn into the first drive I see and continue through to the alley to return to the crossroad where I started. I should presume my condo is in enemy hands. Time to move to option two, off to Harvey's office.

The ride is quiet. I have no desire to listen to the radio. I need quiet to think and plan. Harvey will be scared, but I doubt they will have agents posted there. They know I have little respect for the man, so it's unlikely I would head to him for help, for protection, for ideas. They might expect I would contact one of my team. I won't. They can't be trusted any longer. I have no doubt the cars outside my condo are manned by former members of my team. Better to assume they were never my team, but more just loaners. They were bodies that did as I ordered, only as long as the Committee told them to obey me. I never really had power. I suspect Harvey is realizing this, too. He has the power the Committee gives him. In other words, he has no power.

I park in one of the outdoor pay parking lots, those that are filled with tourists in the summer, but almost empty in the winter. This lot is close to empty. I park my car close to the exit and back into the slot. I might need to leave quickly when I get back from Harvey's, so may as well be prepared for any potential eventualities.

I pull my pistol from the glove box and push it into my holster. It is almost invisible under my coat. I won't worry about the security check entering the building; I have no desire to enter. I will text Harvey on his personal cell and wait. I'll use the coffee shop on the corner as an observation point—which should already be filled with my agents loading up on their caffeine for the day. I'll tell Harvey to meet me just outside the office doors. If he shows, I'll give him another text to invite him for a cup of coffee at my table. Of course, I won't be waiting in the shop, but his coffee will be, along with a handwritten message giving him directions to my car. We are going for a short ride. I hope he puts on a coat or he's going to get mighty cold. It will serve the prick right. Somehow, I know he must be behind all the shit that is now in motion with the Spokesman. He needs to help me put a stop to it.

I am in luck with the coffeehouse. People are lined up for their coffee, their lattes, their breakfast sandwiches, but no one is at the tables. That will all change in the next thirty minutes or so. By then, the tables will be filled with underemployed millennials sharing lies about their job responsibilities and how their bosses suck, or mentally deficient Gen X-ers pretending to be working on their PCs … so sad. I represent a third group: the loner just looking for a place to sit for a while.

I text Harvey. Meet me outside, wait. Ged.

What the fuck was I thinking? I would never refer to myself as Ged. Harvey will know this is odd, though it might pique his interest enough to get him moving. I need him to act quickly, before the Spokesman realizes I've moved on from my home. I'm in luck. Harvey just stepped outside, cell phone in one hand, coat in the other. He is pulling on a coat as the door closes behind him.

I text again. Turn to your right and walk.

He pulls the phone up close to his eyes and turns abruptly to his right and walks. He is headed my way, but on the opposite side of the street.

He stops and is typing on his phone. I don't know if he has contacted the Spokesman until my phone comes alive, vibrating. He is texting me. Where are u?

What the hell is he doing? He is going to screw this up. I text, Just keep walking. Don't stop till I say to. I watch until he has passed by me and continues to head away.

I leave a fresh coffee and an unwrapped breakfast pastry on the table, along with my gloves. I do not want anyone taking my table until Harvey gets here. I send my last text as I exit the shop and begin running to my car. Cross the street to the coffee house, third table from the door next to the window—note for you. Don't forget my gloves. Hurry.

I can't know if Harvey sees me running, and I don't care. I need him to hustle. If the Spokesman understands what is happening, Harvey will be stopped, and they will know where I'll be waiting. My note, written on the pastry bag, tells Harvey the location of my car. If Harvey fails, we both die. If he succeeds, maybe we still die, but not now.

*   *   *

The door is wrenched open, letting in a waft of super chilled air and pushing out what little warmth I have built up as the car idled with the heater running. I've been watching the street where Harvey should be coming from, but there's been no movement. I turn to my right, coming face to face with B. "Here's your fucking gloves. Too cold to be out without them, you stupid fuck. Drive that way." He points toward the exit, opposite the direction of Harvey's office.

"Where's Harvey?"

"Back where he should be. I sent him to his office and told him to forget you. You're gonna get him killed. He's not a bad guy like you and me. You gotta leave him alone or I'll have to kill him, too."

"So, is that what you're going to do? Kill me? Get in line."

"That's what I'm supposed to do. And I will, too, unless you figure out how to hide from the Committee. For now, all I know is you didn't show for our meeting, and I'm gonna have to hunt you down. This is your warning. I give it to you because you've done good by me. You got me this hot shit job, got me a career, got me lots of money, got me some respect. But I won't let you off again; wouldn't be professional. Drop me at that corner and go find Tau. You remember him? He seems to be pretty good at hiding."

I smile.

"You do remember him. Thought you did. He's a loose cannon, man, but you're gonna need someone like him. That is, unless he kills you first." B stopped and looked at me. "You know where he is, too. I can tell. Now you get lost, and don't be a fucking loose end."

B slid from the seat and out the door. I can almost hear the relief from the car springs. He slams the door and disappears around the corner of a building. I slip on my gloves and feel a piece of paper in the right glove. Pulling it back off, I see an address he has left for me. It's Tau's address here in DC. I guess he wasn't sure I really knew where Tau was. I always know where Tau is. I must. He's been hunting me since he fucked up his last job with the organization. He failed to blow up a speech in San Francisco. How he tracked me here, I don't know. Maybe he saw me on TV or something.

BOOK FOUR

There Can Only Be One Hammer

Ten generations in the making and now we are no longer preparing; we are acting. World circumstances have pushed up our timetable. To some extent, this is good in that the timing of our plans has become somewhat of a joke over the years. We lost sight of the fact that timetables are something to be adhered to. For us, the schedules should have provided some motivation, but they always slipped, at least until now. Now, the emergence of another world superpower and the acceleration of population growth have forced our hand. If we do not seize authority now, the ability to grasp it could slip away forever. Ten generations of accumulating and hiding wealth, ten generations of placing trusted people in power, ten generations of family development ... wasted.

CHAPTER 1: Saviors

They are the saviors of the world. Christ may have saved your soul, but they believe they are responsible for everything else. Christ had it easy. They had spent so many years and generations lying to themselves— that their actions were out of stewardship, not selfishness— that some of the members of their families had begun to believe it. The menfolk of the family miss the point completely. They think this is only about money and capital, thinking the goal is to ensure a well-ordered society in which their family controls all commerce. Foolishness. Greed makes it so easy to manipulate them. Point them in the direction of business monopoly and they are happy, while unwittingly supporting the only real goal: power. Nothing else matters.

In a few short years, this modern matriarchy will control everything. They will no longer rule the "family" as the Committee, as they have for generations. They will rule the planet. They will fix the problems men have been unwilling or unable to address, overpopulation and poverty. True, they are related, but population is the only critical item. The other is merely a symptom of the first. They had solutions, pragmatic and unavoidable ones, that their civilized menfolk were too abashed to consider. It is shameful they must still hide behind a man, their Spokesman, Sir Leroy. That, too, will soon change.

The Committee meets every month on the tenth day at ten a.m., Universal Time, as they have for more than a hundred years. Though the place of meeting varies over time, it is always at one of their many mansions sprinkled around the world, and it had always been face-to-face until the past decade. Attendance is mandatory and there has never been a violation of that overriding requisite. If one dies, a proxy, the next eldest adult female of the family, is expected to attend. The requirement of attendance is drummed into each of them throughout their lives; it is as natural a progression as that of life itself. Not even two World Wars managed to impede perfect attendance.

Over the past decade, virtual meetings have changed everything. The time is still the same and each Committee member still attends, but now they rarely have more than half of the Committee in the same room for meetings. The dynamics are all different. The commitment to the family is waning. Their wealth has become as obesity, caught in an ever-increasing cycle of excess, laziness, and denial. The only constant is their insatiable need for power. If anything, their quest for power has become a depravity. Power is everything, and no action is so vile that it be considered inappropriate, not if it enlarges the family's sphere of control and authority. Only they know what needs to happen in the world. Power is the means to ensure they can implement those actions. Without power and the resulting authority, the world will be doomed. The concept of freedom is overstated and dangerous. Is it not obvious?

Their men counterparts also have meetings, but they are ad hoc and always obsessed with wealth aggregation. Secrecy and collusion are at the center of all their tactics. They collude not only with themselves but also with governments. Governments are easy, so easy, to manipulate. Offer a little and leaders and governments trip over themselves to play with them. True, sometimes the collusion backfires when government officials find they can steal the businesses, but that did not happen often, and usually there is plenty of warning. Their business ownership is always hidden through complex constructs using Committee members and shell companies to disguise their true wealth and reach. They have no concern their wealth is under the control of their wives and daughters. Little do these men know that as patriarchs, they will soon be subordinated. Their desire to hide their riches will ensure they have no riches, except for those given them by the Committee.

Committee members do not have unique roles and responsibilities—other than a specific pecking order that changes only with the death of an established member, the addition of a new member, or the mental incapacity of a member. The pecking order starts with the establishment of the Grand Matriarch by vote of all Committee members, much in the way the Catholic Church elects a new Pope, although the Grand Matriarch is not considered divine. A lack of piety prevents them from bowing to even God Himself. Regarding the voting process, one can vote for themselves, but it rarely happens, as it is considered uncouth, unbecoming of individuals of their stature. As such, in the more than two centuries of Committee existence, no Grand Matriarch has ever received a unanimous vote of support.

Beyond the Grand Matriarch, two levels of members exist. The lowest caste, typically the newest and thereby the least indoctrinated, rarely speak in meetings. They are to listen and learn based on the aligned direction of the more senior Committee members. All decision-making is by vote, but the members of this lowest caste are expected to abstain. The Committee brags to their male counterparts that everyone is equal within their organization, but some are just not as equal as others. The real power is vested squarely in the arms of the Grand Matriarch. She never votes but can veto any decision. She is an emperor. It is her right and responsibility to maintain order and control. The Grand Matriarch can only be removed from her position by unanimous vote, and upon such removal, she is permanently exiled from the Committee. To date, this has never happened. The Grand Matriarch has always stepped down from her position of power prior to a vote. Risking removal is risking death. Removal is a euphemism for execution. One never leaves the Committee alive. They know too much.

During their first hundred years, the Committee made little effort to influence this backward country called the United States. This all changed during the last century. The United States had become too rich, too powerful, and too arrogant. It had become a challenger to the Committee. The Committee began to establish control within the country. Europe, though infinitely more civilized, was no longer their inroad to world domination. In fact, Europe seemed intent on destroying itself, or at least its healthy male population. It was certainly better at destroying wealth and power than it was in creating it—its leaders too doltish to be entrusted with anything of value.

Germany and Hitler looked to emerge into a power that could be harnessed for the Committee until the man developed a God complex. Perhaps his insanity resulted from drug addiction, but the Committee had finally come to think it was the drug addiction that resulted from the man's crazy God complex. In any case, Hitler became self-destructive and ruined another generation of wealth and intellect. The Committee had been right to focus its efforts on the United States and introduced their family into all significant levels of government.

The emergence of China as a rival carries the potential to make their investment obsolete. They need to act now or resign themselves to another hundred years of investment. By that time, it will likely be too late. Too late for mankind? Maybe. Too late for the family? Absolutely.

The past year has been extremely productive. They have successfully sown the seeds of fear, uncertainty, and doubt regarding the motivations of those who cling to their outdated rights. The First, Fourth, Fifth, and Sixth Amendments have been paved over by the passage of Let America Speak and the unwillingness of the Supreme Court to question the legislation. Family in high places helps, but cowards in high places who are unwilling to fight against the family are even better. Those few who dissent have been, or soon will be, moved to re-education camps. Most will never return. Those who do will never represent a threat again.

Their next action will be daring and dangerous. It is one the Committee will implement from the safety of Europe. If they fail, three countries will be devastated. If they succeed, only two will be destroyed. In any case, the world will be forever changed, and the Committee and its Family will pick up all the unbroken pieces.

Today, they start in motion the first of their population reduction actions. Once this is complete, they will move on to eradicate poverty. The solution will not be some liberal program of investment, or some conservative program based on personal accountability; these are too slow. Instead, these issues will be solved through elimination. The principle is simple, either you are an asset to society and to the Committee or you are a liability. Liabilities are to be destroyed. Some will consider their methods inhumane. The Committee thinks them perfectly humane. Man has killed man throughout their existence, typically to steal wealth and to enslave. The tactics of the Committee are just more efficient and the objectives more noble.

They will not waste time attempting to change people's perceptions. People are fickle and selfish. Population is always someone else's problem, '… reduce the population over there. We're fine here.' People are too reluctant to implement any programs that affect themselves, so the problem is always pushed off to another generation.

Population is growing faster than the wealth. Population is growing faster than environmental solutions. Population is the root of all problems. Now the Committee will reduce the number of people with whom they will share the planet. Finally, there will be adequate wealth for all, although there will be more for the Family than anyone else. In the future, all will be assigned roles to ensure they contribute to society. Enslavement? Such a pejorative term. All people are slaves: slaves to their families, slaves to their jobs, slaves to their desires. Now they will be slaves to society, but they will be happy to sacrifice their freedom for safety. Is not that a reasonable trade?

A guiding principle for population reduction is speed. Any actions need to be implemented before society can push back. People will push back if they are to be eliminated, and by the time the Committee is complete, four of every five souls will cease to exist. They will be wiped from the planet. Swift elimination is only humane. Drawing the reduction out over generations is neither effective nor humane. It came with continuous suffering. The Committee is committed to the elimination of suffering. Thermonuclear devices have been placed in urban centers throughout China and India. When detonated, the effect will be devastating, destroying life and infrastructure while plunging a dagger into the heart of the countries' commerce and military.

Military escalations and saber rattling have been increasing at an alarming rate between China and India for years. It is only a matter of time before they result in war. It is hoped each country will focus their responses on each other. If not, the attack will be blamed on the United States. Europe will finally be safe from World War. Within a week, China will be in ruins, India devastated, and America will be hobbled, and the Committee's actions will have reduced world population by a fifth. Within another two months, disease and starvation will reduce the world's population by another fifth.

It is only the start. There are additional plans in place on three continents to reduce population by another two fifths. No longer will rampant population growth be accepted. World population will be maintained at no more than one hundred people per square mile of land. Populations will still be aggregated to best utilize infrastructure, and land use would be defined by the Committee and their lieutenants. And for the poor of the world, well, they will be dead.

CHAPTER 2: Forgiven?

Brandon starts talking before Simon even gets the door completely open. "Look, Simon, no hard feelings. The network wants you back. You even get your own program. Maybe not in primetime, but it's still a great gig. I can produce, just like old times."

Simon debates not answering the door when he sees Brandon's face through the peephole. He had suspected Brandon was dead and spent months hiding so as not to join him. Now here he is, knocking at his door, and seemingly no worse for wear.

Simon opens the door, half expecting Gedeon to be hiding in the shadows of the shabby hallway. Brandon is alone. "You have got to be kidding, Brandon. The man let you go? Just like that? I don't think so. It doesn't work that way. He doesn't let anyone off. I still don't know why one of his goons hasn't shown up here. I can't be that hard to find. I've been waiting to die ever since that night."

"He doesn't care. No one cares. And the station needs to prove somehow that they are an objective voice. That's where you come in. When you disappeared, all shit hit the fan. Gedeon came down hard on the exec producer, saying he blew it, twice: first by pulling you off the show, and second by sending us running. Hell, your viewers thought you'd been killed or something just for pulling that congressman from the interview. They still do."

"But I didn't pull him."

"Sure, but nobody knows that. Everybody assumed you pulled him from the rest of the interview, and he went off on you once the cameras stopped. At least, that's the rumor we started. My idea. Delmonico's career in politics was toast before morning. Gedeon owes me and you. If I say you're back, you're back."

"Back to what?"

"Your new show."

"You've got to be kidding."

Brandon stays silent as he shakes his head side to side, smiling.

Simon finally bites. "Okay, so tell me about the show." He is excited, no, maybe just relieved. It's difficult for him to take in everything Brandon is saying. The emotion of being saved is overwhelming. Brandon has to back up and repeat himself time after time and Simon knows he is getting exasperated, but he can't help it. Before his knock at the door, Brandon had been dead, and Simon might as well have been. Then, when he saw him through the peephole, he thought he was there to tell him how he was going to die, and how Simon had cost him his career, and so on and so forth. But now, this is all wrong. It doesn't make sense. He is offering him a new life on TV. It can't be true, but Simon still wants to believe. He can't concentrate. It's as if he's caught up in an ocean wave driving him into the sand as it ploughs over him. There is nothing he can do but let it happen.

Simon doesn't know when it starts, but he finds tears are running down his cheeks. Brandon stops. He must think he's crazy. Simon realizes he has no idea what Brandon has been saying.

He gets it. Simon knows Brandon thought Gedeon was going to kill him that night. Just knowing his life was going to end violently in the parking lot, and then to get a reprieve, had to be life changing. He waits until Simon dabs the tears away, though he can't stop crying. "You want me to come back later?"

"No, just a sec. You mind starting over? I think I'm okay now.

*   *   *

And Simon is okay. The show, his show, is a pure news program on a network that historically makes its money screaming opinions. He thinks his show is a refreshing change. Sure, it is only an hour a day, and it isn't in a primetime slot, one to two on the west coast, ten to eleven in the east. Most people will never see him, but the program is national, and he gets to call most of the shots on the stories. He does have a new boss. Well, okay, he has a ton of new bosses. They call themselves the Committee and they have this guy, Sir Leroy, who reviews everything he wants to do. He must give his thumbs-up on Simon's coverage. There are a couple of taboo topics, but if he stays away from them, they are pretty much giving Simon full run of the show. If his dad could see him now, he would finally be proud. Simon has become a real newsman, just like him.

The pay? It's nothing like he was getting from doing the fluff stuff at night, but it is more than he needs, although he did have to trade in his home for a smaller, trendy townhome. He's happy. Brandon is, too. Simon doubts he took much of a pay cut and he gets his name in the credits as the producer for a national show. With this on his resume, it will only be a matter of time before he moves on to bigger and better things.

It's a shame, because for the first time they are getting along well. Surviving Gedeon put their relationship into perspective. They need to stick together because there are always scary things out there waiting to eat them up. They need to watch each other's back.

Simon never sees Gedeon anymore, and that's a good thing. He's never liked the guy.

This is Simon's day off. He never works on Saturdays. Tomorrow, he'll jump back into work with a vengeance. He and Brandon will meet for breakfast and go over the stories they want to cover the following day and start the game going with their staff by noon. They will reconvene by five Monday morning at the studio to make the magic happen, but this morning is his. He gets to watch someone else report the news, and he gets to rake it in without taking notes, unless he wants to. Of course, Brandon will be working today; he always works. Simon reports the news as a vocation. For him, it's a passion. So it's not a surprise when Brandon calls and interrupts his love affair with his coffee and English muffin. He rolls his eyes even though there is no one there to see his annoyance.

Brandon's call on his day off is not unique, but it is a relatively rare occurrence. He knows the last thing Simon desires to do on a Saturday morning is to discuss shop, so he'll start off with an apology and then jump into some rhetoric about how he didn't want to interrupt him on his only day of rest. Of course, this is BS. He wants to interrupt him, or he wouldn't have called in the first place, but that is Brandon. Simon should be thankful he is looking out for him, and maybe he is. By the time he answers the call, his feeling of aggravation fades into one of mild irritation.

"Yes, Brandon, what's so important at seven in the morning that it could not wait?"

"Too early?"

"A whole day too early. What gives?"

"You won't believe this. I just got a call from Gedeon."

"And?"

"And he thinks he's going to be sent to a re-education camp."

"He is truly a screwed-up man, getting his thrills from visiting one of his hell holes."

"He's not visiting. He's going to be re-educated."

At first, Simon starts to laugh at the irony, but then it sinks in what this really means. If Gedeon can get a one-way ticket to hell, perhaps any of them can. "What happened?"

"Who knows? He never finished telling me why he even called. But if you were concerned about the guy, well, no more."

"I don't buy it. Who could send him? Secretary Harvey?"

"I doubt it. That guy doesn't get involved in any of this stuff. I think it came from higher than that."

"The President?"

"Maybe. You want to run a story or not?"

"About the re-education camps? Only if I want to join Gedeon in his new luxurious abode for the next, let's say, ten years. No fucking way do I want to run a story."

"Who would have thought the great Simon Cartwright would balk at a story just because it might be a little scary. Shit, Simon, you got the First Amendment on your side. You got a permanent get-out-of-jail-free card. You really can't be touched."

"Yeah, tell that to Gedeon."

"Gedeon isn't the press."

CHAPTER 3: Shhh

"Shhh. They'll hear you."

"What are you talking about, Gedeon?" Tau pulls back the shade just enough to get a good view of the front yard. The moon is shining bright, providing ample light to see the entire lawn, or what ought to be lawn. There is no grass, just weeds and dirt. The trees beyond the dead yard are pitch black. There could be an army hiding in the shadows. Maybe he's getting as paranoid as Gedeon. He lies to Gedeon as much as to himself. "Nobody's out there."

Gedeon shakes his head. "I'm not talking about out there. Your phone, stupid. They listen to us. If you're not using it for a call, leave it in the garage. I told you that, how many times? No more bringing it in here."

"Fuck you, Gedeon. Quit being so paranoid. And I don't need to listen to you anymore, remember?"

"Fine, fine. I got it. You're not afraid of these guys. You're not afraid of anything, right? That shows just how little you know. Just don't do something stupid to get us killed."

"I know. It's just I don't give a shit anymore."

"Tau, did you ever give a shit? About anything?"

"Sure. My gang. They were the only thing I ever cared about, and you guys took them away."

For Gedeon, Tau is simple, always easy to follow, both mentally and physically. He could have taken him out a dozen times after his former captain failed to detonate the bomb at the convention center, and he should have. It was the rule, his rule. Why he did not, he still doesn't know. It just seemed so wasteful and worthless. In retrospect, had the bomb worked, things would have been worse. It would have brought out additional resources to investigate. Not a good thing. The plan was stupid. It was a good thing Tau screwed up and got lost. Gedeon took out the threat to the senator's reelection bid the following week anyway. No foul, no harm. Nobody in the Committee gave a damn about Tau anymore. He was ancient history and easily forgotten even before Aldus' body was buried. Gedeon was all too happy to focus his efforts elsewhere, but he always kept track of where Tau was.

*   *   *

Tau is a foolish, overconfident man possessing little ability or interest to cover his tracks, but he is also dangerous, and without conscience. And Tau hates Gedeon, especially after learning he was the Dark Man. The Dark Man set him up to be killed in San Francisco. Tau would never have known Gedeon was the Dark Man except for that brief time watching the TV news at a bus terminal. Watching the news and waiting, two things he would never normally do had he not been on the run, bus ticket to God knows where in hand. On the TV screen, as clear as day, there he was, the Dark Man with this old guy from Homeland Security. The fucker worked for the government. He was no general, just some bureaucrat.

In that moment, Tau changed from hunted to hunter. He changed his bus ticket to Washington, DC. Killing the Dark Man would free him from hiding, and he had three thousand miles to figure out how.

When Tau's bus stopped three days later in DC, Gedeon had been waiting for him. Tau, no longer the hunted or the hunter, was caught. The game was complete, and he had lost. But it wasn't over. A new phase of the game started that day, and he found himself once again allied with the Dark Man.

They've been together now for a month, hiding from something Gedeon called the Committee. During this time, Tau almost forgot why he'd felt the need to kill the man. The organization, GAL, seemed like ancient history, and the man he was originally supposed to kill was dead. He'd died in some crazy car accident. The senator he'd been running against was also dead. Maybe time had moved on.

Tau's phone rings. He looks to Gedeon, as if asking whether he should answer.

"You're the brave one, right? Too scared to answer?"

Tau answers. "Who the fuck is this?"

"Now is that any way to answer a genial phone call?" Then without pause, the caller answers his own rhetorical question. "I would not think so. If you would like to breathe another breath, I suggest you hand your phone to Mister Rose?"

"Mister Rose?"

"Gedeon Rose. You are trying my patience. Hand the phone to him now, or there will be only a gaping hole where your pea-sized brain used to be."

Gedeon looks at the red laser dot dancing on Tau's forehead. "I think you better give that to me, Tau."

Tau tosses his handset to Gedeon, then he drops to the floor.

"Gedeon, it is so wonderful for you to hop on this call. It has been some time since we last spoke. Perhaps you know that you are supposed to be dead. It is a such a shame when past loyalties get in the way of duty. You can count on that not happening again." The Spokesman pauses briefly, just long enough to let it sink in that he knows Gedeon has been warned. "I never knew you had friends, or should I say a friend, singular. By the way, please note I am using the past tense. From what I understand, B is no longer with us. I could say that he has been fired, but that would be too kind. We decided to send him to one of my re-education camps. Pity he was not successful in his learning effort. Rumor has it he flunked out after just a couple of days.

"But enough small talk, I would like to arrange for you to rejoin our effort. It appears you have some fans in our Committee, and they feel I may have been too hasty in my decision to remove you from the landscape. They are wrong, of course, but I am compelled to honor my employers, and, unlike you, I always will. As such, I am prepared to discuss terms of reengagement."

"And why should I trust you?"

"Gedeon, Gedeon, Gedeon, you saw the dot on Tau's forehead. You know our capabilities are significant. Hell, you are responsible for developing many of them. Do you think I could not have had you killed just now without effort? You should assume Tau was not the only individual targeted. Do you think he fell to ground based on my comments? Of course not. I am pretty sure he saw the multiple red dots lighting on your forehead. You should trust me because you are still alive."

"I would if I thought you had anything to do with it. You made it clear the Committee did not want me dead. You went off the reserve and screwed up. In fact, I'm surprised you're still alive. I'm alive because they want me alive. You have nothing to do with it. You are not allowed to kill me."

*   *   *

Déjà vu. Gedeon can't recall how many times he's sat in the back of a non-descript, dark sedan like this one. He is alone in the backseat, as had been his practice for so many years. The backseat provides him solitude, time to think without interruption. His drivers know he is never to be disturbed. Of course, there are differences to this trip. First, it would be an overstatement to imply this driver is his. He is under the control of the Spokesman, and Gedeon knows the driver doesn't give a crap about his comfort or desires. He is cargo to be delivered, nothing more, nothing less. In addition, the driver is not alone. He has a partner sitting shotgun, dressed almost identically in a cheap shiny suit. They look the part of good FBI clones.

Apparently, the Spokesman thinks Gedeon needs additional care to ensure he makes the trip. In normal conditions, Gedeon would refuse to share the car with anyone but his driver. Under these circumstances, he feels it is better to acquiesce. A second difference for this trip is the fact that he is sans firearm. For the first time in years, Gedeon is without his forty-caliber semi-automatic. It feels strange not having the slight pressure of the pistol leaning into his ribs just below his left armpit. Lastly, he has no idea where they are headed, nor does he desire to ask. This is perhaps the most disconcerting part of the ride. Gedeon can't recall a time when he's ever entered a car without knowing why or where the car is headed. Surprises can sometimes be good. He prefers to think this is one of those times.

They'd left Tau in the apartment. Gedeon assumes he is the target of the Committee and Tau will be safe. In any case, if the Committee wants him dead, he already is. There is nothing that can be done about it, therefore there is no reason to be concerned. Gedeon makes it a point to only be concerned with things he can influence or control.

The car weaves its way through traffic, heading east into the center of the city. The morning sun is blinding as it reflects off the windshield and warms the car. The warmth is welcome. Gedeon leans into the door and closes his eyes, hoping to gain a little rest in preparation for whatever is to come. The car lurches and slides as it passes from one patch of melting, slushy snow to another. It makes sleep impossible.

"Gentlemen, would it be possible to stop for some breakfast before heading to wherever it is you are taking me? I'll be glad to buy." There is no response or acknowledgement from the front seat. "Look, I'd like to eat, so find a place I can get some food. Drive-through is fine." Still no response. "Are you not listening? Did you hear me?"

The clone in the passenger seat turns halfway around to face Gedeon. "We don't stop for nothin'. Just shut your fuckin' mouth or I'll break it. Got it?" The language belies the suit. These are not Bureau folks. They are GAL retreads. They look civilized, but they aren't. They enjoy hurting and killing. Gedeon falls silent. The quiet remains deafening until the car crosses the Potomac and pulls up to the curb in front of the Nebraska Avenue Complex of Homeland Security.

The driver finally utters his first words. "Time to get out, and don't lag, man. We can't hold up traffic."

The suit in the passenger seat is already out and opening Gedeon's door. "Stay with me. Run and I shoot you in the leg. Got it?"

Gedeon looks up into the man's eyes as he pushes his legs out through the open car door. "Got it. And you would do well to remember who I am. You might end up kissing my ass in the future." Gedeon stood up. "Where to?"

"Nowhere. They are coming here." He points to two men exiting the gate from the office complex. Harvey and the Spokesman.

Secretary Harvey is first to speak. "Thanks for the delivery, Agent. You are dismissed." Then to Gedeon, "Nice of you to show. I had a bet here with Sir Leroy that my boys would need to put a bullet between your eyes to get you here. I guess I lost. Leroy, you want to sit up front or back with your pal?"

"I think it best you sit with Mister Rose. I fear he and I will be at an impasse with regard to our relation until we have the benefit of discussing the terms of his reintegration with the Committee."

Gedeon smiles. "Leroy, Leroy, Leroy, why not join me back here. I'm looking forward to understanding what you think the Committee expects of me."

"That sounds like a plan, then," Harvey says as he opens the front passenger door and trades places with his agent.

Sir Leroy glares at Harvey as Gedeon slides back into the backseat directly behind the Secretary and closes the door. Leroy walks around the rear of the sedan to take the only remaining seat behind the driver. "Gedeon, let's see if you are still smiling after meeting with my Committee this afternoon."

As the car begins to move back into traffic, Gedeon says without looking at the Spokesman, "First off, it isn't your Committee, and neither are the re-education centers. You will do well to remember that."

CHAPTER 4: Realignments

The car heads north on the Washington National Pike, leaving the DC traffic and congestion behind. At least the meeting wasn't going to be in the same wasted building that had hosted them the previous two meetings. This time they were meeting in a relatively new concrete tilt-up industrial building a couple of hours' drive north of the capital. As the car pulls into the parking lot, they are greeted by two men who are almost carbon copies of their driver. The first of the two men accompanies Sir Leroy into the building through what appears to be an office entrance. The second leads Gedeon and the Secretary around the corner of the building to a large, roll-up garage door and waits until the door begins to lift open.

"You two stay here. Someone will come and get you when they're ready." Their escort disappears around the corner to the front of the building.

They step through the door into an unlit bay and the door slides closed, cutting them off from the light outside, leaving them in pitch darkness.

"Harvey, what the…?"

"Gedeon, let's not talk now. I think things will be a lot clearer in a moment. Just be quiet while we wait, okay?"

As their eyes adjust to the dark, the thin line of light invading from under the door is sufficient to make out another individual standing next to them. They are not alone.

Gedeon says, "Leroy, is that you?"

"Gedeon, I said to be quiet. That's not Sir Leroy. I don't know where he is, but this isn't him."

"Well, thank you, Director Harvey. It is not very flattering being mistaken for Sir Leroy." It is a female voice. "Perhaps we should move on to our appointment." A flashlight illuminates the floor as the woman leads them through the bay to a set of locked doors and key-card reader. Soundlessly, she holds a plastic card that's been hanging around her neck up against the reader. The lock clicks, and she pushes through without waiting for her two male visitors.

The room they enter is also dark, but not nearly so much as the one they just left. At the center of the room, two seats are situated on one side of a large conference table, facing away from the door from which they have just entered.

"Please make yourselves comfortable. We will begin presently."

Gedeon and Harvey sit, Gedeon ramrod straight with his hands folded on the tabletop. Harvey leans forward with his hands below the table. Bright lights flip on from the other side of the table, silhouetting four empty chairs. Their guide stands at the head of the table, her face now exposed by the light. Her clothes are classical, but fashionable. They look very expensive. She is obviously comfortable wearing them. They are as second nature to her as inexpensive dark suits are for Gedeon. She looks reasonably young, perhaps in her early thirties, but Gedeon suspects she is at least a decade older than she looks.

She faces into the white light. "Ladies, let us get started. I hate to delay these gentlemen."

Four shadows move from behind the lights to sit at the table, the light making it impossible to see any features of their faces. They sit as four shadows and, starting from the right, they provide brief introductions for themselves, limited only to their first names and their roles within the Committee. Once completed, the woman standing at the head of the table merely says, "I am Lynn."

From one of the shadows comes, "I understand we had numerous unfortunate breakdowns in our chain of command as it relates to you, Mister Rose. Please rest assured, this is not tolerated and will not happen again. You are part of our family while you are useful to our cause, and I fail to see how your usefulness has diminished. As such, please consider this an apology from the Committee, and note corrective actions are already in motion. Is that clear?"

"I think so, but may I ask a few questions?"

"Of course, but why not wait until we complete our portion of the meeting to ensure that we do not lose traction? First off, it is critical you understand the re-education camps are progressing wonderfully, and we owe you a debt of gratitude for establishing them. They will be imperative to our plans going forward. I think you will realize their true importance shortly. We will mirror these in the old continent beginning sometime next year, but we had to establish these first in the United States. There are too many sad memories for such investments in Europe. We think the differences will be apparent with their implementation here, making them more palatable for global expansion. Of course, there will be significant differences in them depending on the continent and country. We need to be sensitive to the prevailing culture while still ensuring the objective is achieved."

"I know I set these up, but I am not sure I ever truly grasped their total objective. I had thought they were to ensure that divergent ideas were blunted, you know, to make our actions effective and swift. Is there more to them?" Gedeon asked.

"You are looking at them through a much too limited lens. These camps are ultimately necessary to eliminate poverty off the face of the planet. If we are to save the world, we need to implement drastic and perhaps what some might refer to as draconian actions. The remaining poor will no longer be poor, at least as we have defined them in the past, relegated to substandard health, illiteracy, endless toiling for nothing. In our new world, they will learn and work. They will earn a living, modest, of course, but still a living, all while in these camps. Ultimately, we expect them to exit these camps to positions of value for our society."

"And if they don't or can't?"

"Mister Rose, you are starting to sound as if you have a heart. Please do not disappoint us. We are counting on you for critical influence within your government. Influence of a nature for which you seem most suited."

"And if they don't?" Gedeon pushed.

"That is not an option. The poor will exit, no longer poor, walking with their heads held high, or they will be buried. Either way, they will exit. Secretary Harvey will run these camps."

Gedeon turned his head to face Harvey. Harvey smiled back at him and nodded in acknowledgement.

"So, tell me what type of influence it is that you expect me to provide? I'm not sure I have the ability and skills you think I do."

Harvey spoke up, "Gedeon, don't be so modest. My God, if they need someone to break some dishes in the halls of government, you can do it as well as anyone. They need someone to create fear, uncertainly, and doubt, but mainly fear. They need someone who can back up that fear with some real clout. There is no one I can think of who has more ability to address our needs, I mean the Committee's needs, than you. I will provide the resource and capability through my department, and you will bring the US government to its knees. It sounds bad, but it isn't. This must happen if we are to save the world from itself. The populace can never be trusted to know what is best for themselves. That's the reason monarchs reigned successfully for centuries."

"Did they?" Gedeon stares at Harvey as he speaks, then quietly turns back to the shadow who has been speaking. "I'm on board. I always have been."

The shadow continues to outline the specifics of Gedeon's new role in their world.

*　　*　　*

Harvey and Gedeon are sitting in the rear seat of the sedan, waiting for their return trip to their respective homes. Darkness has fallen and a fine mist of icy snow is glistening in the moonlight.

"Dammit, Harvey, how long have you known what was going on in the camps?"

"Long enough."

"Why didn't you tell me? They are my creation, and I had a right to know."

"First off, you didn't have a right to know, and you still don't. I'm not sure why they even told you, but you should be proud that they have enough confidence in you that they were willing to share their plans."

"But their plans are royally fucked up. Hell, they are demented."

"I think you reminded me long ago that I need to remember who the boss is, so let me now tell you. I am your boss now, and I report to those demented bitches. Remember that."

"Harvey, stop with the chest pounding. You are no more my boss than Sir Leroy. God, what a fucked-up name." Gedeon turns to look out his side window. "Speak of the devil. There's the asshole now. Come on, Leroy, get the hell in here so we can leave," he says to the closed window. "I'm freezing my butt off."

"Calm down, Gedeon, and watch."

Sir Leroy stands in the light that is shown through the front office doors. He makes no movement toward the waiting car. Their driver is standing close to him in the cold. The two are talking, but Gedeon and Harvey can't hear what is being said. Gedeon grabs the handle to open the door and prod Leroy to hurry, but Harvey places his hand on his shoulder and shakes his head. "Best not to hear what is being said. Gedeon, leave the door closed. It's too damn cold."

Leroy turns his face away from their driver, keeping his feet still. Their driver pulls a pistol from his coat pocket and places the muzzle against the back of Leroy's head and fires. The noise is deafening even in the quiet of the car. The night instantly returns to its quiet, having consumed the noise in darkness and death.

"What the hell…?" stammers Gedeon, while Sir Leroy falls to his knees and then topples face-first into the dusting of snow.

"Now do you understand who the boss is?" Harvey smiles and crosses his arms across his chest as the driver climbs into the car. "Let's head home."

CHAPTER 5: Prey to Pray

T au is sitting in relative darkness, one large man to his left, one to his right, the only light being that which leaks around the edges of the steel divider separating them from the driver. Over the next hour or so, the van slows, bounces, and jolts occasionally, but rarely stops. It is cold. He can see their breath. His two guards are bundled in warm parkas, knit hats, and leather gloves. He doesn't have the luxury of gloves. His bare hands are cold, tied together with a nylon cable tie and resting in his lap. He wears nothing but the pair of pants and tee-shirt he was wearing when they broke through the door to take Gedeon. His feet are bare and so cold they are numb. The two men accompanying him don't care.

He has no idea where they are going or when they will get there. It seems to Tau as though they've been driving for more than an hour, but the quiet darkness plays tricks on the mind. He does not know how long they've been driving, but he's had plenty of time to consider his options. He can take whatever awaits him sitting down, placidly let these pricks jail or kill him, or he can fight like the killer he has grown to be. He prefers to fight.

It is two of them against him. The fight won't be fair. They have no place to run, and their guns are holstered. He feels sorry for them. The man to his right is giving in to the monotonous noise and motion of the van. Even in the darkness, Tau can see the guy's eyes moving steadily closed, then popping open, only to begin their slide closed again. When he does act, he will make sure those eyes never open again. To his left, his captor remains awake, but he's engrossed in his smartphone. Not so smart. Awake, but hardly diligent.

Tau turns his body slightly to his left, pretending to be doing nothing more than repositioning for some semblance of comfort. In reality, the movement is not pretending. The hard, cold, steel bench seat is unforgiving and hurts his buttocks. Tau, too, can be unforgiving. He rolls with one motion, standing to his feet while grabbing the flat phone from his first victim's gloved hands. He spins completely around to gain momentum and plants the cell phone into the owner's throat, the power of the push strong enough to cut completely through the skin, severing the trachea. Blood spurts while the guard claws wildly at his neck, attempting to remove the seemingly innocuous device from his throat. He is dead even though he doesn't know it yet. Tau then reverses his spin to drive his elbow up and through the dozing partner's nose, pushing bone into the brain and slamming his head into the hard steel of the cab. They are dead. He is now alone. The van keeps moving as if nothing has happened, and as far as the driver knows, nothing did.

Tau searches his dead compatriots. They were in the same business as him and just doing their job; it wasn't personal. He holds no animosity toward them. He finds a small set of diagonal dikes in the second man's coat pocket and uses them to cut the nylon ties and free his hands. Now that he's free of his constraints, he moves on to his second objective, warmth: liberating socks, shoes, gloves, and a coat. Now he's prepared for his final step. He pulls both men's pistols from their holsters and waits. The next time the van stops or slows, he'll act.

The wait is short. As he feels the vehicle begin to brake, he aims both pistols. One points to where the driver should be sitting in front of the divider, and one points at the passenger, if there is one. He opens fire. The noise is concussive in the small containment. Small beads of light bleed through the holes drilled by the bullets. He fires three rounds from each gun in rapid succession, alternating left, right, left, right, left, right, then stops. The van continues to roll, slowing until it hits something that stops it altogether. All is quiet except for the ringing that won't quit in his ears. He waits, looking for motion, listening for any sound of life. There is nothing.

Tau places one of the pistols in his coat pocket and moves to the rear of the van to check the rear doors. They are unlocked and open easily. He steps out of his steel cave of darkness into the comparatively harsh light of the late afternoon. He's no longer in the city, but in the middle of the country. The van, which had been slowing to turn, rolled across an empty intersection of two country roads before coming up against a reflector sign, bending it over under the weight of the van. The van's bumper barely acknowledged the slow speed collision; van one, street sign zero. There are no moving cars in sight, only the swirling and blowing of powdered snow. The winter has forced life inside.

Tau sees a handful of small homes in the distance, fading into the rapidly approaching darkness of the early winter evening; they are quiet. Either the gunshots were effectively muffled by the van walls and snow, or these homes were empty, their occupants still away at their day jobs. Lucky for them. He did not want to leave any loose ends.

The driver of the van is slumped over the steering wheel. He is alive, his shoulders rising and falling with each labored breath. He is bleeding from a shot that made its way through his neck. The other two rounds must have missed. He will be dead soon. The passenger seat is empty. Those three rounds were wasted. They punctured nothing but the seat, air, and windshield. Tau opens the door and places the pistol muzzle against the driver's head and fires, splattering his brains over the passenger's seat and window. No reason to wait for him to bleed out. He pulls the driver to the ground, checks his pockets, and pilfers another pistol. The other two shots hadn't missed after all. Tau can see the puncture holes in the back of the driver's parka. This man is wearing a bullet-proof vest. The Kevlar armor could protect him, but it didn't save him.

Under the coat, the driver is wearing a sports coat. In its breast pocket, the man's ID. These guys were DHS, Department of Homeland Security. These guys had been Gedeon's. Maybe they still were, but more likely not. Not good. Not good for him or Gedeon.

The Committee is now the government, or at least they control it. Tau drags the body to the back of the van and loads him in with his friends. Before closing the doors, he checks the remaining casualties, ensuring they are dead. He doesn't want any surprises. He pulls the phone from the first dead man's neck and then searches the other two for their phones. He throws two of the three into the snow along the side of the road, keeping the one from the dead man's neck. It's still open to the foolish guard's last internet search. Tau didn't need a password to open the phone. Of course, they can track the van through its GPS, but there is no reason to help whoever might be charged with tracking him. If he wants to lose the van and its unlucky occupants before nightfall, he needs to move quickly.

He closes the rear door and returns to the cab. Time to go, but to where, and from where? Tau checks the map on the third phone. He's a long way from home, more than twenty miles north of Baltimore, and not more than a dozen miles from one of the many Re-education camps Gedeon had created. So, he'd been targeted for re-education. Perhaps Gedeon was, too, but he doubted it. Gedeon was too important. He was always too important. He should have known. Even when Gedeon took the phone he hadn't been concerned. Didn't he tell the caller that he'd screwed up and the Committee would never let them hurt him? Not Tau, just him. Tau's face tensed in anger as he realized Gedeon must have set him up. He'd been the target, the only target. He'd been arrested, not Gedeon.

Instead of looking for a place to dump the vehicle and heading back to DC, he decides to move forward and get his first look at what his supposed friend and ally had created. Reaching underneath the dashboard, he feels around for the GPS tracker he knows will be present. He grabs the little plastic box and yanks it free of the wiring. Now that he knows where he is, he tosses the remaining phone, along with the GPS tracker, out the window. The van will now be invisible to the satellites that keep track of all government vehicles. One would think they would hide the little device better, but the folks in charge must assume the large Department of Homeland Security Re-Education stenciled on the sides and rear of the van will make it less attractive to thieves. Or maybe they just didn't care. In any case, Tau hopes the lost signal won't be discovered until he's escaped this intersection. He will move closer to his enemy. This might sound crazy, and perhaps it is, but it will also be the last thing they expect. They will look for a van escaping, not approaching.

He starts up the engine again and backs up slowly to keep the rear tires from spinning on the half-frozen pavement. Even with GPS invisibility, Tau scans the fields as he drives, looking for a car he can trade for his government-issue traveling morgue. He imagines the folks who might be inhabiting the small homes he passes. They will likely be kind and innocent. They'll never expect someone looking to steal their truck or car. Of course, it really won't be stealing. He'll be leaving the van. And they won't care about the trade because they'll be dead.

Darkness is falling quickly, making his search both easier and more difficult. Easier because the glow of lights tell him where people have returned home for the night. More difficult in that the inhabitants' autos are hidden in shadow. He doesn't want to take any piece of shit. He laughs to himself as he drives. Of course, most of the cars out here are pieces of shit. He'll look for a place with a nice big garage or barn, someplace where he can hide the van. The DHS will eventually find it right under their noses, within a couple miles of their re-education camp. He feels it is ironic that they will struggle to find it because it is too close. He wishes he could watch as they unpack the cargo.

*   *   *

The engine chokes into silence. Steam rises from the hood as the heat escapes into the frigid winter night. Rivulets of white frost weave their way across the windshield as cold leaks through the splintered bullet holes. Tau surveys the small home and yard through his rapidly fogging window. This is the place: darkened yard, curtains open, no fence, so no dogs, separate garage, and most importantly, a moderately new Jeep parked out front. It looks like the only car around.

He curses himself as he opens the door, the dome light illuminating not only the car but himself. He wants, no needs, his visit to be a surprise. He exits and closes the door quietly, relieved when the light extinguishes. There is no noise, no door opening, no dogs barking. He's still invisible. He marches to a side window, not wasting time with stealth. It's too cold. The window has cheery floral drapes, the kind he imagines must clothe every small kitchen window in mid-America. No shadow extends from the window into the snow outside, so nobody is standing at the sink. The last thing he wants is to peek into the window only to come face to face with someone cleaning dishes. He moves his eyes up over the sill to peer inside. The kitchen is filled with bright light, probably the best lit room in the small house. Beyond the light, the rooms are dark, but silhouettes from a TV show dance against the walls. The kitchen is empty save for one lone soul, his back to the window, sitting at a green Formica and steel table, eating dinner. The table is ancient and chipped. Little did this old fart realize that the table he sat at was worth a hell of a lot more now than it had been when it was brand new. It was what millennials called 1960s chic, and something they happily paid top dollar for back in the city. For the man eating, it's just a table, probably something he purchased decades ago for almost nothing and just never considered replacing. He can't imagine this simple piece of furniture is something young folks yearn for. The entire kitchen looks like it came right out of the sixties with its faded mosaic-tile-pattern linoleum floor, robin-egg-blue counters and oven, undersized refrigerator, and pine cabinets. The man looks so lonely staring at his plate, his only company being that provided by some mindless TV show. Time has left him behind. Tau will be doing him a favor by ending his life tonight. It is a rare thing that he will do good while doing what he loves. He moves from the window to the front door and knocks.

It is only a moment before the door opens, only it isn't the old man who answers. Instead, the face that greets him is that of a little girl, not more than six or eight.

"Ellie, don't open the door. I'll get it."

"Too late, Grandpa. I got it."

Behind the girl, Tau sees the old man approaching the door. "God's sakes, girl, it's darn cold out there. Close the door."

"But Grandpa—"

"Never mind, honey, Grandpa's got it. Go back in and watch the movie." He waits while the girl scampers around to the left into a darkened room, lit only by the television.

"Son, why in the world are you out and about tonight?"

It's obvious the man is not going to invite him in from the cold. The old bastard will pay. Tau doesn't bother pulling the pistol out of his pocket to threaten and force his way in through the doorway. He just leaves his hands inside his coat, toasty and warm, wrapped around the pistol grip, and fires through the lining. The bullet catches Grandpa in the gut just above his belt buckle and knocks him back against the wall.

Tau enters and bends to the left, pushing the door closed behind him. He fires twice more. Ellie and her little brother never get to see the end of the movie. They'd probably seen it before, so no big loss.

He returns to the old man, who lays struggling in pain as the reddish black blood streams onto the floor. Tau watches his victim pull himself into the kitchen toward the phone, leaving a smear of color across the linoleum behind him. The phone is mounted chest high on the wall. He'll never be able to reach it. "What a stupid fuck, but I give you an E for effort. Grandpa, where are the keys to your fancy-ass Jeep and the garage? Tell me now and I'll save you some pain, kill you quick like. If you don't, I'm gonna drag your ass back into the TV room to show you what I did to those cute grandkids. Well, they ain't so cute now. What's it gonna be?"

The old man whispers, "On the counter … by the phone." He breaks into tears and pulls his hands together in front of his face, mumbling something Tau can't make out, but he understands anyway.

"Gotcha. Only God ain't gonna save ya now." Tau smiles and walks into the kitchen to grab the keys, then leaves by a side door. Fuck the old man. No reason to waste another bullet.

Tau fumbles through the keys until he finds one that unlocks the garage. He'll hide the van inside. Who knows how long it'll take before DHS find it, maybe hours, maybe days? He cracks open the door and reaches inside, groping along the wall, searching for a light switch. There it is, presto. *Fuck, fuck, fuck!* he yells silently to himself as he stares at a mountain of old boxes, papers, wood, tools, and just plain old crap. The place is packed, no room for the old man's Jeep, let alone an extended cargo van. He flips off the light, then closes and relocks the door.

He returns to the van, debating whether to leave it parked beside the road or to move it behind the garage, hoping it'll take a while before being discovered. He decides on the latter and hops into the driver's seat, cranks up the engine, and pulls into the driveway, then he turns into the snow-covered lawn to maneuver around the Jeep. This was stupid. The tire marks will provide a drawing line to where he hid the van. If they know the old codger, the empty driveway and tire tracks will certainly attract the attention from passers-by. It's too late to change plans. The tires slide in the snow as he circles the barn. At least the Jeep will handle better in the icy conditions.

He imagines continuing to Gedeon's re-education camp, not as a prisoner, but as a destroyer. Killing the old man and kids had excited him. He's hungry for death and vengeance. Even if it gets him killed, he relishes the idea of taking out more of the DHS wannabes. He'll make sure Gedeon remembers him. But he doesn't want Gedeon to just remember him. He wants Gedeon to die looking into his eyes. He wants Gedeon to be helpless, to feel fear. Tau scraps the idea of approaching the re-education camp. There's no time. He'll return to DC tonight. He doesn't know whether he should run at or from Gedeon, but he's on his own.

CHAPTER 6: Free to Agree?

For a second time, Brandon reviews what their investigators found regarding the re-education camps. If education is their true purpose, someone screwed up in the design. These are hardly schools. They are closely guarded centers for brainwashing combined with the hard-labor punishment he associated with centuries past, hardly with today's more enlightened prisons. The last word is the most important. These are prisons. No, worse than that, people die here, lots of people.

He reviews the proposed outline of the story a second time before calling Sir Leroy to get permission to run with it. He knows Leroy will try to nix the story, but eventually he will cave; he always did. Brandon pushes the speed dial for the Committee number, knowing Leroy will be the only voice heard. Brandon hates these calls. They were always the same: first a series of disparaging comments focused on him and Simon, then an exasperated request to get on with whatever it was he wanted, then the complaining and threats, and finally, an acceptance of the storyline. Sir Leroy never turned down a story. Quite frankly, Brandon doubted he ever listened to, or understood anything, about what they planned to report. The call had become nothing but a formality, a wasteful formality, seemingly intended to do nothing more than drive home who was boss.

The phone rings and rings, failing to push over to voice mail. Good thing because Brandon hates to leave requests via voicemail. He worries that he won't get a response before running with a story. The phone finally answers. "Who is this?" The voice is not Sir Leroy.

"Umm, this is Brandon. Is Sir Leroy available?"

"Son, you got the wrong number."

Brandon looks at the number again to confirm he didn't push an incorrect speed dial. "No, I don't think so. Put him on, please. I need to get his approval before running a news story."

"A news story? Who is this again?"

"Look, I'm calling for Simon Cartwright. He does a national news show. He's kind of a big deal. Just ask Leroy, he knows."

"Sir Leroy is no longer interested in the news. Maybe you should pass your request on to me."

"That doesn't sound too rational to me. Tell me why I should give a rat shit about what you think?"

"Maybe you shouldn't, Brandon. This is Secretary Harvey from Homeland Security, and I really couldn't care less about what your Simon Cartwright has to say as long as he stays on the farm. Understand?"

Brandon is dumbfounded. "You're Secretary Harvey? And you know Leroy?"

"Yes, I knew Sir Leroy. Let us say he's had an unfortunate breakup with the Committee. I assume you know of the Committee. Of course you do. They call your shots, don't they? Well, back to Leroy. He's retired, permanently. I have his phone, but it probably would not be appropriate for me to tell the press what to say, given my role in government, so to speak."

Brandon wrestles with what this conversation means. "Sure, so to speak, a free press wouldn't be very free if you got to tell me what to say."

"Exactly. So I won't, but I won't leave you hanging either. I'll have a Mister Gedeon Rose get back to you on your story.

"Gedeon?"

"Yes, why?"

"Mister Cartwright and I have worked with Gedeon in the past."

"Good, then there won't be any misunderstandings. I suspect you know Mister Rose hates misunderstandings. By the way, not that I care, what is your story about?"

"Well, it was kind of going to be about Gedeon, and the re-education camps."

Harvey now cares as he hangs up on the call.

*   *   *

Gedeon sits, staring placidly across the desk at the wall above Harvey's head as the Director rails on at him for not shutting down Simon Cartwright and his producer.

"What in God's green earth were you guys thinking to allow him to continue reporting?"

"It wasn't my idea, Harvey. I'm merely controlling him to make sure he doesn't screw up and get in the way of what the Committee wants. My role is to ensure no story damages our cause. To that end, there will be no story about me or the re-education camps. I made that clear. We have nothing to be concerned about."

"Are you kidding? We have everything to be concerned about. I can't allow this to go on. Screw the idea that they pass their investigations by you before reporting on them. You're DHS, for God's sake. There can't be a link between you and the news reporting. There must be at least an appearance that the press is free. Having DHS in the approval process makes a mockery of our Constitution. Get yourself out of the approval chain."

"Easy for you to say. You put me there. How do you propose I extricate myself without having to crush the entire news program?"

"Pass it on to their effing network chief. Tell the network bosses I got places reserved in the re-education camps for them and their families, all expenses paid. The tickets are one way. They will get the point. Tell them to put the kibosh on anything that makes DHS look bad. If they let anything through that even gets close to damaging or outing the Committee, they're on their way to hell. Do it now."

Gedeon smiles.

"What's so funny? There is nothing funny about any of this."

"Just looking at the sign there on the wall, behind you. 'Our Mission: With honor and integrity, we will safeguard the American people, our homeland, and our values.' Sound about right to you?" Gedeon stands and leaves Harvey's office, the Secretary glaring at his back as he exits the room.

CHAPTER 7: Changing Positions

Tao sits motionless in the dark corner on the floor with his legs pulled up to his chest. In his hands he holds a gun, pointed outward into the empty room. The lights are out, window shades drawn. He is invisible. He has been here before. He knows this corner is safe from the motion detector. He reset the security system and positioned himself before it had a chance to arm. The fool will pay for not having reset the code. He concentrates on controlling his breathing, forcing himself to focus, to relax, to be aware … of everything.

He hears a drop of water fall against the bottom of the stainless-steel sink in the kitchen. It will come again, one, two, three, four "thud," like a slow, monotonous drum, constant and never ending. Listen, here it comes again, "thud." Gedeon ought to get that fixed. His senses are elevated in the quiet. He can hear everything. Even with the insulated walls and windows, every car announces itself as it passes by in the street, the water being pressed from under its tires telling him how close and how fast it is moving. Even the cold has its unique sound: creaking and groaning of wood, the tapping of metal as it contracts and expands as heated water courses through the radiators. He smiles. The sounds of darkness are loud if one listens.

He has been waiting for hours and will wait for several more if need be. Gedeon will return home soon. They have much to talk about, and Gedeon has much to answer for, but he doubts he will take the opportunity to do so. Gedeon is too cunning. Talk just gives him time to develop an escape plan; no reason to give him the opportunity. Tau knows Gedeon is smarter than him. He is smarter than everyone. Tau's only advantage will be that of surprise, and Gedeon will be surprised. How can he not? He'll think his visitor should be dead by now. Tau is a loose end, and this loose end has become tangled before it could be snipped away. Gedeon should have known better. This loose end will strangle the man who sent him to the re-education camp. This loose end survived. He is resurrected. He will be unforgiving. Gedeon will feel the wrath of Tau.

*   *   *

Harvey is mindlessly flipping through pages of some report left on his desk. He pretends to read, but Gedeon knows he is not. It's just an act. Gedeon has seen it before. Harvey hates being made to wait. It bothers him more when he's forced to do so in the company of someone he dislikes, and Gedeon fits that description perfectly. Harvey puts up with him because he has no choice. He watches as Harvey shuffles the papers around on his desk. Reading will be impossible, Harvey's mind too consumed with their upcoming meeting. The words on the pages in front of him will be nothing more than jumbles. Gedeon smiles from his chair in the corner of the office. He toys with the idea of saying something, anything, to distract Harvey, to help while away the time, but he doesn't. He enjoys seeing Harvey stressed.

This meeting has no agenda as far as he knows. In fact, the Secretary has not shared with Gedeon who they will be meeting with. He can only surmise the meeting is important to Harvey, and therefore should be important to him. Apparently, his attendance has been specifically requested.

There is a faint tap and the office door opens. The President pushes in and closes the door behind him, leaving his security team outside in the company of Harvey's administrative assistant. "Gentlemen, how are we this evening? Never mind answering. Let's be honest, I'm fine, it's late, and I really do not give a damn how you two are doing. Let's get down to more important affairs."

Even though Harvey is familiar with the President's boisterous way of running things, this lack of tact takes him by surprise. Gedeon never moves or responds.

"I'm just kidding, Harvey. How the hell are you?" The President holds out his hand. Harvey obliges, moving from behind his desk to shake the hand of the man he has reported to for the past three years.

"And Mister Rose, right? How are you doing?" Gedeon nods in acknowledgement but doesn't in any way answer the man's question, nor does he make any effort to offer his hand in greeting. The President seems not to notice and doesn't offer his hand to shake. "I've heard much praise for you, Gedeon. You seem to have a lot of supporters in high places. Good for you.

"Harvey, you mind if I take your desk chair? It looks a hell of a lot more comfortable than these pieces of shit." He motions toward several wooden armchairs facing the desk. Actually, the armchairs look, and are, extremely comfortable. It's obvious that if this is a pissing contest, the President is going to win. Harvey moves to the side.

The President sits down in Harvey's seat and kicks his feet up onto the desk. He waits with his hands laced behind his head until Harvey gives up and sits down in one of the chairs intended for visitors.

"That's better." The President drops his feet back to the floor with a bang and aggressively leans forward, pushing both of his hands palm down on the desktop. "I really appreciate you making your office available for this little impromptu meeting, Harvey. I didn't want to have this discussion in the Oval Office. Too many ears, prying eyes, and such. You get my drift? What goes on here stays between the three of us. It doesn't go any further. Got that?" He stops for effect, but it's also obvious he's not going to continue until he gets an acknowledgement from both parties sitting across the desk from him. Harvey and Gedeon both nod.

"Good. Gentlemen, you may not be aware, but I, too, have a relation with something you refer to as the Committee, albeit my relation has been somewhat longer. You see, I have known some members of the Committee since I was a child. They have been integral in determining my life's direction for as long as I can remember. It is now time for my purpose to be fulfilled. You should be proud of being part of this movement. We are at the point where we will finally be able to say adieu to the problems that have plagued the world for generations.

"There are going to be some major events taking place over the next several weeks. They will seem stochastic, but they are hardly so. They are planned and their outcome is known, preordained, so to speak. The Committee has left little to chance. It is now time for the final phase of preparation on my part."

Gedeon stands and leans forward, his hands also on the desk. "What are the problems we are resolving?"

"Come on, Gedeon, get with it. We are solving the issue of world population growth. It's been out of control for God only knows how long and the problem is accelerating. It needs to be stopped."

"Sure, but what has that got to do with us? You've got a lot of power, but I don't recall world domination being in your job description."

"Very true, Mister Rose. Let me remind you, we are all cogs in a much bigger set of wheels that are already set in motion. My job is not to screw it up. You should be happy that you are also considered an important cog. If you weren't, you and I would be having a very different conversation." The President pauses. "That brings me to why I am here." He pulls a plain white envelope from his breast pocket and places it on the desk, pushing it toward Gedeon.

"This is a list of those who are not cogs. Go ahead, Gedeon, look and then pass it over to Harvey. He might be interested, but you are responsible for making sure each person named is eliminated, whether by getting them safe passage to one of our re-education camps or any other means. I'll leave that up to you." Harvey reaches for the envelope. The President slams his hand back on top of the envelope. "Mister Rose first," then he hands it to Gedeon.

Gedeon opens the envelope, pulling from it several sheets of handwritten paper. "This looks to be something like a purge, something I would have expected from a Stalin. Are these people who oppose the movement? Hell, most of these folks are members of Congress. Are you sure?"

"I am always sure, and this is nothing like Stalin's purge. I could add you to the list for that type of comment. Stalin was a crazed individual who desired power for power and greed. He was a paranoid murderer who would kill his mother if he thought she wanted a share of his power. Rest assured, I am not that type of man. I have no desire for personal power. I am only concerned for the good of the world. Back to the list. Sure, some of them are … contrarians, but most have been supportive of the cause. They've just outlived their usefulness, or they might have some reservations about our means. At this point, they can do nothing more than gum up the wheels. I cannot allow that to happen, and you can't either. There should be no surprises. Please make sure these are taken care of tomorrow evening. I assume you have resources in place to handle this?"

Gedeon reads through the entire list of names and raises his eyes to meet those of the President's, then hands the sheets to Harvey.

Harvey quickly scans the sheets. "My God, you can't be serious. These are good people. I won't let you do this."

"That is not your choice, Secretary Harvey. Please read on and read them closely."

Harvey continues through the pages until his face turns white and he drops the pages to the floor.

"You see, you've been added to the list, Harvey. Thank you for your service, but I have no need for your contribution anymore. Gedeon, you can take care of this?" Without waiting for an answer, the President walks from the office and closes the door behind him. A sharp crack is heard from behind the door. The door opens and Gedeon exits. He walks by the President without a word, leaving the door to Harvey's office ajar, the sulfur odor of gunpowder instantaneously filling the room. The office is left dark and quiet.

CHAPTER 8: Better to Swim with the Current

"Are you kidding?" Simon slams his phone onto the table. This investigation would have been award-winning. It would have awoken people. It was important, and now it would die. Brandon said he went to bat for him. Bullshit. He probably backed off the first "no" he got.

He redials Brandon. "Look, sorry I yelled at you. I know you got my back, but it's bullshit, and you know it. Who's putting the brakes on it?"

"Simon, it's not what you think. I went the distance for you. I hear the stop came from all the way up, from the network chief."

"Fuck him. Call Leroy. It's his call."

"Not anymore."

"Huh?"

"It's Gedeon's. I think Leroy is gone, for good. You know, murdered."

"Damnit, Brandon, quit with the hyperbole. Give it a break for once. Why would anyone want Leroy dead?"

"Why would Gedeon be back? Something happened, Simon. Something bad. We really shouldn't push too hard."

"Aren't you the one who was trumpeting the First Amendment shit? What gives? You seem to have lost your sense of perspective, boy. Gedeon's not going to kill us over our story."

"You got it wrong, Simon. It's all stories. We are effectively shut out on this. I think we're going to get stuff spoon fed to us again, and you're going to report it on the air just like it was our idea, our work, but it won't be. Gedeon wouldn't tell me who was providing the information, just that we'd get it every morning and he expects us to run with it."

"It's never going to happen. I report what I want. That's the agreement."

"Yes, but with approval."

"Sure, approval, not absolute control. I'll leave the show first. Did you tell him that?"

"Of course not. I can't speak for you."

"Brandon, you do all the time. You just chickened out this time. How do I get hold of Gedeon?"

"I don't know. He called me. The number was blocked. I have no idea how to get hold of him."

Simon slams the phone down again. "Fuck you, Gedeon."

The phone rings. "Brandon? you got the number?"

"This is Gedeon, Simon. I understand you would like to speak with me."

"Gedeon, I'm going to do a report on the re-education camps and I want yours and the Committee's approval."

"No"

"Just like that?"

"Just like that."

"But this is big. You haven't seen what we plan to report."

"I don't need to."

"Of course you need to. This isn't fucking fair."

"Nothing is fair. I do not recall seeing 'fair' being in your contract. All I recall is the explicit requirement that you get the Committee's approval prior to airing stories."

"Okay, let me speak with the Committee."

"You are speaking with the Committee. I am their representative in this matter, so drop it and go to bed. It's late."

"Fuck you, Gedeon."

"Simon, Simon, Simon, you never have gotten it, have you. You need to listen to me and respect me. I'm going to keep you out of trouble if you let me. The last thing you want from me is corrective action. I can be very vindictive when crossed, and you are pushing me. I'm putting you on notice. It is the only warning you are going to receive. Give this story up and try reporting on the stock market, the weather, the fucking color of the Pacific, anything, but stay away from this story. Do you understand?"

"I understand that you don't understand."

"Understand this then. Your show is cancelled."

*   *   *

The hour hand rolls past midnight and is approaching one as the gate rolls up to let him enter the parking garage. Thank goodness for reserved parking places. He's tired and has no patience to look for a slot. That said, his neighbors always do a shitty job of parking. They always squeeze into his parking space from both sides. Any tighter and he wouldn't be able to open his door to get out. Fuck them. If they're still there in the morning, he'll key their cars.

He squeezes out and opens the trunk to get his briefcase. It seems stupid to lug this around with him. He rarely accessed anything in it, only the charger. The only things he really needs are his phone, which is always in his sportscoat pocket, and his Glock, which rests in the holster tucked under his left armpit. He smiles, tosses the briefcase back into the trunk and slams it shut. Time for some shut eye.

It has been a wonderful day. It didn't start out that way, but things got appreciably better as evening approached. The best part was putting that bullet into Harvey's forehead. He now has faith in the movement. The Committee is serious and willing to do what needs to be done. It's about time. Of course, putting Simon in his place was fun, too. He just wished he'd been paying attention to the monitor to watch his face when heard he was fired. The press never got it. They were important for a time, but that time was past.

But the best part is kicking off his plan to fulfill his obligation to the President and the Committee. There are more than a hundred names that he will sweep away and forget by tomorrow evening. It will reestablish his position of importance with the movement.

Even as he climbs the damp, gray, concrete steps to his second-floor condo—he'll have a much nicer place once the Committee takes over—things have been set in motion. By now, a couple dozen late-night visits have already been made to the homes of those deemed no longer needed. It's not good to no longer be needed. He imagines how the visits will work. There will be no lights or sirens; these are to be stealth attacks. There will be no pleasant knock at the door or warning. Instead, they will pick the locks and sneak in. If that doesn't work, they'll crash and rush. He wants the attacks to be surprises. No reason to provide the targets the chance to escape or defend themselves. The targets won't be handcuffed and carted away to a re-education camp as the President may have assumed. That led to risk and loose ends. No, these individuals will never leave their homes alive. Sure, his teams will be heavily armed with fully automatic weapons, but if things work well, the only weapons required will be silenced .22 caliber pistols. They'll make almost no noise and will allow them to terminate the individuals with a minimal mess or disruption for the neighbors. The muzzle will be pressed against the forehead and there'll be a quiet "snap" and that'll be the end. It is a kind way to dispatch someone. They should be grateful for the mercy.

The police have been warned. There will be no response to nine-one-one calls. If there are family members in the house, they will be dispatched, too. They may not have been on the list, but they will talk. Let America Speak gave his team latitude. He is sure the President will understand and approve. Hell, he will applaud.

Tomorrow morning, they will move on to the remaining names. These will be easy. They are all members of Congress, and they will be in session, sitting in their seats, pretending to be important … or interested in some speech. Neither will be true, of course. They are fat, dumb, and happy, just waiting to be taken by Gedeon's teams.

There will be two DHS teams, one for each chamber. Their objective, winnow those on the list from the rest of the herd without them knowing it. A fictitious bomb scare will be the catalyst to get them moving. The team will funnel them to safety through the halls, picking off the poor chosen few as they pass to redirect them toward a separate "safe" conference area for a briefing. It is amazing how the desire for safety trumps thought. Gedeon has no doubt they will follow his team's instructions without question. There are a few individuals who will express concern and try to question what is going on. They are leaders. Thank goodness the halls of Congress don't have many. If they get in the way, his team is to shoot them, whether they are on the list or not. He is not concerned with losing control. Fear is even more effective than the promise of safety in controlling most people. It will be no different in Congress. The members of Congress who are on the list are lucky in that they'll be spared the humiliation of being made a spectacle as they're loaded onto busses bound for re-education camps. It will drive home to the world that nobody is beyond the reach of the law ... except, of course, those who enforce the law.

Gedeon smiles. By the time the clock's hour hand passes its apex a couple more times, he will have accomplished his task. He never fails. The Committee will respect him. He will continue as a critical cog in this new machine. It will be simple. There are lots of folks who will need re-education in the new world order. Hell, he might even get a chance to live in Europe. Asia, probably not. He expects that the population control in that region will be more ... aggressive.

He unlocks his door and enters. He keys in his alarm code out of habit without looking. It is funny, he could not recall the code if someone asked, but his muscle memory never forgets. He makes a mental note to change the code since he had shared it with Tau. It's the same mental note he made yesterday but forgot. It's not urgent. Tau is being re-educated. He'll never see the man again.

There is no reason to turn on the lights. He knows the layout perfectly. Moving in the dark is a game he plays, something to keep his senses sharp. Operating in complete darkness challenges him. He will first place his briefcase on the kitchen counter. Well, there's a change for the game tonight—his case is in his car. Then he'll move to his bedroom, remove his clothes, placing his shoes on the floor and hanging his suit on the right side of the closet, waiting with two other suits to be sent to the cleaners. His socks and shirt will be balled up and thrown across the room into an open hamper. Only when the lights went on would he see if he made a basket with his shot. Tonight, the game will not end until he returns to the kitchen and opens the refrigerator to pull out the chilled gin he typically reserves for guests. He'll make himself a rare martini in the dark. He needs a brief escape and will risk clouding his judgement with alcohol. Only then will he turn on the lights and prepare a late dinner. The night will end with some reading.

He stops. Something is wrong. It's not something he hears. It is something he smells. He knows the odor. "Tau, where are you?"

CHAPTER 9: We Are All Nails, a Postlude

Had Simon stayed in San Francisco, he'd be nothing more than ash. Perhaps he's lucky. The bombing was terrible. In one day, the US lost more than twenty million souls on the west coast alone. In the same respect, they largely escaped the devastation that crushed three other continents. That same week, the rest of the world lost more than a hundredfold the lives they lost in the States. Only Europe was spared. It was said to be the first phase of several that would be necessary to control population.

They are being told the world is now a better place. It doesn't seem so to Simon.

It's dark in here, but Simon is not alone. All his friends are with him: producers, reporters, camera operators. He should be grateful. Brandon sits next to him. His co-patriots smile and nod to him as they are loaded. Loaded? That sounds bad. He doesn't mean to imply they are being treated as cattle; they aren't. They each have assigned seats. Of course, there are no seatbelts. Safety must not be a high priority for them. They have become expendable. They are one of many busloads of relocated press members. They should have warned the world, but now it's too late. They got caught up with ratings and riches and forgot how to investigate. They forgot how to think for themselves.

Simon rocks back and forth as the bus bounces along on its journey. His head bangs into the hard steel wall with each bump in the road. It hurts a little, but he no longer cares. The little pain reminds him that he is still alive, that there is hope.

He wonders if Dad would be proud of him now. Doubtful. He would have been out in front of this from the start, fighting against the bad guys all along the way. Simon chose the easy way. He took the money, the fame. Now he has neither. And he fears the bad guys won.

The bus stops and the door opens to a blinding light. They are to be re-educated.

Thank you for choosing to read "NAILS." If you enjoyed it, please consider telling your friends or leaving a review on Amazon, Goodreads, or the site where you bought it. Word of mouth is an author's best friend and much appreciated.

ACKNOWLEDGEMENTS

Although *Nails* is completely fiction, it provides a salient warning for all who are complacent with a steady erosion of rights. A portion of the early readers of *Nails* initially viewed it as a pointed comment on contemporary political movements. To an extent, they were right, but they soon realized it was not so limited. It is a commentary on power in general, at its seductive nature undermining those with even the best of intents.

The inspiration of *Nails* came from the significant totalitarian movements the world experienced in the twentieth century: fascism, socialism, and communism. Unfortunately, individuals today throw these terms around without understanding consistent, basic underlying aspects of all of them. A minority imposed its will on a passive majority through fear and intimidation. The minority consolidated and controlled all power. The individual lost all rights … and it happened quickly.

Lastly, those who were the hammers in these movements often became nails that were pounded into submission or bent and disposed of.

One should not think of *Nails* as being rightest or leftist. Both positions have significant blind spots related to the slow erosion of our rights. Both sides should consider this a warning.

I would be remiss to not acknowledge and thank the many who have been instrumental in the creation of *Nails*. First off, my wife, Caylor, and my family's continuous support, along with honest and direct feedback, have been instrumental in making the story better. In addition, I am eternally grateful for the suggestions my two friends and writers, Wes Brustad and Rick Stepp-Bolling, provided. It is tough providing criticism to friends. I cherished their inputs. I would be remiss to not recognize Denna Holm, who along with being a tremendous writer, was my editor extraordinaire on the book. Lastly, to Carly McCracken and the entire Crimson Cloak Publishing team; it could not have happened without you. Thanks.

To the reader, enjoy and please do not hesitate to pass on your comments to me or Crimson Cloak.

ABOUT THE AUTHOR

M.D. Nuth, after growing up in Colorado, resides in Southern California, his adopted home of the past three decades. Before turning to his passion for writing, M.D.'s professional career spanned for-profit and non-profit organizations that enabled him to work with a diverse set of people that included international business leaders as well as the poorest of the poor. In both his personal and professional life, he remains grounded through family, faith, music, and writing.

Life experience gives M.D. a unique perspective and knack for storytelling, providing him insight to illustrate the human factors that affect all of us. His writing transcends socio-economic status to speak to each of his readers on a personal level, unifying them through life events in which all humankind can relate.

https://www.mdnuth.com